Mystic Harmony

MIDLIFE MELODY, ACT THREE

PHOEBE RAVENCRAFT

COLUMBUS, OHIO

Mystic Harmony: Midlife Melody, Act Three

Copyright © 2022 by Phoebe Ravencraft

All rights reserved.

No part of this book may be reproduced in any form or by any electronic or mechanical means, including information storage and retrieval systems, without written permission from the author, except for the use of brief quotations in a book review.

ISBN: 979-8358148451

Also by Phoebe Ravencraft

MIDLIFE MELODY

Accidental Mystic

Mystic Attunement

SWORD & SASSERY

Sleeping Dragons

High Stakes

Personal Demons

Silver Bullets

Forbidden Magic

Divine Favor

For my mother. Thanks for teaching me to be a hero.

Mystic Harmony

One

Coffee is my very best friend in the world. Okay, so it's not exactly a person. But if you think about it, it makes perfect sense. When I first wake up in the morning and I'm feeling like shit, coffee is there to make me feel better. It opens my eyes and helps me face the day. It soothes my frazzled nerves when they're out of control. It gives me the pickup I need when I'm dragging in the middle of the afternoon. And on a cold day, it warms me up like a cozy blanket.

No one in my life has ever performed all of these services on a regular basis. I sometimes think my marriages failed, because I expected my husbands to live up to the standards that coffee set, unrealistic though they may have been. Whatever problem I was having, coffee could help make it just the littlest bit better.

And there was no better coffee on the face of the Earth than at Drogo's Diner.

I pulled up to the restaurant and put my trusty Ford Escape in "Park." The previous week's cold snap was over, but it was still chilly outside. A shiver ran down my body when the March wind kissed my cheek, and my craving for Drogo's special java increased.

When I walked in, Drogo himself was working behind the counter instead of his usual role of cook. His face beamed with beatific light, and his silver eyes twinkled with their customary happiness. His gorgeous, Middle Eastern features warmed my nether regions, and not for the first time, I wondered if angels ever dated mortals.

"Ah, Bethany Parker," Drogo called in his melodic baritone. "So nice to see you this morning. We are very busy today, but I can offer you a seat at the counter. Or, if you don't mind waiting, I'm sure someone will leave soon."

"Thanks, Drogo," I replied, "but I'm just here for a coffee-to-go."

"Give me just one minute while I get this gentleman's order, and then, I will take care of you."

Tearing my eyes away from the ruggedly handsome celestial, I stared across the diner. The place was in chaos. Not the usual harried efficiency of the breakfast rush, but rather, everything seemed completely out of control. Every one of the booths was occupied. A winged child who bore a strong resemblance to Cupid slid from booth to booth carrying a tray of dishes that seemed impossibly heavy for him to support, before returning to the kitchen. Where was Mona?

"Now then," Drogo said as he glided over. "What can I get you with that coffee?"

"Oh, nothing," I answered. "I don't have time to eat."

He threw me a reproachful look, and his silvery gaze made me feel as though I'd just been caught doing something very naughty.

"Bethany Parker," he said in a mock-scolding voice, "breakfast is the most important meal of the day. You should not be skipping it. Just as your SUV cannot run on an empty fuel tank, you need a full stomach if you wish to accomplish all you desire."

I smiled in spite of myself. He sounded like my mom, but his beautiful, angel's face made it sound so much more appealing.

Just then, Cupid emerged from the kitchen carrying another tray of dishes. He stopped at one of the booths, hovered like a hummingbird, and set meals down in front of a man and woman who looked to be in their sixties. The man eagerly dug into his pancakes. But no sooner had he put a bite into his mouth, then he spit them out all over the woman across from him, who screamed as though she'd been burned.

"You idiot!" the man snapped at the floating child. "These are supposed to have applesauce, not Tabasco!"

The youthful server blushed literally from head to toe. Drogo simply smiled and snapped his fingers. The food vanished from the woman and the hot sauce transformed into applesauce.

"Helio," Drogo said, his voice soothing as silk, "why don't you bring our guests two of our blueberry muffins on the house?"

Helio nodded and flew back to the kitchen.

"He tries very hard," Drogo said. "But food is not his specialty."

"Pardon me for asking," I said, throwing Drogo a concerned look, "but where is Mona?"

Drogo gave me another of his beatific smiles. I felt urges in my loins. Damn, but he was beautiful.

"I made her take a vacation," he replied. "She would work every day, twenty-four hours a day, if I allowed her to. She hasn't taken time off in two years and thirty-six days. I decided it was time. She needed a rest."

I looked around the restaurant. The usual happy smiles and casual conversation I was accustomed to seeing at Drogo's was absent. Everyone seemed on edge and unhappy.

"How long will she be gone?" I asked.

"Who can say?" he said. "I told her to take sufficient time to recover."

"Recover?"

"She was tired and overworked. She needs time to rest, relax, and feel her best self again."

My eyebrows raised. Mona had always seemed harried, but she was also incredibly efficient. In fact, before today, I'd never seen anyone else waiting tables at Drogo's. And she always had a smile and a pleasant attitude, no matter how busy things were. If that was what she was like when she was stressed out and overworked, what was the real Mona like?

"So you really don't know when she'll be back?" I asked.

"No, Bethany Parker," he said with a chuckle. "But do not worry. She always returns when she is ready."

"How long was she gone last time?"

"Seven months, thirteen days, and two hours."

My eyes about fell out of my head. She'd been gone more than seven months last time?

I gazed around the diner again. Helio buzzed over to the table with the Tabasco pancakes and put down a go-bag of blueberry muffins. The man acknowledged the delivery with a gruff frown.

"These eggs were supposed to be over-easy," someone called from an adjacent booth. "Not hard-boiled and served upside-down."

Helio slid over to the new table, collected the plates, and zipped back to the kitchen.

"Well," I said, "hopefully she won't need much time."

Drogo smiled again, and his eyes twinkled with mirth. He could read the concern on my face, but he only acknowledged it with a grin.

"So tell me, Bethany Parker, what must you do that prevents you from eating breakfast?"

"I'm having guests over at the manor tonight. I'm serving a roast, and I need a few things – potatoes, onions, rutabaga, and a couple other items."

"You couldn't have these things delivered?" he asked.

Since I'd arrived in Enchantment two months ago, I'd only gone shopping a few times. It was easy enough to order things and have them magically delivered to the kitchen. The convenience of it was amazing, but it took some of the fun out of it.

"Not if I wanted to stop here for coffee," I answered.

Drogo smiled broadly. I really needed to stop gazing into those sorcerous eyes of his. He was going to charm the pants off me right here.

"Well, I am glad you decided to stop by. The morning would not be the same without you."

I blushed. Suddenly, I was uncomfortably warm. It wasn't a hot flash. I opened my mouth to try to say something, but I discovered my throat had gone dry, and no words would come.

"We do offer catering," he said. "It is a bit short notice, but I'm certain I could accommodate you if you told me what you needed."

Now, it was my turn to smile. Drogo really was the best. There was no better food on Earth, and he was kind and generous. I supposed I should have expected nothing less from an angel.

"Thanks," I said, "but I haven't cooked for a while, and I kind of miss it. I used to make dinner every night for my whole family, and it was fun, particularly when I was making something special."

A sudden wave of sorrow broke over my heart. Jess and the children had never expressed any real appreciation for my cooking, and the kids always complained about having to clean up after dinner. It was one of the many things that led to my resentment.

But I still missed caring for them. Jess may have made all the money, but I provided the things everyone needed on a daily basis. Though I was much happier now, a twinge of regret mixed with pleasant memories forced me to swallow hard and blink back tears.

"I understand completely," Drogo said. "Cooking is among the most pleasurable of arts. And just as a sculptor likes seeing their work in a museum as people admire it, a true chef takes pleasure from the enjoyment of their food."

I nodded. He'd summed it up perfectly. I'd always thought this but never been able to articulate it quite so well.

"Wait here one moment," he said.

He disappeared back into the kitchen. Helio delivered to another table. A woman stared at the meal for a moment, a sour expression on her face. Then, she directed her attention to the Cupid look-alike and hit him with her best death-glare.

"Not chicken eggs," she seethed. "Chicken-fried steak and eggs!"

Helio gazed on her, confused.

"Take it back!" she shouted.

This was a command he seemed to understand, for he swept the plate back up off the booth, and flew back into the kitchen just as Drogo returned from it. I shook my head. I wasn't sure Drogo was going to be able to stay open for very long if Mona didn't come back to work soon.

The angel approached me with a jar of brown liquid and a tiny cannister of some sort of herbs. He pulled a go-bag out from under the counter, shook it open, and set it down on the counter in front of me.

"This is the best *bouillabaisse* you will ever taste," he said, holding up the jar and then putting it into the bag. "And this, sprinkle on your potatoes before baking them. You can use the rest in your gravy. Your guests will find it all ... magical."

He put the cannister into the bag next to the *bouillabaisse*. Then he grabbed the coffee pot and poured out a large go-cup for me. I paid for the coffee and was about to pick things up when he raised his index finger and stopped me. He went to the pastry case, withdrew two blueberry muffins from it, and dropped them and a napkin into another go-bag and passed it across the counter to me.

"I only paid for the coffee," I protested.

"Yes, I know. Consider these a gift. One should never skip breakfast. Nor is it wise to go grocery shopping on an empty stomach."

I sighed heavily and took the bag from him.

"You sound like my mother," I said.

Drogo shrugged.

"Your mother is clearly a wise woman."

"She'd be grateful to hear you say that," I said with a smirk.

Unable to resist, I quickly imagined my mother saying, "I told you so," to me. Yes, Mom, you told me.

I gathered up my things and was about to leave, when a sudden thought occurred to me. I turned back.

"Drogo, you haven't seen any vampires lately, have you?"

He cocked his head, as though that was the most unusual question he had ever heard. Curiosity danced in his silver irises.

"Not this morning," he quipped. "Why?"

"Well, we've been expecting Marcel Truffaut for over a week now," I confessed. "In fact, that's why I'm having friends over tonight: We're planning to discuss what to do about his absence. I was wondering if maybe he'd been by the diner?"

Drogo nodded sagely, as though all this made complete sense to him. I was reminded of how he had known exactly what I'd planned to do before leaving for Cincinnati. Once again, I wondered just how much he knew.

I have only seen Dien Bao Pham once," he answered. "It was shortly after he first arrived in Enchantment a few weeks ago. I don't serve his usual fare."

"Dien Bao Pham?"

"That is his true name – the one he was born with. Before he adopted the identity of his former master."

I frowned. How did Drogo know all this about Truffaut if the vampire had only been to the diner once? And there was something else.

"If he chose Marcel Truffaut as his name, isn't that his true name?"

"Celestials address the soul inside the vessel, Bethany Parker. We don't acknowledge other identities. At his birth, he was named Dien Bao Pham. That is how I see him."

Something about that pissed me off. It was a strange sensation. Drogo's company had only ever filled me with tranquility. But this definitely made me angry.

"You're an angel," I said. "Isn't free will a thing? Self-determination? Weren't Adam and Eve punished because they chose a different destiny than what God intended?"

"All that you say is true," he answered.

"Then if free will and self-determination exist and can be invoked, why can one not choose a name that is more reflective of who they believe themselves to be? If Marcel Truffaut changed his name because he felt it suited him better, doesn't that make it his true name?"

Drogo stared at me in wonder. I watched as he tried to process these ideas.

"That is an excellent point, Bethany Parker. I shall have to give this great consideration."

Great consideration? How male of him.

"All right," I said, "while you're pondering the truth of someone having the right to change their own name, I've got to get going. Lots of shopping to do. Thanks for the ingredients and for breakfast."

"My pleasure, Bethany Parker. Thank you for stopping by today. It is always an interesting conversation with you."

I wasn't sure how to take that, but I suspected he intended it as a compliment, so I decided to let it pass.

"Bye, Drogo," I said. I cast one more gaze around the restaurant. Someone else was complaining to Helio about the food they'd been served. "Good luck."

I turned and went out. Drogo's presumption aside, I was deeply concerned about the fact that he hadn't seen Truffaut either. And since he seemed to know a lot about the vampire, my concern about Truffaut's absence grew stronger.

Two

Ninety minutes later, I'd finally made it home with everything I needed. But no sooner had I pulled into view of the house than I saw Paul Hernandez's car parked out front. I swore to myself immediately. Paul's visits were never good. He always wanted something.

And he always lied about whatever it was.

With a heavy sigh, I shut off my vehicle, got out, and grabbed as many of the groceries as I could. Then, setting a grim look on my face, I made my way to the manor.

Dorigen met me at the door, dressed in her usual long, black dress. Her wrinkled face had extra lines of worry, and her hazel eyes burned with irritation.

"He's in the library," she said without preamble.

I frowned.

"What's he doing there?"

"No idea. That's just where he said he'd wait for you."

Something about that alarmed me. I couldn't imagine why Paul would be poking around in my home, but, given that it was the house of a long dead magician who'd tried to make himself immortal, I couldn't think of a single good reason for Paul to be investigating.

"Did he say what he wanted?" I asked.

Dorigen scowled at me. As usual, she had all the fearsome visage of an angry grandmother.

"Heh," she spat. "Probably came to collect on that date you promised him."

I sighed. She was probably right. I'd promised Paul I'd buy him dinner in exchange for him digging up information on Sheriff Mueller for me. That intel had helped me save the sheriff's life. But I'd had to pay a high cost for it.

"There's a few more things in the car," I said. "Would you mind getting them for me?"

"Sure, Missy."

She started to move past me but made sure to say, "Good luck," before she was out the door. I couldn't tell if it was sarcastic or sincere.

Desperate to put off the latest confrontation with Paul as long as possible, I went to the kitchen, and put away the groceries. Then I took off my coat, tossed it on a chair, and fixed my hair before sighing heavily again and swallowing hard. Summoning my courage, I headed for the library.

When I got there, Paul was walking around gesticulating broadly while speaking to Lucius. My cat-familiar sat on an end-table, his inky-black fur puffed up in suspicion and his green eyes watching Paul's every move with great scrutiny.

"What I find so fascinating," Paul was saying, "is that Alexander Ellington was a summoner. The entire manor is really a giant summoning circle, if you will. So the question is, if that's its purpose, who or what was it built to summon?"

"Spirits, one presumes," Lucius answered.

"Except that's not the way that the artifacts work," Paul said. "They open a portal to the spirit world, so that the undead can be pulled through it. So, what was it that Alexander Ellington wanted or was expecting to summon with this house?"

Lucius frowned. I could tell he did not like this line of thought.

"Some questions are best left unanswered," he said.

"Agreed," Paul replied.

"Ignorance isn't bliss," I said. "I know from experience."

"Ah, there you are," Paul said.

He immediately switched on his oozing charm. Thin, with a receding hairline and dark, Hispanic features, he leered at me with brown eyes through thick glasses while covering his words with honey. He wore his usual khaki pants, brown shoes, white shirt, and brown, patterned tie that had gone out of style at least twenty years ago. His brown overcoat was tossed over one of the red-leather chairs. He fixed me with a smile, as though his invading my residence was completely normal.

"What are you doing here?" I asked, unable to hide the suspicion in my tone.

"I came to see you," he replied smoothly. "You weren't home yet, so I thought I'd explore the library."

I crossed my arms and threw him a penetrating stare.

"Why?"

He smiled, clearly amused by my question. It made me want to smack him.

"I may be a techno-mage, Bethany, but I'm also a librarian. Alexander Ellington's library is filled with old books on a broad range of topics. It's fun for someone like me to lose myself in the stacks."

"I've been keeping him company," Lucius said, making sure I knew that he was on the case. I nodded.

"Why are you here?" I asked.

"You promised me dinner in exchange for information on Sheriff Mueller," he said. "More than a week has passed since the arrest of Karl Markiewicz. My information bore fruit. I have upheld my end of the bargain.

"But you have not called to make arrangements."

So, Dorigen had been right. He was here to schedule our "date."

For a moment. I tried to think of an excuse for why I couldn't pay up. But despite my having opened my Third-Eye Chakra and therefore being able to see the wisdom of the universe, not one damned idea would come to me.

"Sorry, I've been busy."

"Of course!" Paul replied. "So I've come to see when would be convenient."

Bullshit. He could've called. Why was he here?

"Well, not tonight," I said. And then, I couldn't help but twist the knife a little. "I'm having people over."

"Tomorrow then?" he asked, his eyes narrowing.

Once again, I tried to come up with any reason why tomorrow would be a bad time. But the universe offered nothing.

"I suppose that'll be fine," I answered with a resigned sigh.

"Terrific!" he said. "I'll make reservations – Titania's Garden, seven o'clock. Dress elegantly."

I had no idea where Titania's Garden was. I presumed it was somewhere in Enchantment, since, when I'd set parameters for this dinner, I'd told him I wasn't road-tripping. But while I'd been in town for several months now, I had not come across such a place.

"Uh, okay, sure," I said.

"Excellent. I'll show myself out."

He scooped up his overcoat and cruised past me as though this were the most ordinary thing in the world.

"Until tomorrow night," he said as he left the library.

I didn't answer him. I just let him walk down the hallway. When I heard the front door open and shut, I turned back to Lucius.

"What did I just agree to?"

"I don't know," the feline familiar said. "He's up to something. I overheard him tell Dorigen he'd wait in the library for you. That seemed suspicious, so I followed him. I watched for a minute or so as he studied the shelves. He seemed to be looking for something in particular."

"That can't be good," I said.

"I agree. You should be cautious on this date."

"It's not a date," I said, fixing him with a withering glare.

"Does he know that?"

"He'd better," I said. "If he doesn't, he's in for a rude surprise."

Lucius nodded then hopped down off the table he'd been sitting on. We left the library and headed for the kitchen. I had to get the roast in the oven if it was going to be ready in time for tonight's gathering.

But something deep in my gut told me this wasn't the last I would hear from Paul about the library.

Three

The roast was a huge success. Drogo's seasonings on the potatoes indeed made them magical. I couldn't quite place the flavor. I thought maybe I detected thyme and sage or maybe rosemary. But it was only hints of familiarity – the true taste was altogether different. Who knew what he'd actually given me? Perhaps they were herbs that grew in Heaven itself. Regardless, they made the potatoes taste amazing.

His *bouillabaisse* was every bit as good. It rendered the best, thickest gravy I had ever made in my life. I was a good cook, but gravy had always been my nemesis. I could never get it as thick and rich as my mom made it. But this was even better than anything she'd ever managed.

"Oh, my God, Bethany," Rhoda said. "I don't think I've ever eaten anything this delicious."

Thanks," I said. "It's my mother's recipe."

Growing up, my dad had done most of the cooking – not because he was that interested or good at it, but because Mom was an ER nurse. And in the early days of their marriage, she worked a lot of three-to-eleven shifts. So, if he was going to eat, and later feed a child, he had to learn to make it himself.

But Mom had a couple of her own specialties, and like every East

Coast woman of her generation, she could make an amazing Yankee pot roast.

"Drogo helped a little," I confessed. "Gravy has never been my *forte*."

The rest of my company nodded and grunted their appreciation. Sheriff Mueller had his head down dissecting yet another piece of meat. Secretly, I was amused that the wolf-shifter ate the hell out of the roast but largely ignored the potatoes and onions.

Declan sat quietly across the table from him. He had taken a small portion to be polite. But mostly he sipped from a beer stein filled with blood. I focused on how good the gravy was to avoid being disgusted.

Lucius curled up by my feet. I'd cut up some of the meat and poured a little gravy over it for him. He'd eaten it with as much enthusiasm as everyone else had. Now, he seemed content to have a snooze on my foot.

"What I want to know," Dorigen said as she put down her fork, "is if you can cook this well, why the hell have you waited this long to do it?"

Everyone laughed. I smiled and blushed.

"It took a little while for me to want to again," I said. "After years of making dinner every night and not really being appreciated for it, I'd sort of lost my appetite for cooking, if you will."

Rhoda nodded in understanding.

"All right, Parker," the sheriff said, wiping his mouth. "As good as the food is, that's not what you called us here for. Let's get down to business."

I grimaced. I'd been putting this discussion off all evening so I could enjoy the food and companionship of my friends. But the truth was, we had important issues to discuss.

"Okay, everybody," I said. "I still haven't heard boo from Marcel Truffaut. On a whim, I asked Drogo if he had seen him. He told me that Truffaut had only stopped in the diner once shortly after he arrived in town. So, if he's lurking around Enchantment, he hasn't been to Drogo's or anywhere else I'm aware of. It's been more than a week since he went to visit Paul. I can't help but think something is wrong."

"What about you, McGruder?" the sheriff prodded. "He's your vampire buddy. Any word from him?"

Declan shook his head softly as he sipped some of his blood. He put the cup down and wiped his mouth.

"No," he answered. "I've investigated all the places I thought he might've nested. There's no sign of him."

"Well, I haven't seen him either," Sheriff Mueller added. "Over the last three days, I've searched the town from top to bottom in my cruiser. I can do a more thorough investigation in wolf-form, but so far as I can tell, he's not here."

"Rhoda, you haven't heard anything from Reggie, have you?" I asked. "Would he have been able to detect Truffaut?"

"He could certainly find him," she replied. "But the truth is, I haven't heard from Reggie since we got back from Cincinnati. I'm kind of worried. It's never been this long before."

Shit. When we'd gotten the cane in Cincinnati, I'd used it to compel Reggie to possess. Evan Longfellow, enabling our escape. I'd seen him leave the body, so I knew he wasn't trapped. But aside from the strange visitation I'd had from him a few days ago in my dreams, I had had no contact with him either. I couldn't help but fear there was some connection between Reggie's absence and Truffaut's disappearance.

"Do you suppose that's related somehow?" I asked, terrified of the answer.

Rhoda thought about it for a moment. I watched as the shadow of worry passed across her face and planted seeds of concern in her mind.

"I don't know," she said after a moment. "But the spirits here in Enchantment have been ... agitated ever since we returned from Cincinnati."

"Agitated?" I asked.

"Yes," Dorigen said. "That's the right word for it. There's an ... energy about the manor that I don't understand. But it's palpable and dark."

That unnerved me. Dorigen wasn't magical herself, but she was sensitive to the paranormal. She'd been telling me for two weeks that an ill wind was blowing through Enchantment. I didn't doubt her. I just didn't know what to do about it.

"Damn it, Parker," Sheriff Mueller swore. "What sort of trouble have you stirred up now?"

"I'll remind you that Bethany saved your life with that trouble," Rhoda said.

"Yeah," he retorted, "and I told her to stay out of it. Now, because she wouldn't leave well enough alone, we've got a whole new situation where we don't even know what's wrong."

"Oh, stop it!" Dorigen snapped. "You're alive because she convinced the two vampires to even the odds in a way that wouldn't violate your ridiculous honor code. And she browbeat everyone here into going along with it because you saved us from Maggie Cartwright. Put away the toxic-male, penis-waving act and be grateful for a change."

An uncomfortable silence followed. Dorigen always told it like it was, and though her perspective was both important and needed, she always managed to phrase things in a way that left everyone speechless.

"Let's examine what we know," Lucius said after a moment.

I started. I hadn't realized he'd left sleeping at my foot. Now he was sitting on the end of the table, which, with all the food and dishes seemed incongruous and wrong.

"Marcel had been working with Paul Hernandez," the cat went on. "He believed Paul was holding out on him with the location of Alexander Ellington's pocket watch."

"Right," I said. "And after I gave him the cane, he said he was going to have a long discussion with Paul. And he said he would contact us shortly thereafter. That was the last we heard from Truffaut."

"But today, Paul showed up here and was snooping around the library," Lucius said.

"What did he want in the library?" Declan asked, his brow knitting.

"I am uncertain," Lucius replied. "He was definitely looking for something before I interrupted him."

"What would he be looking for?" the sheriff asked.

"Who knows?" Declan said.

But his voice was far away, as if his mind were engaged in something else entirely. I studied him for a moment with my Sight. He was definitely hiding something. He'd been very unforthcoming about what it was he and Truffaut were doing here in the first place. Well, he told me all about what Truffaut was up to. But he kept his own motivations concealed.

"Whatever is happening," Rhoda said before I could press Declan for more information, "Paul is somehow at the center of it."

"Good thing the sorority girl has a date with him," Dorigen groused.

"What?" Sheriff Mueller said.

His eyes were open wide, his brown irises pouring an accusatory glare into my heart.

"It's not a date," I said.

"What is it then?" he asked.

I searched the sheriff like I just had Declan. Was he jealous? I'd discovered that I was his type. But he never overtly made a move on me, and frankly I wasn't sure I wanted to date anyone ever again. Not after the way I'd been betrayed.

"I owe him a favor," I said with a sigh.

"What sort of a favor? And why?"

The sheriff's police line of questioning was almost cute. It was nice to have attention. But it was none of his God-damned business either. Irritated, I told him the truth.

"I asked Paul to look into your background. I wanted to know what was going on with you, and nobody seemed to know. But I figured that our resident Order representative would be able to find out. The price for that was me buying him dinner."

Sheriff Mueller's fair complexion turned bright red. I could practically see the steam coming out of his years. And I didn't need my mystic Sight to be able to tell he was furious that I had been poking around in his past.

"Damn you, Parker," he said. "What gave you the right?"

"I told you." I answered flatly. "You helped me with Maggie Cartwright."

"So, you thought that made it okay to go digging into my business?"

"Regardless," Rhoda said, lifting a hand and asserting control over the conversation, "Bethany's deal affords us an opportunity."

"What?" I said, throwing her a look.

"Since you have to go to dinner with him, you can question him," she said, as though it were obvious.

My mouth was agape. I blinked several times in utter surprise.

"Who do you think I am?" I said. "James Bond?"

Rhoda smiled that trademark grin of hers that always told me she had something up her sleeve.

"Ply him with wine and appeal to his ego," she said.

"Heh," Dorigen laughed. "He obviously wants you. It should be easy."

"I am not sleeping with him to get information!"

"There's no need," Rhoda said. "Get him a little drunk and start asking him questions. He'll spill."

I reflected that Paul Hernandez did love to feel smart and superior. In fact, I'd appealed to that instinct before to get things from him.

"Where is he taking you?" Rhoda asked.

"I don't know," I said. Someplace called—" I tried to recall the name of the restaurant. "—Titania's Garden, I think."

"Jesus, Parker!" the sheriff practically shouted. "Are you insane?"

I looked at him as though he were high. It was dinner at a fancy restaurant. What the hell was the problem?

"What do you mean?" I asked.

"Titania's Garden is a fey restaurant," Rhoda said. "It's only partially in this realm. All of the food is enchanted, fairy fare. You'll need to be on your guard, Bethany."

He was taking me to a fairy restaurant? And did I hear Rhoda, right? It's not fully on this plane of existence? What the hell had I agreed to now?

"Well done, Sorority Girl," Dorigen barked.

"Boy, you've done it again, Parker," the sheriff said, shaking his head. "You poke your nose in my business where it doesn't belong. And now you've made serious trouble for yourself and who knows who else?"

I was tired of being bullied. And demeaned. I might be ignorant of the magical world, but I was a human being deserving of respect, and this was my house.

"Stop it!" I snapped. "I'm tired of everyone acting like I'm stupid. You were in trouble. You wouldn't tell anyone what was going on. So

Rhoda and I did some digging. I had to pay a price, but I saved your life. That's what friends do. That's what families do.

"And I would do it again in a heartbeat.

"Now, stop scolding me and help me figure out what to do."

The sheriff's eyes flew open wide. For a moment, he looked like a dog that had been hit on the nose with a rolled-up newspaper. Then he glowered at me. He was a former pack alpha and a grumpy man. He did not appreciate being talked to that way. But before he could decide what to say in response, Lucius spoke.

"Bethany, you've aligned your Third-Eye Chakra. As a mystic, you should be able to trigger a vision for what to do."

"Yes, but I usually need something to activate it."

"Perhaps we should move to the conservatory," Lucius said. "Piano always seems to activate your abilities."

"Yes, that's how you were able to guide Marcel and I to aid the sheriff," Declan said.

I considered it for a moment. Music was the key to my magic. But somehow, this didn't feel right.

"I'm not sure," I said. "Music usually triggers something active in the physical world, not a vision."

"What about a tarot reading?" Rhoda offered. "That's worked before."

"Do you have cards with you?" I asked.

"Of course!" Rhoda said. "I always keep a deck in my purse just in case."

"All right then," I said. "But let's move to the parlor. That'll be more comfortable."

"Only if I get the whiskey bottle," Dorigen commented.

I shook my head at my housekeeper's dependence on Jack Daniels. But I supposed if I'd been cursed for fifty years by a mad witch, drinking would be a fine way to soothe the pain. God knows, I'd drunk enough wine to drown my divorce and three other people's since I'd gotten here.

We stood up and put our napkins on the table. I decided we could clean up the dishes later. I wanted to know what was next first.

And I had a feeling deep in my bones whatever it was was going to be bad.

Four

A few minutes later, we were all gathered in the parlor. Rhoda and I pulled a small, round table away from the wall and set two chairs on either side of it. Everyone else gathered around. Declan and Sheriff Mueller dropped into easy chairs nearby. Dorigen sat a little ways away on the divan, her hand curled tightly around a glass of whiskey. Lucius hopped up on the chair back behind Declan so that he could get a clear view of the table.

"Because we're at a critical crossroads and unsure what is happening," Rhoda said as she shuffled the cards, "I'm going to try a spread of my own design. It identifies where the querent stands on the path and the ultimate destiny towards which that road is leading."

I cocked my head in surprise.

"You can make up your own spreads?" I said.

"All spreads came from someone," Rhoda said. "They didn't just magically appear along with the cards. Expert readers are able to design spreads that point to clearer messages. In this case, I have developed this one by working with spirits I've had contact with, including Reggie, who as you know was also a mystic."

I nodded thoughtfully. I supposed that made pretty good sense. Still, it was kind of weird to hear that Rhoda had come up with this pattern herself. I always thought these kinds of things were long-lost fragments of ancient wisdom or ritual.

"All right," Rhoda said as she put the deck on the table in front of me. "Clear your mind."

So far, this was as expected. Rhoda always wanted me to first clear my head and then think of the question. I shut my eyes and did my best to let all my thoughts drain away. As usual, it took a few seconds. Memories of the dinner and of Paul's alarming visit earlier this afternoon competed for my attention. I tried to cloak them in thick, black curtains, so that I could not see them. I listened to the beating of my heart. After a moment, its rhythmic thudding lulled me into tranquility.

"Okay," I said.

"Good," Rhoda replied. "Now, I want you to stretch out your senses to the universe. Feel your connection to it and all of its energy."

At first, it was difficult. I'd only done this properly a few times. The grandfather clock ticked loudly in the silence. I listened to it, mesmerized. Soon, my heart was beating in synchronicity with the swing of its pendulum. Though my eyes were closed, I saw colors – red, orange, yellow, green, blue. They swirled together and washed over my mind like waves lapping on a shore. I could feel the chill of the air outside and perceive the dust on the hardwood floors of the manor.

"Okay," I said. "I think I've got it."

"Cut the deck," Rhoda instructed.

Wordlessly, I reached out with my left hand. Though I did not open my eyes, I could see the cards sitting dead-center in the middle of the table between us. It glowed with soft, golden light.

But as soon as my hand touched it, my whole body lit up in fiery pain.

Paul sat across from me at the table, leering like a lecherous old man. A horrifying grin spread up his face, and his teeth were yellow and short. His eyes glowed red like two sinister stars lighting up his face.

And then I was looking at Andrew with those same hell-red eyes, dressed in his Lawrence High baseball uniform. He stood with a red aluminum bat and brought it back to strike as though he were swinging for the cheap seats. He brought it around and the instant it connected with me, there was a painful wave of electricity.

Now, it was Rusty Mueller before me with the red eyes. He fell to his knees shaking violently from electrocution. And when the current became too much. He took on Lucius's cat-like body for a brief moment before exploding in a torrent of blood and fire.

I tried to scream, but Declan stood before me with his vampire face on, blood dripping from his fangs and those evil, red eyes glaring at me in delight. He raised his arms and transformed into the giant man-bat figure that had haunted so many of my visions in the recent past. And as I fell backwards, freaked by the presence of this monstrous thing. Then, it exploded into hundreds of bats.

My eyes flew open, and I gasped. Rhoda stared at me in concern.

"Bethany, are you all right?" she asked.

I didn't know the answer to the question. I seemed to be fine. I sat in the chair at the table, surrounded by my friends. And to my great surprise, I saw that I had actually cut the deck and not just touched it.

But I was absolutely shaken by what I'd seen. I couldn't make sense of any of it, but it was absolutely terrifying.

"I think so," I answered, without knowing if that were true or not. "I just…. When I touched the cards, I had a vision."

Rhoda's eyebrows raised. Great. I'd done something weird again.

"What did you see?" Lucius asked.

I opened my mouth to reply, but then I saw my beloved familiar explode again, blown up seemingly by the electricity that had been coursing through Sheriff Mueller. I couldn't bring myself to describe that.

"I'm not sure," I lied. "There were just flashes, impressions. I couldn't make sense of them."

That at least was true. Aside from everyone seeming to meet horrifying fates, I had no idea what any of it meant.

"Perhaps the reading will clarify your vision," Declan offered.

The memory of him standing over me with blood on his fangs sent shivers down my spine. Was he going to betray us all? Would he become the monster Dorigen had warned me so many times about?

"Yes," I said. "That's a good idea."

I looked forward to this reading like I had no other in the past. If Declan was going to betray us, I needed to know.

"All right," Rhoda said, "here we go."

She flipped the card off the top of the deck and put it down directly between us. The illustration showed some sort of prince riding on a horse. He held up a long staff with a wreath over the end of it, and in the background others held up similar staves. The dude definitely looked righteous, and I couldn't help but think even the horse had a smug look on its face.

"This card represents the querent," Rhoda said. "This is you, Bethany."

I smirked. The idea of me riding a horse was outrageous. But being all done up like some sort of royalty and carrying a staff made me want to laugh.

"This is the Six of Wands," Rhoda went on. "We often see a recognition of personal achievement in the Six. But it's important to remember that while one person is the hero, everyone benefits from whatever they have accomplished. This seems like a good representation of where you're sitting right now."

"How so?"

"You have accomplished a great many things since coming to Enchantment," Rhoda explained. "You've quite literally saved the life of every person in this room. All of us benefit from the things that you've accomplished."

"Oh, great," the sheriff commented. "You're gonna feed her ego and make her stir up more trouble."

"Quiet, Rusty," Rhoda said. "The card represents where the querent stands right now on the crossroads. Bethany has accomplished much, but there is a path before her she has still to walk."

I nodded. All of this made perfect sense to me. In fact, I found myself understanding in a way I never had before. Maybe that was because my Third-Eye Chakra was in alignment and I was seeing so much more now.

"The next card represents the past," Rhoda said.

She turned it over and then placed it beneath the six of wands and to the right so it sat diagonally to it. The theme of imperious dudes continued. This card showed a king holding up a sword in his right hand and a scales in his left. Two pillars rose around him, and at his feet was the word, "justice."

"Justice," Rhoda pronounced as if I couldn't see it myself. "This card indicates that the consequences of your actions are at hand."

"Now *that* I understand," Sheriff Mueller said.

"Shush," Lucius scolded.

"In the past, you have taken actions that have brought about the need for justice," Rhoda went on, ignoring the sheriff. "However, we need to remember that this card is neither sinister nor hopeful. It's balance. It reminds us that all should be treated equally and impartially. As a result of the actions you've taken, you've been offered a gift."

"A gift?" I asked.

"Yes, a gift of entry into a new realm of understanding. As a result of the judgment, you have come to learn in new ways how the universe works."

The consequences of my actions were at hand. That summed up how I'd gotten here perfectly. I'd messed up in my marriage until Jess and the kids couldn't take it anymore and threw me out. That had landed me here, where I had awakened to my mystic powers. Six of my seven chakras were open and in alignment. I was seeing in ways I never had before – both magically and mundane. I had no idea where this reading was leading us, but I could feel its truth deeply.

Rhoda drew a third card and placed it beneath the Six of Wands and across from Justice leaving a space between the two. The card showed what looked like a compass, with sigils at each direction, riding on the back of a jackal. A sphinx sat atop it. In each corner of the card was a creature – an angel, a griffin, a winged lamb, and another sphinx – and all of them were reading books. But it was the name of the card which caused me to giggle.

"Wheel! Of! Fortune!" I said and then laughed again.

Rhoda smiled broadly and shook her head.

"Bethany, your sense of humor never ceases to amuse me."

"Tell me what I've won, Pat," I said in my best gameshow announcer voice.

"You haven't won anything, silly," Rhoda said, laughing herself. "The Wheel of Fortune indicates change is at hand. It could be random change, or it could be premeditated. But its message is that we must work with the cards that fate deals us and remember that what goes around comes around.

"This card is in the position of the foundation. The past delivered justice and created a foundation of change. Now, as the wheel turns, fate is at hand."

I was still amused and imagined Vanna White turning letters to spell out my destiny for me. But once again, I found the message of the card resonating within me. When I closed my eyes and stilled my heart, I could practically feel the turning of The Wheel of Fortune. What I didn't know was whether it was spinning me towards the top or down to the bottom.

"Our next card indicates the situation in the present," Rhoda said. "It lays out the conflict and gives us a hint of what may happen next."

She turned over the card and set it directly above The Wheel of Fortune and higher than the Six of Wands so that she now had three points of an "X." I gasped when I saw the card. It showed a heart being stabbed through the center with three different swords, and above it, three clouds produced torrential rain.

"Oh, shit," I said. "That doesn't look good."

"Well, keep in mind that we need to avoid attaching emotions or judgments to the cards, especially prior to seeing the entire spread. All the cards give us is a message. They don't portend darkness or light."

"Bullshit," Dorigen said. "I'm not a fortuneteller, but I know the Three of Swords means nothing good."

I could not help but agree. Maybe it was my Sight, but I knew that this card was ominous.

"What does the Three of Swords mean?" I asked.

"Its base meaning is sorrow caused by knowledge," Rhoda said. "You have learned something, and whatever it is, is terrible. This knowledge causes a wound on our heart, and a piece of us dies as a result."

If that card had landed in the past, I wouldn't have been as worried.

After all, this entire journey had started with the Three of Swords – I had learned what my family truly thought of me. I had had to start completely over, and I was definitely not the same person anymore.

But looking at it in the position of the present worried me deeply. Rhoda had said that this was the situation at hand, and that it offered hints of what is to come.

"The card frequently indicates heartbreak, loss, and betrayal," Rhoda went on. "But I need to emphasize that we don't necessarily know that is bad."

"Come on," Dorigen said. "Tell me when in your life heartbreak, loss, and betrayal were good things."

"Sometimes, a betrayal leads us to getting out of a toxic relationship or discovering a new friend," Rhoda said, her tone terse.

I nodded again. As devastating as Jess's betrayal had been, it had liberated me. I was so much happier and better off now. Still, I was very concerned about this card appearing in the present.

"What's next?" I asked.

"The direction," Rhoda said. "Our next card will give us an indication of where the road is leading and if you should walk that path or turn aside."

Rhoda turned over the next card and put it down directly across from the Three of Swords completing the "X." It showed a man with his head bowed, wearing a black cloak. The sky was gray, and at his feet were five golden chalices. Three were overturned, having spilled water and possibly blood, since some of the liquid was red. The other two stood upright behind him.

"The Five of Cups," Rhoda pronounced. "This card generally has a pretty simple meaning."

"Which is?" I prodded.

I could tell from Rhoda's grim expression it wasn't good.

"Grief and loss," she answered.

"Shit," I said.

"I told you," Dorigen said.

"The path that you're walking, the direction you're headed, Bethany, will bring you grief," Rhoda said. "You're going to lose something."

"We're doomed," Sheriff Mueller said.

Rhoda didn't look as angry as I expected her to. I could see irritation crowding her eyes, but I also could tell she thought the sheriff was correct.

"Okay, well," I said, trying to interject some humor into an otherwise gloomy situation, "at least we *know* something bad is going to happen. Maybe it will mean Paul loses his sanctimonious attitude."

Rhoda smiled thinly at my joke. She swallowed hard and tried to put on a brave face.

"As I said before, we need to remember that no matter the cards in the spread, they are only bringing us a message. We need to be careful not to oversimplify this and assume darkness will befall us.

"Note that three of the cups are overturned. These are the ones that are in front of the figure on the card. His head may be bowed in sorrow, but we could also view this as him being focused solely on what has been spilled. He only sees the loss. Behind him, though, there are two upright cups. If he would but turn and look, he would be able to see them. This indicates that all is not actually lost. There is still hope for the future."

I thought about that. The end of my marriage was the perfect expression of the meaning. When Jess threw me out, I'd been lying on that hotel bed, wishing I were dead. I could only see the three spilled cups – Jess, Ariel, and Andrew. But there was something else behind me. I just needed to turn around and see it. And eventually, I had. I left Lawrence and wound up here in Enchantment. I had a new family, and they loved me in ways my old one never did.

"I don't know, Rhoda," the sheriff said. "Seems to me you're trying to ignore the obvious, you're not looking at the things right in front of you."

"No, she's right," I said. "And particularly since this card sits in the position of the direction, we only know that I'm moving toward grief and loss. We don't know the exact nature of whatever it is, nor do we know what new beginning, what new resources may be available to me when I arrive."

No one said anything for several seconds. Rhoda's eyes were open wide in wonder. At first, I was surprised that she would react that way, but it occurred to me that she was unaccustomed to seeing me accept this sort of thing right away. I had always been such a skeptic that it must have seemed awfully strange for me to be embracing it so strongly.

"That's remarkable, Bethany," Lucius said.

"How so?"

"You've changed. You're not the cynical, depressed woman I met a few months ago. You are becoming an awfully powerful mystic."

I nodded. It felt good. It was as though, not only was I really, truly healing, but I could feel the wounds sealing, the flesh becoming whole again. It was such a magnificent sensation.

"One card left," Rhoda said. "Destiny."

She turned over the top card of the deck and placed it above the present and the direction and in line with the querent. My eyebrows raised as soon as I saw it. This was the second time I'd seen this card: The Lovers.

"Do not tell me that I'm going to come through this whole ordeal to hook up with somebody," I said, unable to keep any sense of disappointment from my tone.

Both Sheriff Mueller and Declan looked uncomfortable at the presence of The Lovers in my destiny. I'd already surmised the sheriff had a thing for me, and I had been attracted to Declan from the moment I'd first spoken to him. But no matter how fulfilled I felt, no matter how much healing I'd done, I just really was not ready for romance in my life. The wounds from my divorce were still too fresh. And as much as I liked both men, I just couldn't see myself with either of them.

"We had this same argument the last time The Lovers came up," Rhoda said. "It does not necessarily mean you're going to hook up with anyone. The Lovers *can* mean that you will enter into a relationship with someone, but only when that is the question posed in the reading.

"The true meaning of the card is that a decision looms. Two opposite things will come together. You'll recall that the first time we saw this card, you had to figure out how to balance your skepticism and your faith. Clearly, you have another decision to make. The present and the direction both show us where you're going. The Lovers is your arrival. Whatever loss or betrayal you experience as a result of the direction, Bethany, The Lovers indicates you will bring two things together and as a result, they will make your heart glad.

"I don't know what sort of sorrow you will have to endure to get here. But I do know that you will come through it stronger and happier."

I thought carefully about the fact that Rhoda hadn't asked me to pose a question when she began the reading. She'd just told me to clear my mind and reach out to the universe. But ostensibly, this reading had been about what to do about Paul Hernandez and Marcel Truffaut. Everything surrounding the reading was ominous – consequences of my actions being at hand, change on the horizon, sorrow caused by knowledge, and betrayal and loss. But it was leading me towards something that would make my heart glad.

The reading itself didn't tell me anything. It was all too vague to make any clear sense of. But the vision I had prior to Rhoda turning over the first card seemed to indicate great tragedy of some variety. Rusty electrocuted, Lucius exploding, Declan in his whole horror-flick, vampire form. And all that set against the backdrop of tragedy the cards seemed to predict. The only consolation was that I would come through it happier. But I couldn't imagine what sort of loss I was going to have to endure to get there.

"So, now what?" the sheriff asked.

It was a good question. Despite my Sight, I wasn't sure what to do. The reading was supposed to give us some sense of direction. But I wasn't convinced it told us anything more than we knew at the beginning.

"It seems to me that Bethany must meet with Paul Hernandez," Declan said.

Dorigen cocked her head and threw him a sidelong glance.

"Why?" she said.

"Our discussion after dinner indicated that Mr. Hernandez is at the center of this mystery," he explained. "The reading indicates that Bethany is walking a path through darkness but will emerge into the light at the end. Therefore, it stands to reason that Paul Hernandez must be confronted. And Bethany has already made arrangements to do so."

"That's mighty brave of you," the sheriff said.

"What do you mean?" Declan asked.

"You're volunteering her to walk into the heart of danger. I don't see you putting yourself at risk, Mr. McGruder."

"Well, how is that any different than before?" Dorigen asked. "This has been Bethany's show since the get-go. She's the one who makes all the moves. We're the ones who have to live with them."

I turned and looked at Dorigen with a look of surprise on my face. I couldn't understand what she was upset about. I'd released her from the curse. I'd released them all from the curse. But she was clearly haunted by something. I couldn't make out what it was, but there wasn't malice in her words so much as fear.

"Well, while I hate to put my friend in danger," Rhoda said, "I'm inclined to agree with Declan. Bethany has been walking this path since she arrived in Enchantment. One only need look at the past and the foundation in this reading and know her own story to see that all of the events of the past few months have been leading her to this moment. Even if she wanted to – and I doubt she does, though I won't speak for her – I don't believe she can turn from this path."

I thought about that. Everything she said had already occurred to me. I'd seen the divorce in the past and its implications in the foundation. There didn't seem to be any escape from this conclusion. As devastating as the betrayal by Jess and the kids was, it had catapulted me here, which had allowed me to break the Curse of Ellington Manor. The last vision I'd had – that of Reggie being chained before transforming into the terrifying man-bat – told me that it was not over. I had more to do.

"What do you suggest?" Lucius asked.

"She has a date with Mr. Hernandez," Declan said. "She should keep it and use it as an opportunity to learn the fate of Marcel Truffaut."

"Yes, but you'll need to be subtle," Rhoda said. "Let's not forget the ominous nature of most of the cards in the spread."

"Weren't you the one telling me that we weren't supposed to impose value judgments on the cards?" I said, raising an eyebrow.

"Yes," she replied. "But I believe we need to consider Paul a very dangerous man. He is the last remaining connection to Marcel Truffaut. And Declan, wouldn't you agree that by this point, we have to presume something's gone wrong?"

"Yes," he said, frowning. "Marcel is mysterious and operates according to his own agenda. But it is not like him to just vanish into thin air."

"And, given that Paul Hernandez was here this very afternoon poking around the library and clearly looking for something, we need to approach him with caution," Lucius added.

Great. I already didn't like Paul. His condescending air, and his obsequious charm irritated the hell out of me. And he was a classic mansplainer. The thought of him as dangerous conjured images in my head of a serial killer. Was I walking straight into his den?

"Well, someone needs to keep an eye on her," Sheriff Mueller said. "If she's going to walk into a meeting with this guy and we're afraid he's the spider at the center of a dark web, then she's gonna need backup."

I smiled at the sheriff's police language. He was clearly hiding behind cop-talk to tell me he was worried and wanted to protect me. It was sweet.

"You can't go in with her, Sheriff," Lucius said. "It'll look suspicious. Paul will be on his guard."

"Yeah?" the sheriff replied, "that doesn't mean I can't stake the place out."

He got up, fished in his pocket, and pulled out a business card. Then he walked to the table and set it down in front of me.

"That's my number," he said, his voice grim. "I'll be right outside. You call if you get nervous. I'll be in in a heartbeat."

"Okay," I said, my voice slightly choked from the gesture.

I'd never been more nervous for a date in my life. But for all I knew, this one could be the last.

Five

I woke the next morning filled with a strange sense of dread. I had no idea what was causing it. Mercifully, I hadn't dreamed the night before, or if I had, I couldn't remember anything.

But there was something in the air – something palpable, something I could practically taste – that filled me with a deep sense of foreboding. This must've been what it was like for Dorigen when her sensitivity to the paranormal told her an ill wind was blowing. I didn't like it.

As I got out of bed and headed for the bathroom, it occurred to me that it was probably driven by my trepidation surrounding my dinner date with Paul. I had no desire to meet him tonight, and, given that I was now on a secret mission to find out what he was up to, I felt even more nervous about it.

I suddenly realized that I was thinking of it as a "date" now. I needed to put that thought out of my head. I didn't care what anyone else said; that absolutely was not what it was.

After I did my business, brushed my hair, and threw on a pair of jeans and a sweater, I went downstairs for some coffee. Nothing made here was even close to what I could get at Drogo's. But maybe because I was feeling unsettled or maybe because the events of the night before left me feeling overexposed to company, I had no desire to go out.

Dorigen had made a pot of coffee that was still mostly full. I pulled down a mug from the cabinet and poured myself a cup. Then I went over to the table, sat down, and rubbed my forehead. I sipped some of the delicious brew. It definitely was not like Drogo's, but it still soothed. Coffee really was my best friend in the world.

I pulled out my phone and texted Rhoda to let her know I was skipping our usual breakfast get-together. Then, I drank some more java and tried to figure out what to do with myself today. I had no appetite. For the second day in a row, my stomach was disinterested in food. So instead, I poured out another cup of coffee and then shuffled out of the kitchen, looking for a distraction.

Remembering Paul had told me to dress "elegantly," I sighed heavily and then trudged back up the stairs to look for an outfit.

In the bedroom, I set my mug down on the nightstand and made my bed. I needed a surface to lay things out on, and rumpled covers drove me crazy. I don't know what it is about making the bed, but a room always looks clean afterwards. There could be crap all over the floor and dressers, but if the bed was made, it didn't look like a mess. Likewise, an unmade bed in an otherwise spotless room looked shabby.

With everything in order, I had a little more coffee. Then with a deep sigh, I went to the wardrobe and threw it open to search for something I would feel comfortable wearing to my not-a-date with Paul Hernandez.

I still hadn't fully unpacked. I'd only been in Enchantment about two months, and I'd sort of been busy breaking curses and finding magical artifacts. The wardrobe was largely a storage locker, containing hanging clothes I rarely wore. I was a casual girl. I owned some evening gowns and a few formal things, but a sweater and jeans with either boots or sneakers was my preferred look. And I definitely did not want to invoke any feelings of attraction from Paul with my outfit.

So I quickly zipped through the things hanging up and found nothing I wanted to wear. Truthfully, most of it didn't fit anymore. Like every woman my age, I was a bigger girl than I once had been. And though I had never acquired the extra weight from carrying babies, I still wasn't the athletic twenty-something that worked her butt off trying to make it as a singer while waiting tables. Most of these things I hadn't worn in five years or more. And in addition to not wanting to give Paul any ideas, I didn't really want to suffer through the humiliation of trying on something that would no longer flatter me.

Sipping more coffee for comfort, I turned away from the wardrobe and looked at the stack of boxes I had yet to unpack. Most of them were open, having been rifled through as I searched for something to wear on previous mornings. But there were a lot of things I had not yet gone through, and again, I hadn't really made time to empty them.

Over forty-five minutes, I opened one container after another and rummaged through the clothing inside. Anything I thought might work, I pulled out and tossed onto the bed. By the time I was done I had several stacks of clothes. Finishing the last of the coffee, I set my jaw and began trying things on.

It had been a long time since I'd put myself through the torture of trying to find the perfect outfit for a date. I had forgotten how absolutely miserable this experience was – put on some clothes, stand in front of the full-length mirror, hate everything about your appearance, and then tear it off and start over again. Ironically, most of the things I tried on that fit well made me look too good. Instead of hating my appearance because I thought I was unattractive, I would look at an outfit, think, "too sexy," or "too refined," and take it off. Twenty-three-year-old, Bethany would have been stunned that I was trying to find something that made me look good but not attractive.

As if to make this task even more unpleasant, my body decided it was the perfect time for a hot flash. As long as I was in my underwear, I felt cool enough to continue. But as soon as I would try something on, I was baking at nine thousand degrees. Sometimes, I truly hated being a woman. Why didn't men have to deal with this shit, too?

I don't know how many outfits I went through, but I eventually settled on an oversized black, cowl-neck sweater with sequins to make it appear shiny. I paired it with black slacks that were maybe half a size too tight but otherwise fit okay. And since the sweater dropped just below my groin, I wouldn't have to worry about Paul being able to stare at my butt in them. I briefly contemplated a pair of silver heels, but I decided they were too sexy and opted instead for simple, black pumps. I still needed to figure out what to do with my hair, but that could wait for later. I had no desire to continue this torment any longer. I needed a break. So, without putting anything away, I grabbed my empty mug and went downstairs.

Back in the kitchen, I was somewhat relieved to see that there was still coffee. Dorigen was not as passionate about it as I was, but she drank her fair share of java. With the amount of whiskey she consumed every night, I suspected she needed the coffee in the morning to help chase away the hangover. But despite the fact that I'd been upstairs for nearly an hour-and-a-half to two hours. There was still enough in the pot for one more serving.

I refilled my mug and had a sip, grimacing. The last cup in the pot was always bitter from having sat on the heat forever. But I needed a jolt to snap myself out of whatever funk I was in.

Unable to think of anything better to do, I went to the office to manage the estate. There wasn't a lot to do as caretaker of Ellington Manor, but I did have a few tasks to ensure the house was stocked and the creditors were satisfied. I sat down at the computer and sipped coffee while I searched for jobs that needed my attention. Sadly, there were only a few bills to pay, and by the time I had finished them, a mere ten minutes had passed. Unwilling to give up just yet on this distraction from my general boredom and dread, I opened my email.

My eyes opened wide in surprise. There was a message from Andrew, subject line: "Bethany."

The overpowering sense of something wrong I'd been feeling all morning suddenly kicked into high gear. Was this what had been driving it? Why would Andrew be writing to me? I thought he hated me. With my hands shaking, I clicked on the message and read it:

Bethany,

I'm sure you're alone in your big house in Ohio (Ohio? Seriously?), crying your eyes out. Good. You deserve it.

You probably don't even know why. Well, let me tell you. You made all of us miserable. We all had to walk around on eggshells, fearing one of your explosions, never knowing what would set you off. We all had to put up with your constant singing and piano playing – even Ariel got so sick of it. And the constant reminders that we weren't good enough: "Pick up your clothes!" "Wash the dishes!" "Your room is a pigsty!" "I won't live in this filth!"

The house wasn't filthy. You wouldn't let it be. All we wanted to do was relax on the weekends. That's what weekends are for. But you always had to make them about cleaning. I was embarrassed to bring my friends over for fear you'd yell at me for something I hadn't done. That maybe you would make them help clean, too.

And why? It's not like you had a real job. Dad made all the money. All you had to do was make dinner and take Ariel and I to school. If you didn't want to "live in filth," why didn't you clean house during the day like other stay-at-home moms? Probably because you were too busy singing and wishing you'd become a pop star instead of the loser you are.

Poor Ariel. She wanted to be just like you. She wanted to sing and dance and be famous, because you told her that's what she should do. You filled her head with impossible dreams that could never come true. She tried so hard to live up to what you expected. And when she realized she couldn't do it, she wanted to die. She didn't want to major in music and theater. But when she was applying to colleges, she realized she couldn't do anything else. She'd spent four years doing all the plays and musicals and show choir, so that she had nothing else on her résumé. If she wanted a scholarship, it was musical theater or bust.

As soon as she heard Dad threw you out, she quit the music program. She's so much happier already.

Well, I'm not going to make the same mistake she did. I quit the baseball team. All those schools recruiting me? I told them to go to hell. I hate baseball. It was the only way to make you happy, and now that I don't have to anymore, I'll never put on a glove again. I don't want to be reminded of you every day of my life.

The day you left town, we had a party. Dad ordered pizza, Ariel came home from KU, and we drank name-brand soda – not the store-brand shit you always made us drink to save money. And we laughed at you, Bethany. We laughed at all your stupid rules and the fake way you would talk to our friends and the way you dress. And we recalled every hurtful thing you ever said.

Dad kept apologizing to us. He'd say he was sorry he ever let you in the house, and he cried when he thought about how unhappy we'd been.

I think that's what makes me the maddest. He was good to you. You had no prospects when he met you. All you could do was wait tables, and you weren't even working full-time. You were so depressed because you couldn't have children. Any kids you could have had are lucky they didn't have to have you as a mom.

But Dad took you in. He let you parent us. He gave you a place to live and the children you couldn't have yourself. And were you grateful? Were you kind? Were you loving? No. You just made a bunch of rules we had to follow and yelled whenever we weren't good enough. And you made us live your dreams instead of letting us find our own.

You're a terrible person, Bethany. We needed someone to love and take care of us, because our real mom had died. Instead, you were a tyrant. Ariel and I were just waiting for me to finish high school. Then we were going to tell Dad to divorce you. We were waiting because we thought he needed you. But it turns out he didn't. He never needed you. So thank God you acted like a total bitch on your birthday. I got to be rid of you sooner. We all did.

I hate you, Bethany. We all do. And we're so very glad you're gone. I hope you're miserable for the rest of your life. I hope every day you wake up and think about how you blew the best deal you ever had. And every time you think about me or Ariel, I want you to remember that all we wanted was a mom, and we got you instead. You ruined our lives.

Go to Hell, Bethany. Go to Hell and stay there. And burn for all eternity. It's what you deserve.

Sincerely,
Andrew

P.S. (My mom is ten times the woman you are, and she's not even alive anymore. That's how awful you are.)

. . .

I blinked in stunned amazement. They'd had a party to celebrate my leaving town? I deserve to be miserable?

They had all made it perfectly clear that they hated me. But the sheer vitriol, the impassioned attacks on my person in that email simply blew my mind.

I tried to breathe, but I couldn't get the air to come into my lungs. It was like I was in a vacuum, inhaling desperately but unable to draw life from the airless void. Spots swam in my vision. My head spun. And I felt my heart shatter into billions of tiny pieces. All the king's horses and all the king's men would never be able to find them all to reassemble it.

For a moment, I blacked out. I floated in darkness. And then, as though someone had pushed a reset button, my body started breathing again. With a huge gasp, I gulped in oxygen and returned to consciousness.

I was numb. My body may have been breathing again, but I couldn't feel anything. It was as if my brain had redirected all available power to life support and turned everything else off.

Unsteadily, I rose from the chair. I had to lean on the desk to keep from falling over. Noticing my throat was dry, I started towards the kitchen.

My legs were like rubber. It was difficult to walk. I shambled more than strode, like an old lady whose bones hurt so badly she can barely get around.

I stumbled into the kitchen and crossed the floor towards the refrigerator like a zombie. My eyes were blank, hardly seeing. I opened the fridge door on autopilot and extracted a bottle of water with the same absent indifference to my environment. Blankly, I untwisted the cap and poured some of the cold liquid into my mouth.

It shocked me back to myself. The chilly sensation on my tongue was like a hard slap to the face. I blinked several times, and suddenly I could see again – really see.

But my heart still hurt. There was physical pain in my chest as though I were having a cardiac incident. Briefly, I wondered if I was about to die. But the pains weren't sharp or stabbing. It just throbbed with dull, aching soreness. I couldn't actually sense my heart like I'd been able to after awakening to my powers, and I couldn't help but wonder if the shattering sensation I felt after reading Andrew's email was real, that my heart had actually exploded and now there was a hole in my chest where it was supposed to be.

Unsure what else I was supposed to do with myself, I turned and went back out of the kitchen. I had no idea where I was going, my feet were in charge of locomotion, but they had been given no instructions on where to go. Dorigen nearly ran into me as I was exiting.

"What's the matter with you?" she said, her brow furrowing in concern. "Looks like you've seen a ghost."

"Yeah," I said, without slowing my gait.

"Are you all right?" Dorigen asked, cocking her head.

"No."

"What's wrong?" she said to my retreating form. "Bethany? Bethany?"

But I had no ability to answer. I just stumbled out of the kitchen on whatever path I was walking.

Unsurprisingly, I found myself in the conservatory. Music was my security blanket when I was hurting. And Ellington Manor's Steinway grand piano had enabled me to process so much of the grief I'd experienced as a result of my blindside divorce.

I sat down at the piano and lifted the keyboard lid. And then I just stared at the ivory and ebony keys. I couldn't remember how to play. I put my hands in the ready position and stared. But the instrument offered nothing, as though it were speaking Chinese or Hindi or Arabic or some other language I didn't know. How did I do this again?

Tears formed in the corners of my eyes, but they did not spill. They simply blurred my vision, so that I couldn't see what I was doing. I blinked them away and then forced my hands to work.

It took me a moment to recognize it, but the song coming from the piano was "Race You to the Top of the Morning" from *The Secret Garden*. Archibald Craven's storybook goodbye to the sleeping Colin, brimming with regret and self-loathing, opened a door in my mind, and memories spilled out of it:

. . .

I stood on the pitcher's mound of the dusty ballfield at Andrew's elementary school. He was nine. He stared back at me with those sparkling, brown eyes he shared with his father. Eagerness covered his face, but a cloud of worry hung over his head.

"Ready?" I said.

"Uh-huh," he replied, sounding not-at-all ready.

"Okay, watch the ball. Close everything out of your mind and just focus on the ball and bring your bat around to meet it. You don't have to swing hard. Just bring it around and make contact with the ball. Got it?"

He nodded. We'd been at this for approximately ten minutes. Every pitch had gone by him. I could see that he was closing his eyes when he would swing, terrified of being hit by the pitch.

"Remember: Keep your eyes open so you can see the ball."

He nodded again. I threw a pitch – soft and lazy. He panicked, stepped forward, and swung with all his might well before the ball arrived.

"That was better," I said. "Your eyes were open. You saw the pitch. Now, you need to settle down, and wait for it to arrive."

He nodded again, clearly frustrated, but not wanting to admit defeat. I smiled sympathetically.

"Just breathe, Andrew. You can do this."

"You got this, Little Bro," *Ariel called from the outfield, where she waited to shag any balls he hit.*

"Okay, get in your stance," I ordered. "Here we go."

I picked up another ball, waited for him to get set, and then delivered the pitch. He waited half a second, then stepped forward with an intense look of concentration plastered on his face and swung the bat. It was his best swing yet, but he missed. The ball hit the backstop with a rattling clank. Andrew beat the end of his bat in the dirt.

"Hey, hey, hey," I said, taking a step forward. "You're okay. You're doing fine."

"No, I'm not!" he shouted. "I missed! I struck out like ten times now."

I walked over to where he stood pouting, his shoulders slumped, his gaze aimed at the ground. I put a hand on his shoulder and rubbed his back.

"Andrew, this is not an easy thing to do. The best ballplayers in the world are considered good if they can get a base hit one time in every three at-bats. Think about that. It's the only sport in the world where being successful one-third of the time means you're good.

"You can get this. I know you can. You just have to stay focused.

"That was a very good swing you had. Now, I want you to tell me something."

"What?" he said, anger dripping off the word.

"Did the ball go over the bat or under the bat?"

He looked up at me confused. I could tell he didn't know what I was trying to teach him. But my father had given me this very same lesson, and it worked like a charm.

"When you swung the bat, you missed the pitch," I said. "But did the ball go over the bat when you swung, or was it under the bat?"

I watched as he tried to recall what happened. His gaze drifted out of focus as he returned to the previous moment in time.

"Over the bat," he said.

"Good," I replied. "That's right. Do you know what that means?"

"That I suck at this, and I'll never be any good."

I smiled in spite of myself. He reminded me so much of a younger Bethany, wanting desperately to get it and being frustrated that it just wouldn't come.

"No," I said. "It means two things. First, it means you were watching the ball as it came in. You wouldn't have been able to tell me where it was in relation to the bat if you hadn't been watching. Secondly, we know that if you swung under the pitch, we can adjust to make sure we hit the ball next time."

I gave him an encouraging smile and then walked to the backstop to collect the balls that had gotten past him. I scooped them up and started heading back towards the pitcher's mound.

"Okay," I said, "let's try it again."

He looked at me doubtfully. But he returned to the batter's box and set up in his stance again.

"Ready?" I said.

"I guess."

"No, don't guess. You have to be sure. If you're not sure, you will psych yourself out and miss the pitch again."

"Okay," he said, clearly not believing me.

"Are you ready?"

"Yes," he answered, gritty determination underneath the word.

"All right, here we go."

I tossed another soft, lazy pitch to him. Andrew's face turned red, and his eyes lasered in on the ball as though it were his worst enemy. Then he stepped forward, brought the bat around, and belted the ball into left-centerfield.

The ping of the bat making contact resounded across the field. Andrew's jaw hung open, staring in stunned silence as the ball rocketed out of the infield and Ariel chased it down.

"Yes!" I crowed. "Good boy! I told you you could do it, Andrew. I'm so proud of you."

As I started the second verse of the song, I tried to close my mind off to that perfect moment. He'd been so happy, so overwhelmed by the sense of his own accomplishment. And I'd been thrilled for him. He never understood how, like any parent, my pride in his accomplishments had nothing to do with me. I was only pleased to see him get what he wanted.

It was the top of the ninth inning. Lawrence High was down three to two. There were two outs.

Andrew stood in the batter's box, facing down an oh-two count. I sat in the stands with my fingers knitted tightly together, squeezing hard, praying he was going to be okay. The home crowd at Free State High School jeered at him. They told their pitcher that he just needed one more and everyone could go home. I watched as the guy dug into the mound and smirked, confident he was going to rob my boy of any chance at glory. Lawrence High had runners at first and second. Andrew just needed to get aboard without causing anyone else to be thrown out.

The pitcher drew back, wound up, and launched a breaking ball in the direction of the plate. The pitch was off from the moment it left his hand. It was already outside. And then it broke the wrong way hitting the dirt well past the umpire and spinning towards the Lawrence High dug out. The Free State catcher scrambled to locate the ball as Andrew's teammates took off.

The catcher managed to scoop up the ball before it could roll out of play, and with a brilliant, sidearm throw zipped it to the third baseman right on time. But the throw was high, and Andrew's teammate slid into the bag.

"Safe!" the umpire cried.

The Lawrence High faithful stood up and cheered. Now, the Lions had two runners in scoring position. A contact single would at least tie the game.

"Okay, Andrew," I shouted. "You've got him!"

The Free State pitcher looked rattled from the wild pitch. I knew in my heart he was going to throw a fastball. He'd want to make sure he recovered his poise, and he was afraid that if another pitch got past the catcher, the tying run would come across home in another stolen base.

Andrew looked perfectly calm. He was down one-and-two in the count. He had no margin for error here. And he seemed completely unfazed by it. I knew then, he was going to be a hero.

The pitcher went into his windup, and just as I'd predicted, he threw his best heater. Andrew stepped in, brought his bat around, and sent the ball screaming into left-centerfield.

Everyone cheered. The left- and centerfielders raced towards each other. Andrew was already halfway to first. The runner at third flew for home like his life depended on it. I held my breath, praying the ball would not be caught.

It landed between both outfielders with a soft thump on the grass and rolled to the warning track.

I screamed so hard I thought I would lose my voice. Both runners made it home. Andrew reached second for a stand-up double. Lawrence was ahead four to three. And that would end up being the final score.

Andrew's ninth-inning heroics were all anyone could talk about. The other Lawrence High parents clapped me on the back and congratulated me. But I just shook my head. I hadn't done anything. It was all Andrew.

. . .

As I went into the song's final chorus, tears were streaming down my cheeks like someone had turned on a faucet. My voice choked with each word, and I struggled to sing the high notes.

"Climb hills to remind you," I croaked. "I love you, my boy at my side."

My hands were unable to finish the song. I tried so hard to play the last few measures, but I just couldn't. My chest was on fire, and my face was flooded. My phone rang. Without even thinking to check who it was, I picked it up and answered.

"Hello?" I sobbed.

"Bethany?" my mother said. "Honey, what's wrong?"

"Mom ..." I began, but the rest of the words stuck in my throat.

"Bethany, honey, what's the matter?"

"Mommy," I said.

I couldn't remember the last time I'd called her, "Mommy." Dear God, Andrew's email had completely gutted me.

"It's ..."

And yet I still couldn't make myself say it. I sucked in a huge breath, trying to get my crying under control enough to be able to speak.

"It's okay, Bethany," my mother said. "I'm right here. Tell me what's wrong."

"Andrew... He... He sent me this horrible email," I confessed.

"Oh, my God," my mother said.

"He told me how much he hates me. He told me I deserve to be unhappy. He said they had a party when I left town."

I started sobbing again. My mother listened in stern silence for several seconds.

"I knew it," she said.

As overwhelmed as I was with emotion, that caught my attention. What did she think she knew now?

"Knew what?"

"I had a bad feeling in my stomach today," she answered. "You were on my mind yesterday, and when I woke up, I had a strange feeling that something was wrong. I finally decided to call you to see if you were okay. Obviously, you're not."

My mom had a premonition that I was going to get bad news today?

For just a moment, I considered the possibility that I had gotten my mystic powers from my mother. She'd never shown any indication that she believed in magic, beyond taking me to church on Sunday. But she did seem to have an uncanny sense of danger and suspicion that something was about to happen, usually something bad. Maybe she had True Sight but had never been taught to develop it or her other abilities.

"I have to say, Bethany, I already had a very low opinion of those children. But for him to send you an email just to hurt you makes him even worse than I believed."

"No, Mom," I said. "He's a kid. He doesn't know what he's saying or doing."

"Bullshit, Bethany," my mother said, invoking a rare curse word. "He's seventeen years old. His brain may not be fully developed yet, but he is more than capable of taking responsibility for his actions. I don't care how badly you hurt him; that doesn't give him the right to torture you like that. Especially since you worked your butt off for those children and gave them everything you had. If that's the way he thanks you, then he's a dirty, little scoundrel who deserves every bad thing in the world."

"Mom," I begged, "please don't say things like that."

"Why not? Why can't I defend my daughter? They abused you, Bethany. They took advantage of you at every turn. And as soon as their rotten father didn't need you anymore, he threw you out. They are horrible people, Bethany."

Tears continued to stream down my face. I didn't want to hear this. I knew my mother was trying to help. I knew that she loved me. But her stern, callous judgment of everyone who didn't meet her standards was not what I needed right now. I just wanted her to sympathize with me, not vilify my children.

That was not my mother's way, though. She was the first person you'd want on your side in a crisis, because she was matter-of-fact, and her brain would focus on everything that needed to be done. But if you just needed a hug and some sympathy, Mom was not a good person to ask for it from.

"Thanks, Mom," I said. "I appreciate you being on my side."

That was the closest I could come to acknowledging her comments in a positive manner. We were wired differently, my mother and I. And though it was entirely unhelpful, it was nice that she was willing to pick up her sword and cut down anyone who messed with her baby girl.

"Honey, is there anything I can do? Do you want us to come out there?"

"No!" I said quickly.

The idea of my parents even trying to find Enchantment was ludicrous. And I could not imagine how either of them would view my friends and the strangeness of the town.

"No, Mom, I'll be all right. You just happened to call right after I'd read it, so the emotions were really raw. I'm going out with a friend tonight for dinner. That'll cheer me up."

Heh. That was a damned lie. Paul Hernandez was neither a friend, nor was he likely cheer me up. But I didn't want my mother worrying about me.

"Well, if you say so," Mom replied.

"Seriously, I'll be okay. Promise."

We talked for a few more minutes as the tears finally subsided. But the pit in my stomach did not close. Anger, pain, and self-loathing had a kegger inside my body. I hung up with Mom as quickly as I could.

"I'm so sorry, Bethany," Lucius said.

I whipped my head in his direction. He sat on the back of his favorite chair, as he usually did when I played piano. I should've expected as much, but I hadn't heard him come in, and I didn't know he was there while I was talking to my mom.

"Jesus, Lucius, you're going to give me a heart attack."

"Forgive me," he said. "I heard you playing, so I came to listen. After your mother called and I heard what happened, I thought you might need a friendly face."

"That's eavesdropping," I said as I wiped away tears. "But thanks."

He hopped down off the chair, strolled over to me, and leaped into my lap. I started stroking his ears immediately. His fur was so soft, and though I'd never really been a cat person, I found him incredibly comforting.

"What is wrong with me, Lucius?"

"What do you mean?"

"Why do they hate me so much? How could I have been such a bad person that he would send me such a vitriolic email? I mean, he really hates me, Lucius. He made sure I understood that."

"You're not a bad person, Bethany. You were with the wrong family. You're with the right one now. You are loved and appreciated for who you are by everyone here."

"Maybe you just don't know me well enough yet," I said, unable to keep the bitter tone from my voice.

"You saved everyone here, Bethany. You didn't do that because you were evil. You didn't do it because you thought it would be fun or because you wanted to. You broke the Curse of Ellington Manor and protected Sheriff Mueller from Karl Markiewicz because it was the right thing to do. You knew that, and you acted because you could.

"I honestly don't know what could've happened with your former family to have made them revile you. But I do know that those people did not appreciate who they had. No matter what you did, casting you as a monster is wrong."

I sniffled and stroked his head some more. I wanted so very badly to believe him. I had indeed tried my best to give Jess, Ariel, and Andrew everything they needed. But somehow, I'd gotten it all wrong. And given the way I was raised, I could only interpret that as me being a screwup. Thanks, Mom.

I sighed heavily and stroked Lucius's head a little more. God, I just wanted to feel good. Why was that so hard for me to maintain over an extended period of time?

"Thanks, Lucius. I appreciate you looking after me."

"Any time," he replied.

I stood, spilling him back to the floor. He didn't complain, just wound himself around my legs. Truly, the best part of my divorce had been acquiring a cat.

"Come on," I said. "I'm hungry. And I think there is some tuna fish in the pantry.

"Right behind you," he said.

We set off for the kitchen, me feeling marginally better. But the pain in my chest had not really subsided, and I struggled to believe I would ever be whole.

Six

I met Paul in the parking lot for Titania's Garden. It was large and mostly empty. There was only one other car – a nondescript blue Chevy, which I presumed was Sheriff Mueller's. But otherwise, the place didn't appear to be busy tonight.

As soon as I put my vehicle in "Park," I got nervous. I couldn't actually see the restaurant. The only thing besides my vehicle and the sheriff's was an enormous oak tree growing in the center. This felt like a setup.

Paul showed two minutes later, parked in the space next to mine, and got out. A lump formed in my throat, and I couldn't help but feel nervous. Was he planning to kidnap me? Murder me? Get me to follow him me to some secret location, where my friends couldn't help me?

With a heavy sigh and swallowing hard, I opened the door. Paul looked me up and down after I exited the SUV and smirked.

"I thought I told you to dress elegantly," he chided.

I contemplated giving him the finger, but since I needed information from him tonight, I decided to pretend to be polite.

"Sorry, it was the best I could do. I'm still unpacking."

"Well," he said, "I'm glad you could make it."

Yeah. I bet he did, since he was expecting me to pay for this.

"Shall we?" he said and indicated we should walk towards the tree.

There wasn't very much lighting in the parking lot, and every fear a woman has about walking in darkness without someone she knows and trusts leaped immediately into my mind. I wanted to believe I was safe, but I didn't trust Paul Hernandez one whit. I flicked my eyes over to the Chevy, hoping to see the sheriff sitting behind the wheel. But it was too dark. I couldn't tell if the car was occupied or not.

When we made it to the enormous oak, I saw no doors. I looked up into the branches but couldn't make anything out.

"Please tell me this is not a treehouse that we have to climb up to," I said.

Paul chuckled. A condescending smile slid up his face. I desperately wanted to smack it off.

"No," he said.

He reached up and knocked on the trunk of the tree – knock-knock, knock-knock, knock-knock. Then he waited. A moment later, pink light formed in a rectangle on the tree in front of us. With a loud click, the bark swung outward, forming a door. Inside, was a space that was too large for the tree to have reasonably contained. I remembered Sheriff Mueller telling me that Titania's Garden was only partially on this plane of existence. It seemed that "partially" meant the door was here, and everywhere else was … elsewhere.

Cold panic hit my heart. The sheriff had promised to watch my back. If I was stepping into another realm, how was he supposed to do that?

Paul made another sweeping gesture, indicating I should step inside. My hands shook, and I had to swallow twice to summon up the nerve to move forward. For the gajillionth time in my life, I heard my mother say I would be found dead in a ditch somewhere. Sucking in one more breath, I stepped across the threshold.

The interior of the place was vast. It was warm and humid and covered in dense foliage. Despite the fact that we had just stepped inside of a tree, there were bushes and trees and vines everywhere, as though this were some great, temperate wooded grove. Paul stepped inside and shut the door behind him. Suddenly, I felt trapped, cut off from the world I knew and understood – strange and magical though Enchantment might be.

A *maître d'* stood in a powder-blue tuxedo straight out of the Seventies. He was short – only about five-six or five-seven – but he was absolutely beautiful. His skin was so fair it reminded me of snow. A light dusting of freckles ran across his upper cheeks and his nose. His hair was black as night, a stark contrast from his pale skin. But his most entrancing feature was his eyes. The irises were a soft shade of lavender. Unlike Drogo's silver eyes that I could drown in, these unnerved me. They were bewitching, but in a frightening way that warned me to watch everything I said.

"Do you have a reservation?" *The maître d'* asked in a voice that was both musical and threatening.

"Yes," Paul said, stepping forward. "Paul Hernandez, reservation for two, seven o'clock."

The *maître d'* dropped his lavender gaze to the reservation book in front of him. He scanned it briefly, before returning his attention to us.

"Yes, I have you right here."

He reached under the podium and withdrew two leatherbound menus. Then he fixed us with a smile that looked more like a leer.

"If you'd care to follow me?" he said.

He turned and set off into the heart of the restaurant.

I'd never been any place like this before. I could not see the sky, but I definitely felt as though we were outdoors, or at least in some giant arboretum. Everywhere I looked, there were trees and bushes. We walked along a path that, so far as I could tell, was made of dirt. It wound around the bushes and between the trees, and in every little alcove and clearing, there was a table with seated diners. In fact, every single table seemed to be occupied, and I heard snatches of conversations in English, Spanish, French, Japanese, and one or two others I didn't recognize.

As *the maître d'* led us deeper and deeper into the forest, strange insects larger than dragonflies zipped back and forth in great numbers. The air was so warm and thick that, in my sweater, I quickly became overheated. I was definitely wishing I had worn a dress.

At last, our guide through this vernal realm turned sharply to his left, and we found ourselves in a tiny clearing. A table of natural wood stood before us. It was asymmetrical, giving me the impression it was made of driftwood. But it was polished to a fine sheen as though some skilled artisan had fashioned it into this very shape on purpose. It sat under an enormous tree, whose branches overhung it, forming a canopy. Globes of soft, white light were suspended from the branches, but I could detect no electricity or other power source for them. I couldn't help but feel as though I were about to dine in some storybook, enchanted forest.

"Here we are," the *maître d'* said, pulling out one of the chairs for me.

"Thank you," I said.

I was barely settled when he pushed it in, his thin body apparently hiding considerable strength. Paul seated himself across from me, *the maître d'* put the menus down in front of us.

"Your server will be with you momentarily," he said.

Then he turned and vanished into the thicket.

I glanced around. It was difficult to see the rest of the restaurant. Each booth seemed to be secluded by natural vegetation. I suspected many of the patrons who dined here appreciated the privacy.

"Half of Enchantment must be here tonight," I commented. "I only saw one other car in the parking lot, but every table we passed was full."

"So far as I know," Paul said, opening his menu, "we are the only ones here from Enchantment. The restaurant itself is located in the fairy kingdom of Avalon. There are entrances all over the world. The portal through which we entered is only one."

As much as that made sense to me, I was still absolutely stunned by it. I was in another world for real? And not just any world: Avalon, the home of fairies? It suddenly occurred to me that Titania's Garden was no mere name. Assuming that Shakespeare had got it right and Titania was indeed the queen of all fairies, perhaps I was out about to have dinner in her actual home.

"What if we leave by the wrong door?" I asked, suddenly worried. "Could we, like, end up in India or Russia or somewhere?"

Paul flashed me the condescending smile an adult gives a child. It was all I could do not to smack him across the face with my menu.

"Don't worry," he said. "The fairies ensure everyone leaves by the same portal through which they entered."

I nodded. It really didn't give me a lot of comfort, because I was still relying on people I didn't know to do the right thing. My mother's hypervigilance suggested that was a bad idea. But I was here now. It wasn't like I had much of a choice.

Five of those strange insects suddenly flitted over to the table. But they weren't insects at all. They were fairies. They hovered at the edge of our table, four of them holding up a tray with two glasses of water on it. The fifth tapped a wand on the edge of the tray, conjuring pink sparkles into the air. A moment later, the glasses levitated and floated gently to the table in front of us.

I had to admit that was a pretty good trick.

"Greetings," the fairy with the wand said. "I am Merrylaugh. I will be your server for tonight."

I studied her for a moment. She was every bit as beautiful as *the maître d'*. She stood, maybe a foot-and-a-half to two feet high, with gossamer insect wings sprouting from her back and beating swiftly to hold her aloft. She wore a shimmering dress of green that sparkled in the light. Two antennae sprouted from her head, which was adorned with long, golden hair. Her skin was fair, and her eyes were oblong and black – alien-looking with no whites or irises.

"We have two specials tonight," Merrylaugh went on. "The first is an enchanted ribeye steak, braised with red-apple jelly and topped with blue cheese crumbles. It is served with potatoes au gratin and buttered asparagus.

"The second is a Cobb salad with enchanted ham and turkey, dressed with magical raspberry vinaigrette. Are you ready to order?"

"I think we'd like a moment to look over the menu first," Paul said.

"Very good, sir," Merrylaugh replied. "I will return shortly."

With that, she and her assistants flitted away. I shook my head.

"I'll give you credit, Paul, this place is something else. "

"Well, I couldn't very well take you somewhere pedestrian like Drogo's."

"Ha! Especially since I'm paying?"

He smiled and shrugged. I grabbed the waterglass and had several big gulps. Partially, I didn't want him to see me scowl. But I was also overwarm from the humidity.

"What did she mean when she said, 'enchanted steak'?" I asked after I set the glass back down.

"Fairies do not believe in killing and eating animals," Paul answered. "However, human customers expect to be able to order gourmet meat dishes at an upscale restaurant. Since fairy magic is largely illusion and glamour, they enchant edible plant material to taste and look like the food their patrons desire."

Once again, I found myself utterly amazed. Plant-based meats were all the rage in the vegan community of the mundane world. But fairies apparently took it to a whole other level.

Nevertheless, I was alarmed. Before I left for the dinner, Dorigen had stopped me in the foyer.

"Here," she said, thrusting a pendant at me.

I'd taken a moment to examine it. It was a small, flat stone with a hole in the center of it that a black cord had been strung through.

"What's this?" I asked.

"It's a self-bored stone," she answered. "The hole in the center was made by water erosion, not a drill. It's supposed to ward you against fairy magic. Might work; might not. Especially since you'll be surrounded by it. But since you are no doubt walking into a trap, or at the very least, a giant mess you've got no idea how to deal with, maybe this will offer you some protection."

I was touched. Dorigen had been angry at me ever since March began. Then she'd been downright furious when I traded Alexander Ellington's cane to Marcel Truffaut in exchange for his rescuing Sheriff Mueller. But ever since I'd arrived in Enchantment, she'd treated me like she was my mother, or at the very least, my grumpy, old aunt. She cared about me, and despite the fact that I knew she objected to me undertaking this mission in the first place, she was trying to help. I was reminded of Lucius's words earlier in the day, when he told me everyone loved and respected me.

Speaking of my cat-familiar, he had also waited at the door to send me off.

"Good luck, Bethany," he said. "Be careful. And maybe don't drink any ambrosia."

"What's that?" I asked.

"Magical fairy wine," Dorigen said, her tone covered in scorn. "If you thought the night you got sick on whiskey at a frat party was bad, Missy, you surely don't want to be messing with ambrosia."

I nodded. Suddenly, this whole date sounded even more dangerous than I had already believed.

"Thanks," I said.

Back at the restaurant, I flipped my menu open. Hopefully, there was some sort of vegetarian dish I could eat that wouldn't trigger Dorigen's ward.

But everything was written in a strange language I didn't recognize, let alone could read. Because of course it was. Why should this be easy?

"What language is this?" I said.

"The menus are written in Gaelic," Paul answered. "But they're enchanted so that the words appear in whatever language you read. Can you not see English in yours?"

"No," I said.

Vaguely, I wondered if the self-bored stone was defeating the magic, or if there was some other issue I needed to be worried about.

"Here," Paul said, "let's trade menus. Mine seems to be working."

He passed his across to me, and I handed him mine. But when I cracked it open, I still saw only Gaelic.

"This one's not working for me either," I said.

Paul cocked his head. A perplexed look landed on his face as he knitted his brow.

"That's very strange," he said. "I've never heard of that before. Perhaps your Sight sees through to the true words instead of the illusion."

That was a good theory. I wasn't convinced it was right, but whether it was that or Dorigen's pendant, the menu might as well have been Greek to me. And since Paul was willing to pass it off as my powers, I let it drop.

"It's no problem," I said. "I'll just have one of the specials."

No sooner had I said that, than Merrylaugh appeared at the table as though I had summoned her. Perhaps I had.

"Are you ready to order then?" she asked.

"I am if you are," I said.

"Certainly," Paul replied.

"What can I get for you, ma'am," the fairy asked.

"I'd like the Cobb salad," I said. "But could I have that without meat?"

"Very good, ma'am. And you, sir?"

"Enchanted Chicken Parmesan, with Italian dressing on the salad."

"And to drink?" Merrylaugh prodded.

"A bottle of ambrosia," Paul said.

"I'll just stick with water," I said.

"Very good, folks."

She withdrew her wand and tapped my glass. It magically refilled to the brim. Then, she zoomed away again, sounding very much like a giant bee.

Suddenly, I found myself unsure what to do. Now that the food was ordered, it was time to get down to business. But I had no idea how to begin.

"I want to thank you again for looking into Sheriff Mueller's background for me," I said, hoping stroking his ego would be a good start.

"Well, that's what this dinner is all about."

God, he was irritating. All he needed to say was, "You're welcome," or "My pleasure," or some other polite thing. Instead, he reminded me I was in his debt. What an asshole.

"Yes, but it really made a difference," I said, trying to keep my temper under control. "If I hadn't known about Karl Markiewicz, I wouldn't have been able to save the sheriff."

"*You* saved him?" Paul said, raising his eyebrows. "He told me he was rescued by a pair of random wolves."

I couldn't tell if that remark was misogynist disbelief that a woman could have fixed the situation, or if he just thought I was a total rube incapable of rescuing a wolf-shifter in deep trouble. Regardless, it pissed me off. I decided to show a little of my hand.

"Yeah, well," I said with a small grin and a shrug my shoulders, "I arranged that."

Paul's eyes opened wide at that remark. Was he was feigning surprise, or was he genuinely impressed?

"Really?" he said. "Do tell."

And just like that, I was on the defensive. God, I was such a horrible spy. I'd let him bruise my ego and reacted by giving him information I didn't want him to have.

"Not tonight," I said, sipping some more water.

This time, he genuinely *was* surprised. He probably wasn't used to being spoken to like that. Good.

"Why, Ms. Parker," he drawled. "So cagey."

I arched an eyebrow at him, reasserting control over the conversation.

"Very well," he conceded. "Another time, perhaps."

"Perhaps," I replied, but I was thinking there was no way in hell that was ever going to happen.

"Well," Paul said, after sipping his own water, "if there is ever anyone else you need me to snoop around on, please don't hesitate to ask."

He couldn't have set me up better.

"Actually," I said, "there is someone."

"Oh?"

"Yes, what do you know about a vampire named Marcel Truffaut?"

Paul didn't answer right away. He simply stared, his brown-eyed gaze attempting to penetrate my smiling *façade*. I blinked and had a few more sips of water.

"What about Marcel Truffaut?" he asked at last, suspicion dripping from every word.

I put my water glass back on the table and shrugged.

"He claims he got you your job," I said. "And that you're supposed to be helping him acquire one of Alexander Ellington's artifacts. He didn't say which one. Or why."

The corners of Paul's mouth turned down in a sour frown. I could tell I'd hit a nerve even without my Sight.

"I have a Master's degree in Library Science," he growled. "I'm a professional archivist. I'm also an accomplished techno-mage. No one 'got me my job,' Bethany. I earned it."

"Of course, you did," I assured him, reveling in turning the tables on him. "My impression of Marcel Truffaut is that he thinks very highly of himself. He takes full credit for things he only had a partial hand in, when truly, he's at best a behind-the-scenes manipulator. He's arrogant and overconfident."

Naturally, I was really describing Paul. Some of what I said did indeed apply to the arrogant vampire, but my words were intended to hurt my dinner companion. It wasn't exactly nice, And I thought to myself that I should probably lay off if I really wanted information from him. But I was so tired of his condescension that I could not resist getting a few licks in.

"How do you know Marcel Truffaut?" Paul said, lasering his gaze at me as if it could strip me of my secrets.

"He's an old accomplice of Declan's apparently," I answered. "The two of them were cooking up some plan for Ellington Manor before Maggie Cartwright enacted her curse, taking Declan out of the picture.

"He stopped by the house the other day and asked a bunch of questions about you, spun that fanciful tale about how he got you your job, wanted to know what you were doing, and told us you were supposed to be helping him."

I let that land with the weight of a brick. Neither Paul nor I truly knew what the other person's involvement with Truffaut was. But I'd made it plain that I knew Truffaut, and I was beyond certain, based on his reaction to my making the claim, that Marcel Truffaut had indeed gotten him his job. Whatever else the vampire had told us, that part of it was true. And unless Declan had lied to me, I could be certain that their quest to acquire all of Ellington's artifacts was also true. So, it was logical to assume that everything I just put out there was accurate. For his part, Paul did his best to hide the truth from me. But I knew he was lying.

"What was this 'plot they were cooking up'?" Paul asked, clumsily attempting to learn just how much I actually knew.

"I couldn't say," I answered. "They wouldn't tell me. But if they're searching for any of Alexander Ellington's artifacts, it cannot possibly be good.

"You don't know anything, do you?"

I blinked innocently at him. He continued to probe me with his gaze, but I was fully in control of the conversation. I gave him nothing.

"I know Marcel Truffaut is a very dangerous vampire," he answered. "And if you have any suspicions about him, Declan, or anyone else for that matter, seeking or recovering any of the artifacts, you need to report it to me immediately."

I threw him the mommy look Ariel and Andrew knew so well. Anyone who had been a parent for any amount of time developed a finely tuned nose for bullshit. Nothing indicated a child trying to cover something up better than misdirection about the shape or subject of the conversation. So, I did what I always did with the kids: I restated the facts and invited him to try again.

"I'm telling you everything I know right now," I lied. "And Truffaut said you were helping him with the artifacts."

"I'm the Order representative in town, Bethany. Those artifacts are extremely dangerous. The Order wants possession of them all, so they can be locked away in a safe place where they won't do any harm. Any interest I have in them is purely Order business."

I smiled. Andrew was a better liar than this. I was kind of offended that Paul thought I couldn't see through him. He'd clearly never had children.

"If you say so," I said, making certain he knew I thought it was bullshit.

"I'm serious, Bethany. Don't play games with this. If you hear or see anything to do with Alexander Ellington's artifacts, you need to tell me immediately."

Fury ignited in my heart. I was damned sick of the implication that I was playing some sort of game. I *knew* this was serious business. And I knew his ass was deep in it. I was tired of being patronized.

But before I could lay into him, the food arrived. Ten fairies carrying two trays flew into view and hovered at the edge of the table. Merrylaugh zipped behind them and tapped the plates with our entrees. The dishes glowed with magical light before lifting themselves into the air and floating gently to rest in front of us. I couldn't help but think of "Be our Guest" in *Beauty & the Beast*.

She waved it again, and two wine glasses materialized on the table. The winged servers brought the second tray forward. An intricate, green-glass bottle sat on it. Merrylaugh tapped her wand to the top, and the cork rocketed off it with a loud pop, reminiscent of champagne. But the contents didn't fizz over. Instead, the bottle levitated off the tray like all the other food had and gently filled the first class with a rich, amber liquid that looked like a combination of sparkling wine and brown ale. I could see bubbles dancing in it, but once again, there was no foam.

With the first glass filled, the bottle moved to the second.

"None for me, please," I said.

All ten fairies looked at me in shock.

"You have to try little," Paul said.

"You're not getting me drunk tonight," I replied.

Merrylaugh tittered.

"I wouldn't think of it," Paul said.

Bullshit, I thought.

I should've told him when he ordered a bottle I wouldn't be drinking any. But after telling Merrylaugh I'd only wanted water, that should have sent the message.

"Regardless," Paul went on, "to refuse any is to insult their hospitality. It won't go well if you do that."

God damn it. One more thing I didn't know about the magical world. I couldn't tell who was worse – me for continuing to blindly stumble into these problems, or my friends for not arming me with critical information.

"Just a small glass," I said.

Merrylaugh nodded and tapped the bottle with her wand. It tipped and filled the glass as full as Paul's. I sighed.

"Thank you," I said, trying to sound sincere.

"Of course!" Merrylaugh said.

And then she and her cadre of fairy servers flitted away, chuckling as they went. I threw Paul a cross look.

"You should've said something before it arrived," I said.

"Forgive me," he replied, "it didn't occur to me you wouldn't be having any."

"No, damn it, I do not forgive you. You were paying attention when

I told Merrylaugh I wouldn't be having anything to drink besides water. You're manipulating me. Just like you always do. I've really had it with your attitude."

"My *attitude*?"

"Yes!" I said. "You're sanctimonious and always act like I'm stupid. You and everyone else in this damned town want to treat me like a child, because I wasn't raised in the magical world. I may not have grown up with all the things you did, but I am an intelligent woman who has lived a lot of life. And I have done things here no one else has been able to do. I broke the Curse of Ellington Manor without you even knowing about it. I may have needed information from you, but it was me who saved Sheriff Mueller.

"So put away your bullshit condescension and start treating me with respect."

Paul had the decency to look shocked at my outburst. Honestly, I wasn't entirely sure where it came from. But I supposed that my emotions were still pretty raw after Andrew's devastating email.

"I'm sorry," I said. "It's been kind of a rough day."

"Apology accepted," he replied. "I know you're not interested in drinking tonight, but can I persuade you to try one sip of the ambrosia? It really is a specialty of the house."

I glowered at him. I was feeling incredibly manipulated. But I thought that perhaps if I did as he asked, I might be able to turn the conversation back in a better direction.

"All right," I relented, "one."

He raised his glass and waited. Good Lord, he wanted a toast as well? Trying not to grimace I raised my glass.

"To you, Bethany," he drawled. "An accomplished woman in her own right."

I clinked glasses with him. Then I had a sip.

The flavor was unbelievable. I was immediately hit with strong notes of apples and pears and … was that licorice? I felt as though I were floating away. My spirit seemed to expand and permeate the entire restaurant. As I swallowed, the delightful elixir left an aftertaste of honey and lilac on my tongue. And every negative thought I'd had only a moment before – indeed, every hurt I'd been dealing with all day –

seemed to evaporate. I couldn't remember such an entrancing sensation.

"If you thought the night you got sick on whiskey at a frat party was bad, Missy," Dorigen said, *"you surely don't want to be messing with ambrosia."*

Oh, shit. No wonder Paul had been insistent that I try some ambrosia. He had known what affect it would have on me. Meanwhile, he let only the tiniest amount of the amber liquid past his lips.

He'd tricked me again. I wanted to be angry. But the aftereffects of the wine were so extraordinary that I had no ability to summon even a tiny fraction of my fury. I took a deep breath in through my nose, the scent of the ambrosia still haunting my nostrils and tastebuds. I put the glass back on the table and pushed it away.

"Potent stuff," I said, an accusatory note in my tone.

"Yes, indeed," he replied.

We ate mostly in silence. Dorigen's charm penetrated the fairy magic just as I had feared it would. Though the "meats" had been left off my Cobb salad, the whole thing had a vaguely woody aftertaste – like sawdust maybe. Perhaps it was the magical raspberry vinaigrette or maybe the fairies used enchanted vegetables, too. Regardless, the eggs didn't taste quite like eggs, the cheese was dry, and even the lettuce tasted like it had been rubbed on the dirt floor. For as much money as I presumed they were charging me, I was terribly underwhelmed. Briefly, I thought of having another sip of the ambrosia to try to sweeten the food. But I worried that if I did, I would be unable to resist drinking the entire glass – and perhaps another after that.

When we did speak. It was small talk. We chatted about how relieved we were that the cold snap that had so afflicted the town had not returned. I mentioned that Dorigen had said it was an ill wind that brought it. Paul smiled as though she were superstitious, but I knew she'd been right.

As I put the last bite of unsatisfying lettuce into my mouth, Merrylaugh reappeared at our table.

"How was everything?" she asked.

I bit my cheeks so as to avoid answering honestly. If they would be insulted by my refusing to accept the ambrosia, I couldn't imagine what the reaction might be if I'd had the gall to admit I didn't like the food.

"Exquisite," Paul said, "as always."

"Agreed," I said, nodding.

Hopefully, Merrylaugh couldn't see through my lie.

"May I bring you anything for dessert? We have a *crème brulé* and a raspberry cheesecake."

The cheesecake sounded divine, but I feared it would be as awful as the rest of the food.

"No thank you," I said, praying I wasn't making a mistake. "I am absolutely stuffed."

"None for me, either," Paul said.

He'd either chosen to be merciful to me by not ordering dessert and making me look bad, or it was actually okay to refuse.

"I think we'd just like the check now, please," I said.

"Very good, ma'am."

With a rapid buzzing of her wings, she raced off to the kitchen.

"What time is it?" Paul said absently.

He reached into his suitcoat and pulled out a pocket watch, flipping it open.

"Here you are, ma'am," Merrylaugh said.

I practically jumped out of my skin, screeching in alarm. One second, she wasn't there. The next she was.

Frightened by my outburst, she flew backwards a bit and hugged the folder with the check in it to her chest like a shield. I blinked several times. What happened? I looked at Paul. He stared back in surprise. Something was different about him, but I couldn't figure out what it was.

"I'm so sorry, ma'am," Merrylaugh said. "I didn't mean to startle you."

"That's okay," I said, my voice, far away.

I felt strange. The beginnings of a headache began to creep around my eyes. Was this the aftereffects of the ambrosia, or something else?

"Here's the check you requested, ma'am," Merrylaugh said as she cautiously flew towards me again.

I reached out and took it from her. I tried to smile by way of apology, but I'm pretty sure it looked more like a grimace.

"Does this include your gratuity?" I asked.

"It does, ma'am. Thank you for asking."

"Of course," I said.

Digging in my purse for my wallet, I pulled out my credit card and stuffed it inside the leather check-holder before handing it back to her.

"I'll return in a flash, ma'am," Merrylaugh said. Then she looked mortified. "But I'll endeavor not to frighten you this time."

"Think nothing of it," I said.

I tried to chuckle, but it came out more as a cackle. Merrylaugh looked concerned for another moment before she flitted away.

"Are you all right?" Paul said.

"I don't know," I replied. "I can't ... I can't remember what I was thinking about."

"The fairy must have frightened it right out of your brain," Paul quipped.

I considered his joke seriously for a moment. No, that wasn't it. I had a very strange sensation in my head, as though there were someone else in my mind.

"Why did she just materialize like that?" I asked.

"I don't follow," Paul said.

"Every other time, she's flown up to the table. Her appearances were sudden, but she didn't just teleport in. Why would she do that?"

"She didn't teleport, Bethany. She flew over from the kitchen like every other time."

Paul looked at me with great concern. I shared it. What the hell just happened to me?

"I would've sworn she wasn't there before she appeared. I was looking in that direction. I should've seen her approach."

"Your mind must have wandered, Bethany. It's not surprising. This place is filled with magic. You've never been here before, and your Sight has been messing with your perception."

I nodded. Yeah, I guess that made sense. But I still felt odd.

Merrylaugh returned, flying slowly and lazily to make certain I would see her approach. I smiled at her to reassure her.

"Here you are, ma'am," she said, setting the folder down in front of me. "Your credit card, and your receipt are inside."

"Thank you," I said. "Sorry about before."

"Think nothing of it, ma'am. It was a pleasure waiting on both of you tonight. Do come again."

"We shall," Paul said.

"The *maître d'* will return in a moment to escort you out," she said.

Then, she dashed away, disappearing into the lush greenery as though she had never existed.

A moment later, the lavender-eyed *maître d'* stepped into our alcove.

"If you'd like to follow me?" he said.

We stood and went after him. This must be how they assured that all guests left through the same door they came in.

As we wound through the trees following the path, I continued to feel disoriented. Nothing looked the same as it had when we came in, and I realized I was sweating through my pants. I was incredibly uncomfortable and a bit unsteady on my feet.

At last, we were back in the lobby. The door opened as we approached it, spilling pink light into the dark parking lot back in Enchantment. We stepped out, and I was immediately assaulted by the chill of the air. It hadn't been especially cold tonight, but the drastic change in temperature from the restaurant to the real world made it feel as though we'd walked out onto the North Pole.

"Thank you again for dinner," Paul said. "I enjoyed every minute of it."

That seemed like an odd remark, since he'd been insulted by Marcel Truffaut's claim that he'd been responsible for Paul getting his job. But my head spun too fast for me to remark on it.

"You're welcome," I said instead.

"Until next time, Bethany."

He got into his car, started it, and drove away leaving me alone. Figures. A real man would've made certain I was safely inside my vehicle before leaving. Not only was it unlikely that Paul had children, it seemed to me he'd never even had sex.

The door of the blue Chevy opened, and Sheriff Mueller got out. He walked straight towards me, steam coming from his mouth.

"You all right?" he asked.

I wasn't sure how to answer. I was mostly definitely not "all right." But I couldn't have told him what was wrong. The headache intensified.

"Yeah," I said.

He heard the uncertainty in my voice.

"You sure? What happened in there?"

"I sweated my ass off, because it was like summer inside," I answered. "Paul was evasive and mostly a dick. The food wasn't very good. So, I guess I'm fine, but I feel like shit, if that makes sense."

He nodded. I read concern in his eyes, but he didn't push me.

"Okay, Parker. Drive safely on your way home. Call me if you need anything."

"Thanks," I replied. "I will."

That was kind of a lie. I couldn't imagine what I might need him for. But I sensed he wanted to feel needed, so I threw him a bone.

I opened my SUV and climbed inside. Unlike, Paul, Sheriff Mueller waited for me to get into my vehicle and start it up. I waved a thanks to him as I put it in gear.

Now that I was outside of Avalon, the headache I'd felt before got going full-blast. It felt as if four or five burly men had set up shop inside my brain and taken jackhammers to my skull. I groaned and started towards home.

It had been a long time since I'd been out to a fancy restaurant with a man. After tonight, I couldn't imagine ever wanting to do it again.

Seven

I walked through utter blackness. I could see perfectly fine. But there was nothing around – just a black floor and a black horizon. I had no idea where I was or what was happening. Yet it all felt terribly familiar.

After an indeterminate amount of time, I could see something up ahead. My steps quickened, as I rushed to get away from this complete nothingness.

Almost at once, I came across an enormous, red-brick wall. It stretched away to infinity in either direction, and it rose so high I could not see the top. Wherever I was, this seemed to be the end.

I turned to my left and was immediately drenched with an overwhelming sense of dread, of certainty that only terror lay that way. I looked to my right, and just off in the distance was Dori.

My eyes opened wide in surprise at the sight of her. She'd been Dorigen ever since I'd broken the curse on the manor. But here was eighteen-year-old Dori in her black housekeeper dress with the white apron, her porcelain skin practically glowing, and her red hair tied back in a tight bun. I was so surprised to see her, I couldn't think of anything to say.

She raised her right hand and beckoned to me. Unsure what else to do, I followed.

We walked a short distance, hugging the impassable wall as we went. And then, we walked into the library of Ellington Manor.

That was only slightly less surprising than seeing Dori. I almost never went into the library, although I'd been there just yesterday when Paul had visited.

Dori walked without hesitation over to one of the bookshelves. There, she withdrew a large tome bound in blue leather. She turned back to me, cracked it open, and flipped pages until she found what she was looking for. The spine of the book read, "William Shakespeare – The Complete Works."

"Beware the Ides of March," Dori read.

I cocked my head. Why was she reading from Julius Caesar?

Then, she exploded into bats, and their leather wings filled my vision.

♪

I woke up the next morning feeling like shit. The memory of the headache haunted my brain and made me feel as though the pain would return at any moment. I was vaguely nauseous, as though whatever I did actually eat the night before at Titania's Garden was plotting revenge against me. My mouth was dry.

With a heavy sigh, I sat up and rubbed my temples, hoping to stave off the return of my headache. My eyes were bleary. Groaning like an old woman, I forced myself out of bed. As soon as my bare feet hit the cold, hardwood floor, I was shocked back to myself. My vision cleared and the threat of a migraine and vomiting receded.

Not that I felt better.

I stumbled to the bathroom, did my business, and tried to remember everything that had happened last night. The disagreeable dinner date with Paul had yielded no information beyond my conclusion that Truffaut had been telling us the truth about Enchantment's Order representative. And then of course, there was the strange sensation of the missing memory and the disturbing dream with Dori. As the image of her exploding into bats flitted through my mind, it occurred to me that it couldn't be coincidence that she had led me to the library. It was a room I never visited. So, between Paul's unwelcome appearance there the day before and last night's vision, I felt certain that whatever Dori wanted me to find was there.

With something resembling a mission to work with, I threw on some clothes and took a few minutes to make myself look presentable. Then I went downstairs. But instead of taking my usual path to the kitchen, I diverted course and went to the library instead.

When I got there, I found Lucius sitting on the back of a red-leather chair and staring intently at a bookcase. It was the exact same thing I'd seen him do a week or so ago. More evidence that I was onto something.

"Good morning," I said. He didn't answer, continuing to stare, mesmerized, at the bookcase. "Lucius?"

"Hmm?" he said.

He turned his head in my direction, and then a look of recognition danced across his face, as though some spell had been broken.

"Oh, Bethany, I didn't hear you come in."

"Yeah, I noticed. What are you doing?"

"Oh, I was just ..." He looked around as though he had walked into the room and didn't recognize it. "I'm afraid I don't know what I was doing. In fact, I don't even remember coming in here."

That alarmed me. Aside from his occasional, comical, cat-like behavior, Lucius was the most stable and sensible person in the house. For him to appear discombobulated and have no memory of how he got here deeply concerned me.

"Are you all right?" I asked.

"Oh, yes ... I just ... I just thought I ... heard something."

"You thought you heard something?" I said, making my skepticism plain.

He didn't answer right away. He seemed to be searching his mind for some answer that made sense to him.

"Yes, I'm sure that was it," he pronounced. "What are you doing here?"

"Looking for a book," I answered, making it clear that I did not believe him.

"Which one?"

"*The Complete Works of Shakespeare*," I said.

"Ah, well, happy hunting." He hopped down off the chair. "What time is it?"

I stopped cold. *What time is it?* That question had a haunting, familiar ring – like it was an important memory. But I couldn't put my finger on what it was, and when I tried, it evaporated from my mind. I dug my phone out of my pocket and checked it.

"It's eight thirty-three," I said.

"Oh, good," Lucius said. "Dorigen probably has breakfast ready."

He sauntered out without saying goodbye or giving any further explanation for his behavior.

I shook my head and returned my attention to my original mission. Crossing the room, I went to the bookcase Dori had been standing near in my dream. Once I was there, I looked around, checking to make sure I was in the exact same spot. I examined the shelves. Sure enough, the blue-leather volume was right where Dori had extracted it.

But there was one major difference: It wasn't Shakespeare.

Instead, the book's title was *Advanced Summoning Practices*. I blinked in stunned surprise. That couldn't be right. I remembered the book and the passage Dori read distinctly.

I looked the shelf over carefully. None of the books on it contained Shakespeare or any other British poet. And *Advanced Summoning Practices* was the only one bound in blue leather.

Confused, I pulled it out and cracked it open. The cover didn't lie. It was a technical manual for how to bring otherworldly beings like demons and djinni to Earth. As I flipped through the pages, I came across a few diagrams and sigils, but it was otherwise nothing but complex spells written in an English dialect that sounded like it had been penned by Jules Verne or H.G. Wells. Out of curiosity, I flipped to the copyright page. The book had been published in 1898.

"All right," I said aloud. "Just what the hell does *this* mean?"

♫

Half an hour later, I walked into Drogo's in desperate need of coffee. As usual, Rhoda had beaten me there and staked out a booth. Not that she probably had to. Despite it being, nine-thirty, the breakfast crowd was pretty thin.

"No!" one of the few patrons cried. "*Poached* eggs. Poached! They don't come in a coach."

"Coming right up, sir," Helio said.

He flitted away to the kitchen. I raised my eyebrows in concern. How much damage was the cherub doing to Drogo's business?

"Oh, my God, what happened?" Rhoda said as I sat down in the booth.

Her face was covered in concern. She looked at me as though I just gone eight rounds with Mike Tyson.

"What do you mean?" I asked.

"You look terrible," she said.

I shrugged as I grabbed the menu.

"I need coffee," I said.

"No, I'm serious, Bethany," Rhoda said. "Your aura is really dark, like you're sick or something."

I raised my eyebrows at that. So far as I knew, I wasn't ill. I felt fine – well, maybe not fine. I was hungry and in dire need of caffeine. And emotionally I was still pretty wrecked. Was that what she meant?

Before I could ask, Helio arrived at the table.

"Good morning, ladies," he said in a cheerful, high-pitched voice. "What can I bring you?"

I couldn't help but think that that was a loaded question, given that you never knew what Helio might deliver to the table.

"I need coffee, stat," I said. "And scrambled eggs with hash browns, please."

"Coffee and a bagel," Rhoda said.

"Be right back with that," the cherub replied.

He zipped away. I said a silent prayer that he couldn't screw up scrambled eggs and hash browns. I wasn't certain it would be answered.

"I wonder what we'll actually get," I said.

"That's why I ordered a bagel," Rhoda said. "I figured if I wasn't specific. He couldn't bring the wrong flavor."

"Assuming he brings a bagel at all," I said.

We both chuckled. Then Rhoda adopted a serious expression.

"All right, Bethany, what happened?" she asked.

"With Paul?"

"With you. Why is your aura so dark? The last time I saw you, you looked great. You had six of your chakras aligned, and there was a general air of hope about you, your worries about Truffaut notwithstanding. What happened?"

I suddenly realized what she meant. I hadn't been thinking about it, because I'd been so focused, first on the mission with Paul, and then on figuring out the strange vision I'd had. But now that I thought about it, a lot of shit happened since last I'd seen her.

"Yesterday was kind of a mess," I said. "What do you want to hear about first?

"Start at the beginning," she said.

"Andrew ..."

Fresh tears leaked from my eyes. Another lump came into my throat, and I found myself unable to continue.

"Andrew?"

"My stepson," I said. Then, under my breath, I muttered, "My boy at my side."

"Oh, no," Rhoda said, putting a hand on mine. "What happened?"

Helio arrived with coffee. I quickly wiped away tears as he set the mugs down in front of us and poured out steaming, black java.

"Your food will be ready in a few minutes," he assured us.

Offhandedly, I wondered if it would be our food that was ready or someone else's. I wrapped my fingers around the warm porcelain, lifted it to my lips, and drank. Helio had brought real coffee, real Drogo's coffee – the very best thing in the whole wide world. It warmed my throat and stomach and soothed just a little of the ache in my heart. Clinging to the mug like a lifeline, I sucked down as much of the hot beverage as my tongue could stand.

"Oh, God," I said. "I needed that so badly."

"There is no more comforting comfort-food than Drogo's," Rhoda commented.

"So true."

"So, what did Andrew do?" she asked, yanking me back to the topic at hand.

"He sent ..." I had to gather my strength before I could continue. It took all the courage I had to tell one more person about this. "He sent me a hateful, horrible email. He told me how much they all despise me and how much better off they are, now that I am gone. He said ... he said they had a party the day I left town."

"Oh, Bethany, I'm so sorry. That's just terrible."

"Justice," Rhoda pronounced. "This card indicates that the consequences of your actions are at hand. In the past, you have taken actions that have brought about the need for justice."

The tarot reading made even more sense to me now. My heart ached with the revelation that I somehow deserved this.

"But I ... I just ... can't figure out what I did. I just don't understand. I get that I didn't notice how unhappy everyone was, but I was with me the whole time. How could I have possibly been so horrible that this is how they act towards me?"

Rhoda took my hands and stroked them sympathetically. She took a deep breath and met my gaze, with love in her eyes.

"Bethany has it ever occurred to you that maybe you didn't do anything horrible?"

"What do you mean? Why would they be so hateful towards me if I hadn't been bad to them?"

"Bethany, I don't know these people. I've never met them, so I can't assess their behavior or how they treated you. But I have known you for the better part of two months. And in that time, I have watched you bend over backwards to help people you have no obligation towards. You were raised in the mundane world and were completely skeptical of your powers. And yet, you very quickly adapted to life here in Enchantment and become a vital part of our community.

"Those are not the actions of a terrible person. I'm no psychologist, but you've told me that the children's mother died before you met. You've also told me that Jess never respected the work you did. Is it possible that you were set up to fail?"

"What do you mean?" I asked, confused.

"I don't have any children of my own, Bethany, but I know that every parent on Earth goes through hell when they have teenagers. If you've been having conflicts with those kids for the last four years or so, that makes you just like everybody else. A teenager's job is to be an asshole and piss off their parents."

I laughed. So true.

"It was always going to be hard when your children became teenagers," Rhoda went on. "Now, let's mix in the fact that their mother died when they were little. You were always going to be compared to her. Because she was dead, none of her flaws were ever going to be taken into consideration. However good or bad a mother she was before she died, the children were always going to worship her as perfect."

My mouth fell open. That thought had honestly never occurred to me. When you become a step-parent you know you're always going to have to compete with the birth-mom or -dad. It comes with the territory. But you also figure that if you do right by them, if you love them with all your heart, they will come to accept you for who you are and be grateful to you for being there when they needed you. Was that *naïve*? Had I been an idiot? Was I actually doomed from the very beginning?

I thought about how readily both children had taken to me. Ariel was outgoing from the moment we met. She was a little chatterbox. And when we connected over music and theater, that formed a bond that felt to me like the kind of mother-daughter relationship I'd always craved.

It'd been a little harder with Andrew. He was much more aloof, much more reserved. But he was into sports, and my past as a softball player for the hometown university had eventually given us something of mutual interest.

Those relationships were real to me. They were authentic. I hadn't been able to get pregnant, but I loved those children as though I had given birth to them. It had never even occurred to me that there was any difference between them and kids I might've created. They were mine. They always would be.

But maybe, that wasn't how they saw it. Maybe they just saw me as a governess – Maria von Trapp or Mary Poppins.

"I don't know what kind of people they are, Bethany," Rhoda said. "But I can't believe that a child who lost their mother would ever be able to take you fully into their heart as their mom. Not until adulthood. The human mind isn't fully mature until age twenty-five. Your stepchildren are still developing. Maybe one day they'll look back on their time with you and realize all the things that you did, that you tried to do for them. But right now, they're sad, angry, confused teenagers. And they have done what they had to to protect themselves. It's unfortunate that those self-preservation techniques have inflicted so much pain on you."

Tears streamed down my face and splashed lightly on my hands. Was that really what this was – a self-defense technique? The kids hated me so that they didn't have to feel regret?

I recalled Ariel's therapist telling me after one particular session that Ariel did not like to sit with her emotions. She was, in fact, afraid of them. I'd been surprised by that, because Ariel always seemed happy, unless the subject of her mom came up. I had always assumed that that was because she didn't want to think about the fact that her mother had died. And it occurred to me now that she had bonded so quickly and deeply with me because she was desperate for a maternal figure. I suddenly wondered if what I had thought was her finding the mother she needed in me was actually her fleeing her own grief. I knew from bitter experience that it was much easier to pretend you didn't feel bad and that you were over something than it was to actually confront it.

Mark had wanted to talk about my miscarriage. But I had refused. I told him he couldn't possibly understand what it was like. And I threw myself into activities with friends and a whole lot of wine to drown the aching sorrow I had no desire to feel.

What if that's what Ariel had done, too? What if she latched on to her replacement mommy so that she wouldn't have to think about the one who died?

And what if that meant that she never truly bonded to me, that however innocent and unknowing on her part, she'd been using me? The pain in my chest deepened. If that was true, and my Sight suggested that it was, then I'd been even more blind than I'd thought.

I picked up my coffee mug and drained it, but Drogo's magic elixir gave me no comfort. Helio arrived and sat our plates in front of us. He'd brought me eggs over-medium instead of scrambled, and an apple fritter for Rhoda.

"Everything look all right, folks?" he asked.

Rhoda smiled broadly and said it was just fine. I don't really like runny eggs, but I decided I didn't want to make things any harder on the poor cherub.

"I'd just like some more coffee, please," I said.

"You got it!"

He fluttered away happily. Rhoda started laughing.

"Bagel, doughnut – they're the same thing," she joked.

"It could've been worse. I said. "He could've brought you Baked Alaskan."

Rhoda laughed aloud.

"Oh, Bethany," she said. "I do so love your sense of humor."

"It's always been one of my more redeeming features," I quipped, wiping the last of the tears from my eyes.

"Are you going to be all right, mama?"

"I don't know, Rhoda. Every single time I think I've got my arms around this grief, some new revelation absolutely destroys me."

"What do you mean?"

"It's just, I suddenly realized that Ariel was running from me the whole time. She was hiding in our friendship, so she wouldn't have to deal with her grief over her mom's death. I thought she really loved me. But I couldn't see how badly she was really hurting. I did everything all wrong with her."

"Bethany, honey, you have got to learn to forgive yourself. You forgive everyone around you, but not you. Didn't you tell me that you'd been divorced and were barely making ends meet, waiting tables at a restaurant when you met Jess?"

"Yeah, so?"

"And that divorce came as the result of you being unable to have children, correct?"

"Yeah," I said bitterly. "That's correct."

"How old was Ariel when you met her?"

"Ten."

"All right," Rhoda said. "Let's think about this. A woman whose husband divorced her because she'd been unable to have children becomes stepmother to two kids. And the little girl who reminds her so much of herself immediately clings to her and is just so happy that her new stepmother likes all the same things she does. Do you think that that wounded woman might have misinterpreted that reaction innocently?"

I furrowed my brow. I could almost figure out what it was she was trying to tell me, but it just wouldn't come.

"I'm not following you," I said.

"Bethany, a lot of parents would have missed that. You didn't know Ariel from birth. By the time you met her, she'd already developed her own unique mannerisms, her own skills at social interaction, and her own ability to keep secrets. You had to learn about her. When you start at age ten, it's a crash course on the individual. That doesn't make it easy to parent, and it certainly doesn't make it easy to catch all the signs of danger.

"That was her father's job. He should have seen the signs that Ariel was ignoring her grief to the detriment of her development as a person."

"Yeah, but Jess was grieving, too. The kids lost their mother; he lost his wife."

"You were grieving also, Bethany. You lost your husband, the man who was supposed to take care of you. You'd lost your ability to make children. That'll do a number on any woman. If it's okay to forgive Jess for missing Arial's emotional needs, why isn't it okay to do the same for yourself?"

She may as well have stabbed me in the heart. I had all sorts of answers for her question. Because my mother had raised me to be more responsible than everyone else. Because Ariel had needed me, and I'd failed her. Because I had done all sorts of reading about children grieving the loss of a parent. I'd deliberately educated myself so that this wouldn't happen. Why hadn't it been enough? Why hadn't *I* been enough?

I picked up my fork and started playing with my potatoes. Helio had at least gotten that part of the order right. I put a bite of them into my mouth. They were buttery and divine, just the way I liked them. Not that I should be surprised. Everything Drogo made was just the way I liked it.

"Let's change the subject," Rhoda said. I nodded gratefully. "Were you able to learn anything from Paul last night?"

"Not really," I said after I swallowed. "I questioned him straight-up about Marcel Truffaut, and he was evasive."

I smiled.

"Boy, did he get pissed when I told him Truffaut had arranged for him to get his job."

Rhoda's eyebrows raised. She swallowed some of her fritter and washed it down with a little coffee.

"I wish I'd seen that," she said.

Helio at last arrived with a coffee refill. I had no idea why it took him so long since we were the only people left in the restaurant. As soon as he flew off, I had another swallow. This time it steadied me.

"Anyway, based on Paul's reactions to what I said, I believe everything Truffaut told us was true – he got Paul appointed to Enchantment so that he'd be able to have access to information on the artifacts. And he was definitely helping Truffaut find the pocket watch.

"But as for Truffaut's location or recent activities, I got nothing."

Rhoda nodded thoughtfully as she ate some more of her fritter.

"So, now what?" she said after another sip of coffee.

"I was hoping you could tell me," I said.

"Well, we did a tarot reading already," Rhoda said. "Have you had any visions or insights?"

"Sort of."

"Sort of?" Rhoda said with a laugh. "What does that mean?"

"Well, I had a dream last night, but I can't figure out how it's even remotely related to any of this."

"In my experience, Bethany, the universe is always telling you what you need to do. Maybe you're asking the wrong question."

"Well, that could be," I said. "It's not like I'm an expert at this stuff.

"I was walking in utter, black nothingness. Like, I could see just fine, but everything was black in every direction. After awhile, I came to this giant brick wall. It stretched to infinity in every direction. When I looked to my right, Dori was standing there."

"Wait, Dori? As in young Dorigen?"

"You got it," I replied. "She beckoned me to follow her, so I did. And she led me into the library at Ellington Manor."

"That seems strange," Rhoda said.

"Well, that's what I thought. I never go in the library. But two days ago, when Paul came to make sure I settled up on the dinner I promised him, he was in the library. He told Dorigen he would wait for me there. When I found him, he was talking to Lucius.

"So I'm thinking that dreaming about the library one night after Paul was in there can't be a coincidence."

"I agree."

I laughed at myself. Forty-nine-year-old Bethany would've said it was absolutely a coincidence. But she didn't know the supernatural was real.

"So what happened then?" Rhoda asked.

"She went to one of the shelves, and she got a book off it. And I can remember this very clearly, because it was bound in blue leather and was obviously a special book, you know?"

"Uh-huh," Rhoda said.

"So, I looked at the spine, and it was *The Complete Works of Shakespeare*. And Dori opened the book up and read the line from *Julius Caesar*: Beware the Ides of March."

"Interesting," Rhoda commented.

"When I woke up this morning, I figured that had to mean something. So I went down to the library to see if the book was there."

"I'm so proud of you, Bethany," Rhoda said, beaming. "Your instincts have sharpened. Only a few weeks ago, I would've had to tell you to go look."

I shrugged. I couldn't help but think of Genie in *Aladdin*: "He can be taught!"

"Well, before I could look for the book, I saw Lucius."

"Lucius was in the library?"

"Not only that, he was just sitting there, staring intensely at one of the bookcases."

"That seems odd."

"Oh, you haven't heard the half of it," I said. "When I asked him what he was doing, at first, he didn't even reply. It was like he hadn't heard me. When I asked again, it seemed to break the spell that he was under. Rhoda, he couldn't remember what he was doing."

"What?" Rhoda said, a shadow of concern passing across her face.

"I asked him what he was doing, and not only could he not remember, he said he couldn't even remember coming into the room. He eventually made up some story about thinking he might've heard something and went in to investigate. But I knew he was lying. Something very funny is going on with him."

"That's disturbing," Rhoda said.

"And Rhoda, this is the second time that's happened."

"What do you mean?"

"A week or so ago, after I'd had a nightmare, he wasn't in bed with me like usual. I went downstairs and talked to Declan. He said he had seen Lucius in the library. So I went to have a look, and I found him just like I did this morning. He was just sitting there staring, entranced."

Rhoda sipped some coffee. Then she put her cup down and stroked her chin thoughtfully. I took the time to eat some of my own breakfast. I had a few bites of my eggs, but the uncooked yolk just ruined it for me. It was the first time I'd ever been to Drogo's and been disappointed in the food.

"I think you're definitely right, Bethany. Whatever is happening, the library seems to be a focal point for it. Did you find the book?"

"Ha! That's the best part. I went over to the shelf that Dori had been standing by, and I found it sitting right there, bound in blue leather just like in the dream. But, Rhoda, it wasn't *The Complete Works of Shakespeare*; it was a technical manual from the nineteenth century on how to summon demons and shit."

Rhoda's eyebrows raised again. I was glad I wasn't the only one who was mystified by this.

"That would be a lot more in keeping with the kinds of books Alexander Ellington was interested in," she said. "But it is strange that in your dream Dori would read you Shakespeare from a book that in real life is a magic tome."

My mind drifted back two days. Paul had been discussing Ellington with Lucius.

. . .

"What I find so fascinating," Paul said, *"is that Alexander Ellington was a summoner. The entire manor is really a giant summoning circle, if you will. So the question is, if that's its purpose, who or what was it built to summon?"*

I shuddered at the idea Dori might be suggesting I needed to summon something. And if it were Shakespearean, what would it be? Ghosts? Fairies? Spirits?

"The Ides of March," I mused. "I mean, it can't have something to do with that can it? It's just too *clichéd*."

"Not to mention too late," Rhoda added.

"What do you mean?"

"The Ides of March were yesterday. They're the Fifteenth of March. Today is the Sixteenth."

"Oh, great," I said. "So my brain decided to give me a warning *after* it would actually have helped. Terrific."

"Well, maybe," Rhoda said. "The Ides are traditionally associated with the middle of the month on the Roman lunar calendar. And a lunar month begins with the new moon, so the middle of the month is the full moon. In the ancient world, the ides of a month are the full moon days."

"But the full moon was a week-and-a-half ago," I said.

"Right. So, there are two possible meanings to Dori's warning. Let's think them through.

"The first is the more common interpretation of the Ides being March Fifteenth. We know that was yesterday, so something significant may have happened we need to be aware of."

"But what could it be?" I asked. "I already told you I didn't learn anything significant from my date with Paul."

I winced when I realized I referred to the dinner as a "date." Damn, Sheriff Mueller was getting in my head about that. I shuddered at the idea that Paul may have thought of it as a date.

"That may not be it," Rhoda said. "Maybe something happened while you were out with him that we don't know about. Or perhaps something happened at dinner you aren't aware of. Or maybe something else occurred during the day. We don't really have enough information to make an assessment yet."

I frowned. The other significant thing that had happened yesterday was Andrew's email. But I couldn't see any way that would be connected to the mystery of Marcel Truffaut. Plus, I didn't want to think about it.

"What's the other possibility?" I asked.

"That Dori meant the night of the full moon in her warning," Rhoda replied.

"The night I saved Sheriff Mueller," I mused.

"Yes. The same night you traded Alexander Ellington's cane to Marcel Truffaut."

Oh, shit. That had to be it. I spent days trying to figure out what the right thing to do was. I'd obsessed and worried that giving Truffaut the cane was the wrong decision. Now, here was the proof.

"Bethany, I can see you jumping to conclusions already," Rhoda said. "You need to remember that we don't actually know what Dori meant. She quoted a cryptic phrase that could have multiple meanings. Beating yourself up because you are assuming the worst possible outcome is the one that's true is a mistake."

I frowned. I supposed she was right. But beating myself up was what I was really good at – it was my true genius. I was convinced that every bad thing in my life had come to pass largely from my own stupidity. How could this be any different?

"What does your Sight tell you?" Rhoda asked.

That caught me off-guard. My Sight? What did that have to do with this?

"Come on, Bethany," Rhoda prodded. "Close your eyes, reach out your senses, and ask the question. See what the universe tells you."

I sighed and sipped some coffee. I supposed it made sense.

"Okay, Mom," I said.

Rhoda laughed. At least that amused her.

I closed my eyes and did my best to flush away all distractions. Then I asked myself, "What did Dori mean when she quoted, 'Beware the Ides of March'?" I waited for the universe to reach out its divine hand and plant the answer in my brain. Nothing happened. I suppose I hadn't really expected it to. But I was still surprised.

"I got nothing," I said.

"What do you mean?" Rhoda asked.

She cocked her head in surprised concern. Those deep, brown eyes of hers held me.

"I mean, I can't feel anything," I said after thinking about it for a moment. "I phrased the question in my mind, but there's nothing. No link, no answer."

"Try opening your Third Eye," Rhoda said.

"That's what I just did," I protested.

"I know. But imagine the eye in the middle of your forehead. Picture it opening up and seeing."

I did as she said. I visualized another eye on top of my forehead, which frankly made me look pretty freaky. But I pushed the judgment away and focused on the image. I tried to make it open.

My headache from last night immediately returned. I moaned softly and put a hand to my head, rubbing my temples. Reaching for my coffee, I took a long sip.

"What's wrong?" Rhoda asked.

"I'm getting a headache," I said. "Feels like a migraine."

Rhoda stared at me in further concern.

"Bethany, give me your hands."

That seemed strange. But if I'd learned anything in my time in Enchantment, it was to trust Rhoda. So I extended my hands across the tabletop. She took them in hers and closed her eyes for a few seconds.

"Oh, mama," she said. She opened her eyes and met my gaze. "Bethany, honey, your Heart Chakra is massively out of alignment."

"What?"

How could that be? I'd gotten it realigned a few weeks ago.

"I mean, your Heart Chakra is really messed up right now. It's completely blocked, Bethany. There's no energy able to flow upwards from your Base Chakra or down from your Third Eye. The misalignment is acting like a dam in a river."

My mouth hung open. I had felt my heart shatter into millions of pieces after reading Andrew's email. I'd gone numb, as though all of my nerve endings had been switched off. I'd wandered into the conservatory and played "Race You to the Top of the Morning," which had only stirred painful memories of Andrew. My mother had called, and I'd had to admit to her what happened. I'd had to suffer one more humiliation.

"Shit, Rhoda," I said. "I think it was Andrew's email that did it."

"That would fit," she said, nodding. "I've watched all morning as you keep reliving that horrible incident and everything associated with it over and over in your mind. I don't know how to help you resolve this, Bethany. But if you don't, you won't be able to realign your Heart Chakra. And as long as it's blocked, you won't be able to access any of your higher powers."

Great. Now, I couldn't even do grief right. By hating myself for what I had done to Andrew and Ariel, I'd taken away my own powers.

And I didn't know how to stop hurting so I could get them back.

Eight

Rhoda insisted I accompany her to her shop, Hidden Wisdom, to pick up some remedies. Why she hadn't offered me any of this sort of thing when I first came to town, I wasn't sure. But she felt that I needed some of her New Age assistance in healing the damage that Andrew's email did to my heart.

She unlocked the front door, turned the sign to "Open", and then proceeded to the counter. I followed her wordlessly, uncertain what to say. I'd been to Hidden Wisdom numerous times since I'd moved to town, but I still didn't quite know what to make of it – shelves upon shelves of herbs and ointments and stones and books and who knew what else. I wasn't skeptical the way I used to be, since I knew that all of this was real. But between my father's strict atheism and my mother's well-honed cynicism and sense of judgment, I still couldn't help but feel weird standing in a place like this. The types of people who had frequented such stores in Lawrence always made me laugh. And not in the good way.

Rhoda was busily pulling ingredients off of shelves behind her. I couldn't help but watch with fascination.

"What are you cooking up there, Teach?" I quipped.

"I'm making you a tincture that will help soothe the agony in your heart and draw in the green energy of the chakra."

"Sorry I asked," I said with a grin.

Rhoda smiled back at my sarcastic humor. She got out a mortar and pestle and then emptied a small pouch of pink leaves into it.

"Rose petals," she said.

Then she set to grinding them up with the pestle.

Of course! Roses, I thought. *That made perfect sense!*

Except of course, that it didn't.

When she had the petals ground into a fine paste, she dropped in ten dried berries.

"Hawthorn berries," she said. "Any part of the hawthorn plant will do, but I believe the berries are little more potent."

"Naturally," I said.

After she ground down the berries. She put the pestle aside and got a rubber scraper out of the drawer. Then she grabbed an empty beaker and folded the mixture into it. Next, she grabbed a small bottle of alcohol and poured in about a teaspoon.

"Now you're talking," I said. "But can you make it a double?"

She laughed again before opening a bottle of springwater and filling the beaker halfway full with it. After that, she reached into another drawer and withdrew a glass stirring rod.

"Now, I want you to add a teaspoon of this to warm water or, better, chamomile tea," she instructed as she whisked the concoction together. "No coffee. We're trying to soothe the heart, not make it race."

"What about wine?" I joked. "That's relaxing."

"No. Alcohol is a depressant. That'll speed the despair, not the healing. Sorry Bethany, but you need to stay away from the booze for a few days."

"This is starting to sound like torture," I said.

Rhoda gave me a smile and then poured the contents of the beaker into a glass vial. Pinkish red in color, it looked like the poison the wicked queen tainted Snow White's apple with.

"So I can't just quaff this whole potion?" I said. "How long am I supposed to dose myself?"

"I recommend twice a day," she said. "Have some in the early afternoon and another cup either after dinner or before bed. And it's not a potion."

"If you say so."

"Now, wait here for a moment," she said.

She went out from around the counter and into the store, stopping in front of a large display of crystals. She looked them over before finding the variety she wanted. Then she selected the biggest one in the basket. Returning, she offered it to me.

The rock was half pink with the rest of it covered in some sort of greenish-brown discoloration that made it look as though it were a gangrenous chunk of flesh.

"This is rhodonite," she said as she forced the stone into my hand. I want you to keep it on your person at all times. Put it in your pocket, so you can't lose it. Better, hold it in your hand whenever possible.

"Rhodonite is the stone of self-love. It helps work through emotional problems, it assists in the healing of past wounds and restores balance to the Heart Chakra.

"Are there magic words I'm supposed to chant over it?"

I felt a little bad. My natural cynicism was oozing from every pore of my skin. I should really show Rhoda more respect, especially since I knew she was trying to help me and that her magic worked. But fifty years of trying to look cool by projecting cynicism didn't die easily.

"No, silly," Rhoda said. "But I recommend meditating with the stone in your hand. That will help activate its power."

She put the vial and the rhodonite into a brown paper bag. I reached for my purse.

"What do I owe you for all this?" I asked.

She thrust the bag into my hands and looked me deep in the eyes.

"Find Reggie and free him from whatever hold the manor has over him," she said.

I nodded. The vision of Reggie being chained to the divan in the parlor raced across my mind. I hadn't seen or heard from him since then, and I was deeply worried what it meant.

"You got it," I said, uncertain I would be able to keep that promise.

"All right, mama," Rhoda said, "you better get out of here. I've got some things I should get done before the real customers show up."

"Thanks, Rhoda."

I turned and left the shop. I had no idea if these things would really help me get my Heart Chakra back into alignment. Frankly, it didn't seem possible, given the wounds Andrew had inflicted on me. But I'd made Rhoda a promise. I owed it to her and to Reggie to do all I could to fulfill it.

♪

Back at the house, I tried to figure out what to do first. I didn't really feel like drinking tea or meditating at the moment. Of course, that told me it was exactly what I should be doing, but since when have I ever followed directions?

I hung my coat on the hook by the door, set the bag of New Age remedies on the stand, and rubbed my eyes. Why did everything have to be so hard? I really tried to put myself in the mystic frame of mind – believe in both myself and in my ability to tap into the hidden messages of the universe. But my heart still ached in my chest, and though I knew what was causing it, and what the remedy was, the icy grip of Andrew's chilling email clutched tightly to my willpower and refused to free it.

Sighing again, I picked up the bag and headed for the kitchen.

But that wasn't where I ended up. Unconsciously, I walked instead to the library. It was as though some force were compelling me, pulling me along, drawing me towards a destiny I did not know that I was supposed to meet. Somewhere deep in my guts, I could feel the inexorable calling. But I struggled to see its intent or purpose.

When I got there, I looked around slowly. The hair on the back of my neck prickled. Someone, something, was in here. A second later, happy humming floated on the air to my ears, as though someone were entertaining themselves while they worked. I turned in its direction.

Dori stood by the same bookshelf from my vision, cleaning it with a feather duster.

My eyes opened wide in alarm. I was awake. Wasn't I? Had I fallen asleep without realizing it? And if so, where was I? I swallowed hard and spoke:

"Dori?"

She turned and looked on me with curiosity. A warm smile lit up her face.

"Yes, ma'am?" she said.

Well, it was definitely her. I never had been able to get her to stop calling me, "ma'am."

"What are you doing here?" I asked.

"I'm dusting the bookshelves, ma'am," she replied as though it were obvious.

"Yes, I can see that," I said. "But ... *how* are you here?"

She smiled sympathetically, as though she were looking at someone with no intelligence whatsoever. But there was no malice in her expression. Just happiness.

"I have a message for you, ma'am."

My blood ran cold. The impossibility of this whole situation caused my heart to race. Dori didn't exist anymore. Once I'd broken the curse, the spell that caused she and Dorigen to coexist, one by day, the other by night, had ceased to work. And since it had been fifty years since Dori first came to Ellington Manor, it was Dorigen who had the final form.

But here was Dori standing before me, saying she had a message for me.

"What is it?" I asked, terrified of the response.

"Find the missing book to read the answer," she said.

I'd gotten use to riddles and cryptic quotes in my visions. The universe seemed disinterested in giving anyone a straight answer. But what the hell did this mean?

"The missing book?" I said. "Which missing book? *The Complete Works of Shakespeare*?"

But Dori simply smiled warmly at me and left the library. For a moment, I stared after her in stunned amazement. She was really just gonna bug out on me like that? Oh, hell, no.

"Hey, wait a minute!" I said.

She ignored me and turned down the hall after passing through the doorway. I raced after her.

"Dori!" I snapped.

I ran to the library door, turned the corner to pursue her, and nearly plowed into Dorigen.

"What the hell are you doing, Sorority Girl?" she barked. "You could've knocked me over."

"I'm ... so sorry, Dorigen," I said, completely confused.

"I'm sixty-eight years old, Missy. My bones aren't what they used to be, and the last thing I need to do is take a spill."

I stood blinking in amazement at her. Dori was nowhere to be seen. But here was Dorigen – stooped, her grey-and-white hair seeming to go in every direction, her wrinkled face seized with irritation, and her blazing, hazel eyes boring holes into me. It was just exactly as it usually was, as it was supposed to be.

"Where the hell were you in such a hurry to get to, anyway?" she demanded.

"I ..." I tried to figure out how to tell her what had happened, but I couldn't think of any reasonable explanation. "You weren't just in the library, were you?"

Her eyes flew open wide for a moment before narrowing with suspicion. She studied me carefully for about three seconds, although it felt like three years.

"I never go in the library unless I absolutely have to," she answered. "It's the one place in the manor that truly spooks me. I don't know what it is, but I can sense bad things happen there."

A shiver ran down my spine. I knew what the answer would be to my question before I asked it, but I still felt compelled to confirm it for myself.

"And you weren't in there just now?" I said.

Suspicion set up camp on Dorigen's face. The intensity of her gaze went up ten notches.

"No," she said. "Why?"

I really didn't want to tell her. Frankly, I wasn't convinced that I wasn't insane.

"I was just speaking to you in the library," I said. "Only you were Dori."

I steeled myself for one of her trademark insults. Frankly, that would've been comforting. But Dorigen looked alarmed, and instead of upbraiding me, she simply took me by the hand.

"Come on then, Missy," she said, "let's get away from here. No good can come from us lurking on the precipice of madness or danger."

She led me wordlessly down the hall. I couldn't think of anything to say to her genuinely frightening response, so I just followed.

In the kitchen, she let go of me, went to the refrigerator, and got out some deli meat, a tomato, and a jar of pickle chips. Withdrawing a knife from the drawer, she quietly cut the tomato into slices.

"Dorigen, are you okay?" I asked.

She chuckled sarcastically. Without answering, she went to the pantry and retrieved a loaf of bread.

"No, Bethany, I'm not okay," she said as she returned to the countertop.

"I've lived here for fifty years, trapped, unable to leave. And this house terrifies me."

"But you're not trapped anymore," I said. "I freed you. You could leave anytime. Why don't you?"

Dorigen's shoulders sagged. She finished putting together the sandwiches and sliced them in half before bringing them to the table and setting one in front of me.

"I don't know," she answered, taking a seat across from me. "Maybe I've been here so long I don't know how to leave. Maybe I've got no idea where to go. But I feel like there is something left for me to do here. As you know, I'm not supernatural myself; I'm just sensitive. I feel like I was drawn to this place for a reason, and it'll let me know when it's okay for me to depart."

Her gaze had drifted off into infinity. She didn't seem to be looking at anything, except maybe a memory. Absently, she reached down, picked up her sandwich, and had a bite. I studied her carefully, wondering if there was some clue here I was meant to uncover. But if there was, it eluded me.

"There's a dark presence at Ellington Manor," Dorigen said. "I don't know what it is, but it scares me. It lurks in the walls and in the air and even in the water in the pipes. I can feel it, Bethany. And more than that, since you broke the curse, I can taste it, smell it. You may have broken Maggie Cartwright's curse, but something else is wrong here. And it wants to escape."

I couldn't help but remember the terrifying dream I'd had a week-and-a-half ago. Reggie Matheson was chained to the couch in the parlor. He begged me to unbind him, and then he transformed into the giant man-bat I'd been seeing since I left Kansas. I shuddered at the memory. I couldn't help but feel Dorigen was right.

There was some darkness permeating the mansion, and it had plans.

Nine

The events of the day haunted me all afternoon, and I ate my dinner absently, taking no pleasure in the food – just fueling myself. I hadn't drunk my potion in the afternoon like Rhoda had instructed, so I begrudgingly forced myself to do it after I washed up the dishes. I found some chamomile tea in the pantry, so I got it out and put the kettle on. I didn't really like chamomile, but I was trying to be good and do what I was supposed to to mend my Heart Chakra.

When the kettle whistled, I poured out a large mug for myself and steeped the teabag. Then I poured some of Rhoda's magic elixir into it, and stirred the tincture into the tea. With a heavy sigh, I went to the study. I could usually find Declan there doing his research on the twenty-first century, and I had some questions for him.

"Good evening," I said as I entered.

"He turned from where he sat at the desk with the computer open and observed me.

"You're wearing a melancholy countenance tonight, Bethany," he commented.

It was true. And even if he had a somewhat pretentious way of putting it, he was right that I felt depressed and didn't feel like hiding it.

"Yeah," I said as I seated myself in an easy chair, "I suppose I am."

"What troubles you?" he asked.

I didn't answer right away. So much troubled me that I had no idea where to begin. I sipped the tea. It needed honey or sugar or something. The berry flavor was sour and combined with the grassy flavor of the leaves, I felt like I was drinking a plant. If it was supposed to soothe my heart, it wasn't working. Setting the cup on the end table next to me, I tried to convince myself that maybe I needed to drink the whole thing before I would begin to feel the effects. God, I hoped not. If I was going to have to drink this shit, I definitely wanted it to have some benefit while I was actually consuming it.

"Can I ask you about the ring?" I said.

Declan frowned.

What do you want to know?" he asked.

"Why did you want it?"

"As I have explained to you before," he said, sounding vaguely irritated, "Marcel and Margaret and I were seeking the four artifacts to power the mansion. The Order representative in Enchantment at the time had the ring, so Maggie and I took it from him."

"Yes, I know that," I said, trying not to sound irritated myself. "What I mean is, why did *you* get it? Based on what I've seen of Truffaut, I would think he would want all the artifacts in his possession alone. So why were you the one to get the ring?"

Declan considered carefully, his gaze drifting out of focus. It seemed as though he couldn't decide what to tell me or how much.

"It was important for me to have leverage over Marcel," he answered at last. "You've no doubt noticed that Marcel is ruthless and dangerous. So, I wanted to be certain he couldn't betray me. I wanted the ring to be magically protected from him."

"Wouldn't you have been better off with the cane? If it has power over the dead, wouldn't that have been more insurance?"

I wasn't so much trying to pin him down as I wanted to figure out how their relationship worked exactly.

"We did not know the location of any of the artifacts, except the ring. But even if I'd have been given a choice between the two, I would have chosen the ring. It's power of protection is passive. So long as you're wearing it, it does not need to be activated. The cane on the other hand, requires direction. Since I was looking to make certain Marcel could not stab me in the back, I wanted the artifact that would make that impossible."

I nodded. That made sense to me. And though I remained cut off from my Third Eye, my Sight gave me the impression Declan was being truthful. I sipped a little more of the potion. It still didn't taste good. I was definitely putting something sweet in it next time.

Swallowing hard, I met Declan's gaze and resumed questioning him.

"You never told me why you were involved in Marcel's quest."

"Yes, I did," he replied, sounding surprised. "The last time we had this conversation, I told you that I didn't feel I had much of a choice. Marcel was determined to teach me how to be a quote-unquote real vampire. I went along with him, because I feared he would turn on me. It's the same reason I made certain I was the one who acquired Alexander Ellington's ring."

I stared at him for several seconds. He was avoiding me. It was obvious from the way he held his head, how he seated himself in his chair. There was a hard set to his face that told me he was absolutely trying to dodge this subject.

"Declan," I said, putting as much honey in my voice I could manage, "that's not what I meant. You came to America with Truffaut, pursuing the Blood Heir legend. But when you got here, Maggie Cartwright convinced the two of you that what you sought could be better accomplished by activating Ellington Manor. You've told me that your goals were not the same as Truffaut's, that you had no desire to establish a vampire or other undead army. But you have not told me what your true motive was. I need to know."

"No," he said flatly. "You don't."

The tea must've been having some sort of a positive effect on me, because I didn't immediately jump down his throat for his insulting presumption of what I did or did not need to know. Instead, I studied him carefully. He definitely didn't want to talk about this. I could see some dark secret hiding behind the veil of his entrancing, blue eyes. Whatever it was, my instincts told me it was important.

"Declan, Truffaut is out there somewhere with the cane and the cigarette case. You have the ring. That's three of Ellington's artifacts we know the whereabouts of. Paul Hernandez has been poking around the library. Something is up, and I don't trust him, especially with Truffaut missing. I need information."

He sprang from his seat in the blink of an eye. I barely had time to gasp before he showed me his vampire face – his eyes red with hate, his skin sallow and papery, and his fangs extended in a wide-mouthed snarl that promised violence.

"Not this information," he growled, his voice completely different from ever I had heard it.

I recoiled into my chair, but the back refused to allow me to escape. The memory of him in my vision sprang to the front of my mind. Aside from blood dripping from his fangs, he looked exactly as I'd seen him – especially the hell-red eyes. Declan advanced on me menacingly.

"Get away from her, Mr. McGruder," Dorigen ordered.

She stood in the doorway of the study, a large, wooden cross in her hand and a stern look plastered on her face. Declan snarled at her and took one step in her direction.

"Don't be giving me any of your lip, sir," Dorigen replied. "Or I'll send you to Hell, where you fear to go."

Declan whipped his red gaze back-and-forth between the two of us, as though he were measuring his chances, considering his options. Dorigen advanced into the room holding the cross out before her. Declan's lips curled in a defiant sneer. Then, he closed his eyes and appeared to be concentrating deeply.

A moment later, he had resumed his human face. He looked angry but no longer dangerous.

"I believe I'll do some hunting," he pronounced. "Good night to you folks."

Dorigen stood aside to let him pass, still brandishing the holy symbol to make certain he didn't change his mind. But Declan simply stormed out as though he had had an argument with his lover.

"This is why you shouldn't be alone with him, Bethany," Dorigen said, lowering the cross and sighing with relief. "He's charming and attractive, but you can't forget he's a wild beast at heart."

"I ... I have never seen him like that. Except for the night I woke him, when he was starving for blood."

My heart pounded in my chest as the adrenaline continued to course through my body. Declan had never vamped out in front of me before. The sheer fury burning in his eyes frightened me. And I couldn't get the image of blood dripping from his fangs out of my head.

"Vampires are emotional creatures, Bethany. Their rage always sits just below the surface, and it's easily provoked. I would've thought you'd have learned that from Marcel Truffaut."

Yes. Dorigen had warned me that I needed to be careful around Declan, that he was every bit as dangerous as Truffaut was. Here was the proof.

"Good thing you had a cross handy," I said.

"We live with a vampire, Sorority Girl. There is nowhere in this house I don't have a remedy within arm's reach."

She turned and left the room. I was left to my astonishment.

Once again, I trudged through the darkness, surrounded by nothing, seeing nothing. And then, just as before, I came to the enormous, brick wall. It extended to infinity in every direction. There was no way around or over.

As I had before, I turned to my left and was immediately overwhelmed with a sense of dread and foreboding. I took one step in that direction, and my stomach became so seized with terror it wanted to drop me to my knees and force me to puke. Not wanting to suffer that fate, I turned back the other way.

Dori stood before me, beckoning as before. A sense of relief washed over me. As though I had avoided the worst kind of disaster and had instead found what I was truly looking for. I followed her again, hoping she would reveal to me where the missing book was and what it meant.

Within moments, we stood in the library. Dori faced me and folded her hands.

"Which book is missing?" I asked her, trying to take control of the vision.

"Please, ma'am," she begged, her voice choked. "Unbind me."

My eyebrows raised when she said the same thing the giant man-bat had said on so many occasions. And before I could ask her any more questions, she once again exploded into bats. They swirled all around me, and the familiar, frightening, red eyes materialized within them.

"Unbind me," a dark voice howled.

🎵

I woke up with my heart racing. Raw fear froze the blood in my veins. Those eyes and that voice made my flesh crawl.

Craving comfort, I reached down to stroke Lucius. But I couldn't locate him. And when I sat up to look, I discovered he was not in bed with me. I still shook from the memory of the vision and didn't want to be alone. And I had a hunch where Lucius might be.

I got out of bed, threw on a robe, and then padded downstairs. I went directly to the library. Every instinct in my soul told me that was where I would find him.

And sure enough, when I went in and flipped on the light, he sat on the back of the same red-leather chair, staring intensely at the same bookshelf.

"All right, Lucius, snap out of it."

As though there were magic in my voice, he blinked three times and then turned to me. A moment later, a look of confusion ran across his feline face.

"Bethany?" he said, sounding very confused.

"Yes, it's me. What are you doing?"

He turned back to the bookshelf and stared at it for several seconds.

"Well, I was just ..."

The same look of worried confusion I'd seen earlier set up shop in his eyes. "Actually, I don't remember what I was doing."

"Do you remember coming in here?" I asked, remembering what he told me earlier.

He thought for several seconds. I knew his answer before he gave it.

"No," he said. "The last thing I remember was curling up on your feet. I was taking pleasure in how warm you were. I felt myself drifting away to sleep.

"But then, I suddenly felt an overwhelming urge to find a clue."

"A clue?" I said. "What sort of clue?"

"I don't know," he said after another lengthy pause. "I couldn't tell you what the clue was or what mystery it would solve. I just felt drawn to find it."

I let that information wash over me. Dorigen had said some powerful force was at work in the manor. Dori kept inviting me to the library in my dreams. And earlier in the day, I found her in here dusting, even though Dorigen had not been in the room.

Now, Lucius had felt compelled to come in here to uncover a clue. He had no memory of entering the room, and he didn't know what he was doing. But it seemed to me that he himself was the clue, that whatever power was behind this mystery had drawn him here, so that I would find him. But why?

Dori had been leading me to the library. What had she said when she was here during my waking hours?

Find the missing book to read the answer.

A sudden bolt of intuition tied several disparate threads together for me. Dori had told me to find the missing book. I'd assumed that it was Shakespeare. But what if that wasn't it? What if instead I was meant to find something else entirely?

"Lucius, which bookshelf do you think contains the clue?"

He looked at me, confused.

"What do you mean?" he asked.

"I mean, you seem to be staring at one particular bookcase," I answered. "This is the third time I've found you in here, sitting on that exact same chair and staring at the same bookshelf."

I crossed the room and pointed to the one in front of him.

"Is this it?" I asked.

"Yes," he said. "I'm still not following you."

But I ignored him. I was laser-focused on finding the missing book now. Starting at the top left, I scanned each item to see if it was what I had been told to find. When I got to the third shelf, I came across a series of blue, leatherbound tomes. They were all titled, *The Complete Encyclopedia of Summoning, Conjuring, and Binding*. There were seven volumes in the series.

Number III was missing.

Ten

Lucius and I spent the next several days, turning the library upside down in our quest for Volume III of Alexander Ellington's collection of summoning spells. It was a slow, and tedious hunt that didn't offer much in the way of hope. The library was huge, and there were shelves upon shelves of books. If the one we were looking for was indeed misfiled, it could be anywhere. And as our search went on, I began to despair that it wasn't in the library at all but lost or otherwise hidden somewhere else within the gargantuan manor.

Dorigen refused to help us, despite the enormity of the job. She was so spooked by my vision of Dori in the library. She didn't even want to be near the entrance. And she was straight-up afraid to go inside. So Lucius and I agreed that I would start at one end and he at the other, and we would work our way towards each other.

Aside from it taking forever, it didn't really matter that Dorigen wouldn't participate, because we didn't find anything. After three days of exhaustively examining every single tome in the large room, there was no sign of Volume III of *The Complete Encyclopedia of Summoning, Conjuring, and Binding*. I tried to figure out what the possible connection could be between that title and *The Complete Works of Shakespeare*. But I remained unable to access my Third-Eye Chakra, and though I dreamed of Dori bringing me to the library from the brick wall every single night, she did not offer any new clues about the object of my quest.

Frustrated, I met Rhoda for breakfast on the morning of the fourth day.

"Still no luck, huh?" Rhoda said after listening to my update.

"Nope," I replied. "If the book is in the house, it's not in the library."

"Have you started looking elsewhere?"

"That's today's project. I suppose I'll start in the attic, since there were a number of Ellington's things collected up there the last time Lucius and I went up. But I don't recall seeing any spellcasting books. Although, I suppose I wouldn't have known one if I'd seen it back then."

"You've come a long way in a short time, Bethany," Rhoda said with a smile.

"Maybe, but I'm stuck on the road now. It's like I've come to a fork, and both paths look exactly the same."

Helio flitted over and poured coffee for the both of us. It had taken him the better part of a week, but he had at last learned that Rhoda and I always wanted coffee and he should just bring it with him when he came to wait on us.

"What can I get you fine ladies this morning?" he chirped.

I looked around. There were five people sitting at the countertop where Drogo spent time taking care of them and cooking food back in the kitchen. We were the only ones in a booth. Poor Helio. No one wanted him to wait on them.

"Blueberry pancakes," I said.

"Two bagels," Rhoda replied.

"Coming right up!" he said cheerfully and flew off to the kitchen. I looked at Rhoda with a bewildered expression.

"You have ordered bagels every single day this week, and he's never ever brought them to you. It's always something else. Why don't you get some order something different?"

"I want to see what he brings me this time," Rhoda said with a smile and a shrug.

"So, it's become a game has it?"

"Of course!"

I laughed. In Helio's defense he'd never brought Rhoda something she didn't want to eat; he just delivered something she hadn't ordered. So, in that regard, Rhoda was playing "Breakfast Surprise."

"Have you had any more visions?" Rhoda asked.

"No. I keep having the same one every night. I come to the brick wall, Dori is standing to my right and beckons to me. I follow her, and she leads me into the library. Then she tells me to find the missing volume. I keep asking her for another clue, but the dream always ends there."

Rhoda frowned and had some of her coffee. I watched as she considered her reply.

"Maybe you need to go left, Bethany," she said at last.

"Every time I turn left, I'm overcome with a terrifying sense of dread. Whatever's in that direction scares me too badly for me to move."

Rhoda studied me for several seconds. I felt like my mom was probing me to see if I had lied.

"Bethany, you've got to realign your Heart Chakra. Until you do, you won't be able to fully connect to your Third Eye. Have you been using the tools I gave you?"

"Yes! I keep the rhodonite on me at all times. I even put it under my pillow at bedtime. I've been drinking that awful potion. The pain in my heart has actually eased, but no matter what I do, I can't get the chakra unblocked."

Rhoda considered for another several seconds. I drank some coffee and felt the warm liquid soothe my soul. It didn't cause my chakra to realign, but it still felt good.

"It's time for music, Bethany. Every time you've gotten a chakra into alignment, it's been at the piano."

"I've tried that," I protested, feeling my frustration rise. "It hasn't worked."

Rhoda frowned again. I could see confusion and worry in her deep, brown eyes. Though I didn't have full access to my Sight, it was obvious I was presenting her with a perplexing problem she didn't quite know how to solve. Right there with you, my friend.

"All right," she said. "Let's turn this into a step-by-step plan."

"Okay," I said, making my skepticism plain.

"First, I want you to drink the tincture. Wipe your mind of all thoughts and just focus on its flavor and its healing energy."

"This isn't gonna work if I have to focus on how shitty it tastes," I quipped.

Rhoda threw me a look of mock disapproval.

"Pretend it's flavor is the magic," she said. "Take your mind off of what you're supposed to be doing and just be in the moment."

"If you say so," I said. "But magic tastes like shit."

Rhoda was unable to suppress a smile at my joke. Offhandedly, I wondered if she'd ever had a student who was as big a pain in the ass as I was. At least she liked me.

"Once you've drunk the tincture, sit at the piano and hold the stone. Clear your mind and focus solely on healing. Imagine that your heart has wounds on it and that you can see them closing."

I nodded. That part seemed easier to do. I could already imagine my heart in tiny little pieces scattered all over my chest.

"When you feel yourself at peace, when your breathing is smooth and even, put the stone on the piano," Rhoda instructed. "Then, start playing. Don't pick out a song; just let your fingers find it."

I thought about telling Rhoda that was how it always happened, that I never chose to play the song that invoked my magic; it just happened. But I'd already been enough of a smartass, so I decided to let it pass. Besides, nothing else had worked. So maybe all this prep work would help.

The bell on the door, jingled, and Sheriff Mueller breezed through it. He saw us immediately and made his way to our booth.

"Coffee and a Reuben to go, Drogo," he called out.

"Ready in five minutes, Russell Mueller," Drogo replied cheerfully.

Rhoda slid over to accommodate the sheriff. He sat down next to her and stared at me.

"Well, there isn't a whiff of Truffaut anywhere in town. I have gone everywhere I can think of in both human and wolf form. But my heightened senses haven't detected him, and no one has seen him at all."

"What about Paul?" Rhoda asked.

"I did a little spying on him," the sheriff replied.

"He hasn't met with anyone other than the people who come to the library. He's always been a loner, and he seems to be keeping it that way.

"I'm sorry y'all, but it looks to me as though your vampire has straight vanished."

I turned the news over in my head. There was absolutely no sign of Marcel Truffaut, but Paul was walking around as though nothing had happened. It didn't add up.

"That just doesn't make any sense," I said. "Truffaut was obsessed. I know neither of you saw him when he came to the manor, but he had the look of a man who was laser-focused on getting what he wanted. And he made it abundantly clear that he wanted Ellington's pocket watch. I just can't imagine why he would suddenly give it up."

"You said the last time you saw him, he told you he was going to meet with Paul, right?" Sheriff Mueller said.

"Yes," I replied.

"Well, maybe the weaselly little bastard gave him a real lead this time. If Truffaut was nowhere in town and Paul survived his meeting with the vampire, then maybe Truffaut is off on a quest to get the piece of the puzzle he's missing."

I shuddered at the thought. If indeed Paul had finally told Truffaut where the pocket watch could be found, then it stood to reason that he was off searching for it. And if Paul had not sent him on another wild goose chase, then he would be returning with three of Ellington's artifacts in his possession. Declan had the fourth. They would be able to finally put whatever their master plan was into motion. I needed to know where the missing book was. God help us if Truffaut or Declan had it.

"What's going through your head, Parker?" the sheriff asked. "I can see the wheels of your mind turning."

I frowned.

"Why do you do that?" I asked.

"Because you're the number one troublemaker in town, and I want to know what sort of fresh hell I'm in for."

"No, that's not what I meant. Why do you always call me, 'Parker,' instead of, 'Bethany?' You're the only person who does that. And I'm the only one you call by her last name. You address practically everyone else by their first name. Why am I different?"

The sheriff turned beet red. Anger and perhaps a note of humiliation flashed in his brown eyes.

"You're the mystic in town, Parker," he said. "Use your magic Sight to figure it out."

"Order up, Russell Mueller," Drogo called from the register.

The sheriff got up and went to pay for his food. My mouth hung open in amazement as he paid Drogo and then left without saying goodbye to us. I turned back to Rhoda in shock.

"What does that mean?" I asked.

Rhoda shrugged. She threw a knowing glance at me, as though she understood Sheriff Mueller perfectly. But with my Heart Chakra blocked and no access to my Third Eye, I had no idea what it meant.

"I'm not sure," she answered. "But that'll give you more impetus to get your heart back into alignment."

I sighed heavily. All I wanted was to figure out what the hell was going on in the house and where Marcel Truffaut was. I really didn't need these other distractions.

♫

Back at the manor, I resolved to get on fixing my chakra straightaway. I really didn't want to go up to the attic to hunt for the missing book, so I figured taking Rhoda's advice and performing a ritual was a great way to put it off.

I had just set the kettle on the burner when my mother called.

"Hi, Mom," I said.

"Hello, Bethany. How are you?"

"Oh, I'm about the same."

"I'm sorry to hear that, honey."

I smirked. I hadn't given my mother any context for what the statement meant, but she immediately leaped to the darkest conclusion. The ER nurse was ever on the watch.

"Oh, it's not like I'm moping around, crying in my coffee," I said. "I'm managing just fine. But I'm not sleeping well, and I just can't get the image of them having a party to celebrate my leaving town out of my head."

"Assholes," my mother said. "After all you did for those children, I'm so angry they treated you this way. They're just awful people."

I sighed. Once again, I knew my mother was trying to help. But equating the children to the worst kinds of people still wasn't what I needed to hear.

"They're kids, Mom," I said. "Not awful people."

"Yes, they are, Bethany. They are rotten, terrible kids. They never ever wrote your father and I thank-you notes for any of the presents we sent them. Ariel only ever emailed me when she wanted something. They're selfish and mean, and they took advantage of you. I don't understand why you can't see that."

My heart hurt at that remark. I truly appreciated my mother being on my side. It meant a lot for someone to have my back. But she just didn't get it.

"Mom, they're eighteen and seventeen years old. Their brains haven't fully developed yet. And they're hurting. They never recovered from the death of their mother. And I am coming to realize that I didn't help them grieve properly. I didn't show them how to embrace the sadness so that they could let it go and move forward."

"That wasn't your job, Bethany! Their father should've done that."

I smiled weakly as my mother echoed Rhoda's sentiments.

"Jess was grieving too, Mom. We all were. Jess lost his wife, the kids lost their mother, and I was divorced for being unable to have children. We were four people who were spiritually broken. And we clung to each other, trying to pretend that we didn't hurt the way we did. Neither Jess nor I helped the kids the way we needed to. And we didn't help each other either.

"You can hate Jess if you want to. But Ariel and Andrew were and are children. It's not their fault that the adults in their lives didn't get them the help they needed."

"You are too forgiving, Bethany," Mom said. "It's no wonder those people were able to walk all over you for years."

That stung me to my core. Mom had always wanted me to be stronger than I was. She'd always believed I was too weak, too accommodating, too spineless. I was fifty years old, and she still didn't think I could take care of myself. Admittedly, she had some reason to think that – I was, after all, twice-divorced.

But it made me angry that she continued to treat me as a failed human being. This wasn't the emergency room. Mistakes didn't cost lives. Indeed, mistakes were critical to growing.

"I'm sorry you feel that way," I said, straining to keep the anger from my tone. "Maybe after some time, you'll come to see that they were just kids who didn't know any better."

"Oh, they knew better, Bethany! They're teenagers. Ariel is an adult. They have to take responsibility for their own actions."

"I'm not talking about responsibility for their actions, Mom. I'm talking about motivation. Everyone acts with the information they have at hand and in the environment in which they find themselves. Ariel and Andrew grew up in a bad situation. They made decisions based on that. They may have been mean and hateful about it, but I'm not sure if I'd grown up in the same environment they did that I wouldn't have acted the same."

"You wouldn't have," Mom said. "You're a better person than that."

The tea kettle whistled. I went to the stovetop and turned off the burner.

"I appreciate you saying that, Mom," I said as I moved the kettle off the burner. "But I have to go now. I've got a whole bunch of things to do today. Thanks for calling and checking on me. I appreciate it."

"I wish you would listen to me, Bethany."

"I know," I said. "But I've got to make my own way, Mom. Talk to you later. Love you. Bye."

I hung up the phone. I wasn't certain we would ever see eye-to-eye on this. But I had no control over that. My mother's opinions were her own. And at seventy-four, she was unlikely to change.

I dropped another chamomile tea bag into a mug and quickly poured the steaming water into it. The tea immediately began dissipating into the water, and I pulled on the string, steeping it as swiftly as I could. With my mother's dark thoughts lurking around my brain, I wanted to get to the healing as soon as possible. I wasn't convinced this was going to work, since my previous efforts have been futile, but I was tired of hurting. Andrew's email had sent me rushing back to the day of my fiftieth birthday – when Jess had told me he wanted a divorce, and Andrew had told me to leave. The wounds were all fresh again, as though they'd just been inflicted. But more than two months had passed since that terrible day. And I was sick of reliving it. It was time for me to get back to moving forward.

After about a minute, the tea appeared sufficiently strong, and I pulled out the teabag and threw it away. Then I unscrewed the top of the vial Rhoda had given me and poured out a double dose of the horrible concoction. Who knows? Maybe it hadn't been working because I hadn't been mixing it strong enough. Stirring the tincture into the tea, I scooped up the mug and set off for the parlor.

Once I got there, I seated myself in my favorite chair by the fire. The mid-March weather was warmer than it had been a few weeks ago, but Dorigen still had a log burning in the fireplace. The heat from it baked into my jeans and my sweater and soothed me.

I closed my eyes and sipped the horrible potion. The strength and taste of the double shot I'd spiked it with made my face, crinkle in disgust.

This better damned work, I thought. *Because I am sick of drinking this shit.*

Realizing that that probably wasn't the right attitude to have if I wanted the magic to work, I tried to flush my brain of all thoughts.

It was difficult. Andrew's email immediately leaped into my mind. The terrible words he wrote solely to hurt me reared their ugly head and mocked me. Without wanting to, I visualized each of them in my mind, and they transformed themselves into knives and flew into my heart, cutting it to ribbons. I started spiraling into depression.

"Stop it, Bethany," I said aloud. "You're here to heal, not to hate on yourself."

I had another long draught of the potion. I lasered in on its awful taste, feeling it on my tongue, focusing on the rose petals and the chamomile. In the back of my head. I contemplated how much I hated herbal tea. I was a coffee girl through and through. If I drank tea, which was rare, I wanted Darjeeling or maybe Earl Grey.

Forcing myself back into the moment, I felt the warmth of the tea in my throat, in my stomach.

I sipped more of the dreadful brew. This time, I focused on the taste of the hawthorn berries. They were more pleasant than the chamomile or rose petals. But only marginally.

Rhoda had insisted that these were all good for the Heart Chakra, though, so I pretended that the magical brew didn't taste like shit and focused instead on the heat it generated inside of me.

With my eyes still closed, the blackness of my vision changed. It became green – dark, deep, forest green. Soon, though, it began to lighten. It shifted first to emerald and then to jade. After several seconds, it was a bright, happy, Kelly green. A smile slid up my face. I'd always liked Kelly green. It just seemed so warm and inviting.

Without opening my eyes, I went to take another sip of the tea and realized I'd already drunk the whole mg. I opened my eyes in surprise and stared into the cup. Sure enough, it was indeed empty. How much time had passed? It felt like only a few seconds. I looked up at the grandfather clock that sat opposite me in the stately room and saw that I'd been drinking tea and meditating for twelve minutes.

"Holy shit," I said.

Still reeling from how long I'd been meditating and how surprisingly tranquil I felt, I stood, set the empty mug on a coaster, and went to the conservatory. As I entered, I withdrew the rhodonite stone Rhoda had given me and squeezed my fingers tightly around it. Then I seated myself at the piano and, just as Rhoda had instructed, I focused on my heart.

As soon as I closed my eyes, my vision once again washed over green. I imagined my heart beating in my chest. As though I were flexing a bicep, I worked the organ pushing not just blood but positive energy out into my arteries so that they would flow throughout my body. The strangest sense of calm and satisfaction settled over my mind. I had no idea what I was supposed to be looking for before I began playing, but this seemed about the clearest sign that I was ready as I could imagine. Reaching out, I gently put the stone on top of the piano and lifted the keyboard lid. Then, without warming up, I started to play.

Rhoda had told me not to pick out a song, to let my fingers find one. And I had expected to just tinkle the keys until something happened, or maybe to play a few Hanon exercises to loosen my muscles and open the pathway to my creative mind.

But to my surprise, I began playing a song almost immediately.

It was "Love on the Rocks" from Neil Diamond's 1980 remake of *The Jazz Singer*. I'd bought the soundtrack album on cassette when I was a freshman in high school, because I'd loved the music so much. I'd seen the movie several times on cable and had enjoyed it. I knew practically every song by heart, and I won my eighth-grade talent show by singing "Hello, Again."

But I hadn't thought about any of these songs in at least a decade, maybe longer. They were a part of my past, of a more innocent time when I didn't understand the emotions the songs were designed to evoke.

And yet, "Love on the Rocks" was absolutely perfect for the moment. When I hit the first bridge, I was singing full-throated, and agony erupted in my chest. Ordinarily, that might've stopped me from performing and worry that I was having a heart attack. But because I was deliberately trying to realign my chakra, not only did I not cease playing, I forged ahead as though this was what I was supposed to have been doing my whole life.

The heat in my chest became searing. Tears flowed freely from my eyes as I continued to sing and play. The image of the Three of Swords from the tarot reading exploded in my brain. But the rain from the clouds on the card washed over my mind, as if to cleanse it of all anger and sorrow. A hand – my hand – curled around the handle of the blade piercing the heart and began slowly withdrawing it.

My voice became choked as I continued to sing. My body shook in anguish as I went into the second bridge. Trying hard not to scream but to keep singing, I focused every thought on getting that terrible blade out of my heart. And as I crescendo'ed into the words, "We all know the song," the tip at last came free.

The worst pain I'd ever felt in my life shot through me, as though my blood were liquid fire launched from a furnace in the center of my chest. If I hadn't been singing, I would have wailed, begging for it to stop.

And then, without any warning, it did. Suddenly, the agony was gone.

I sang the last verse softly, as though I were expressing relief:

"Yesterday's gone, and now, all I want is a smile."

I played the final notes, lifted my hands from the keys, and began bawling. But they were not tears of grief. Rather, this was a happy cry – cleansing like a forest fire burning away all of the dead trees of anger and resentment. I realized for the first time that letting pain go hurt worse than keeping it locked inside. But once it was gone, everything felt so much better.

Was this how grief worked? The only way to move through it was to face that agony head-on and walk through it, like it was a fire? I hadn't felt so good in years, but the experience seemed worse than Jess blindsiding me on my birthday.

My vision washed over green, as though someone had put a spotlight gel over my eyes. I blinked away tears and saw Lucius sitting on his chair, staring worriedly at me.

"Bethany, are you all right?" he asked.

I smiled broadly. My head ached from crying, my nose was full, and my shoulders throbbed. But as I cleared the last of the tears from my eyes, a sense of joy began burning in my soul.

"Yes, Lucius," I answered. "I'm fine. I'm actually very, very well."

Eleven

Once again, I was walking in utter blackness. There was nothing around me in any direction, as though I were in an ocean of darkness. I felt a strange sense of confidence that I had not in any of my previous visits to this dream. I knew where I was going, and I knew what I had to do.

As usual, I came to the infinite brick wall – too high to get over and stretching forever both left and right. As she always did, Dori waited for me. She lifted her hand and beckoned to me like in every other iteration of this vision.

But this time, I did not follow. Instead, I turned to my left. The sense of dread immediately ignited in my stomach. But Rhoda had told me that this was the way I needed to go. I had taken one tentative step forward, when I felt a finger tapping me on the shoulder. I turned around and saw Dori looking at me, an expression of alarm covering her face. Her hazel eyes pleaded with me to turn back, and she shook her head vigorously.

"No," she said, but there was no sound.

Gently, I reached up and took her hands in mine. I bent my head and kissed her knuckles. Then I looked into her eyes and gave her my most reas-

suring smile. Afterwards, I pushed her hands down and released them at her sides. Then, I resumed my journey.

Each step I took filled me with horror. I could perceive on some instinctual level that I was drawing close to a terrible confrontation. I had no idea what monster waited for me at the end of this road, but I knew it was fiendish indeed.

And yet, I was not afraid. With my Heart Chakra back in full alignment, courage propelled my steps. I didn't want to meet whatever darkness awaited me, but I knew that this was the right thing to do. And I did not fear it.

A figure appeared on the dark horizon before me. I couldn't make it out, but it seemed human. I was walking towards a meeting with someone, and I knew again this was meant to be.

But I was stunned when I saw it was Andrew.

He stood casually, wearing his Lawrence High baseball uniform – white cap, with a black bill and script "L" in red; white pants and jersey with black trim; "Lawrence" in red in script on the chest, and a baseball bat above with the famous "Chesty Lion" logo balancing on each end, a clear rip-off of the St. Louis Cardinals jersey.

He held a red, aluminum bat in his right hand that rested gently on his shoulder. His face was a mask of malice, and his brown eyes blazed with promised violence.

"Turn back, Bethany," he ordered.

I blinked in stunned surprise. His presence here in my vision was strange enough. But acting as a guardian completely put me off.

"Andrew?" I said, unable to think of anything else.

"I mean it, Bethany. Turn back."

"What are you doing here?" I asked, my confidence growing.

"If you don't turn back right now," he growled, "I will beat you to death."

My eyes popped wide at the threat. I knew that Andrew was angry with me, and he clearly was capable of malicious action, given the email he had sent. But he was threatening to murder me? What the hell was going on here?

"Andrew, I—"

But he didn't let me finish. He stepped forward swiftly, and with the perfect swing that I had taught him, he brought his bat around and slammed it into my shoulder. I cried out more in shock than in pain.

"Go back!" he roared.

"Andrew, please!" I cried.

His only response was to swing again. This time, he brought the bat low and hit me in the knee. Pain exploded in my leg, and I collapsed to the ground. Then he raised the bat over his head like an axe and brought it down savagely on me, beating me over and over and over again, while I wailed and screamed in pain, begging for mercy.

♫

I sat bolt upright in bed, covered my head with my hands, and screamed and kicked for all my worth.

He was doing it! He was literally beating me to death! With a savage kick trying to escape him, I sent Lucius sailing off the bed. He awoke in mid-flight, his green eyes popped wide in alarm. And then he struck the window, caterwauled, and dropped to the floor.

I had no time to worry if he was okay. Andrew's blows kept raining down on me. Every inch of me screamed in agony. I couldn't get away. Oh God, I couldn't get away!

"Bethany," Lucius called from somewhere far away.

I ignored him. I couldn't escape. Andrew was going to kill me. Dear God, I was about to die.

"Bethany!" Lucius shouted. "Bethany, wake up! Bethany! It was a dream! It's over! You're safe now."

A dream? How could it be a dream? I'd seen Andrew. He was right there, adding the dark red mess of my blood to his shiny bat.

I opened my eyes, praying for some way to escape.

Andrew wasn't there. Lucius had somehow made it back onto the bed and cast a worried gaze upon me.

"Bethany," he said, "it's over. You're safe now."

When I realized it had, in fact, been a dream, I began bawling. My muscles still ached with phantom pain. My bones continued to believe they'd been shattered.

"Oh, my God, Lucius," I wept. "It was so real. It felt so real. "

"But it wasn't," he said. "Whatever you were dreaming, it was all in your mind."

I continued blubbering. I thought I'd healed the pain of this earlier in the day when I'd realigned my Heart Chakra. But apparently there were still ghosts working in my brain, waiting to harm me.

Dear God. I realized I'd foreseen this before the tarot reading. Andrew had stood before me in his baseball uniform just like in the dream. He'd attacked me. With Declan's terrifying transformation a few nights ago and now this, two of the images from that horrible vision had come to pass. What did it mean?

"What was your dream about?" Lucius asked.

"I ... Andrew was beating me to death with a baseball bat," I confessed.

"That's terrible," he said. "I'm so sorry, Bethany."

He came forward to nuzzle me, but after only one step, he stopped and winced in pain. The image of him flying off the bed and into the window suddenly leaped into the forefront of my mind.

"Oh, Lucius, I'm so sorry," I said. "You poor baby."

I gathered him up and drew him to me. He groaned again.

"Here," I said.

Then I massaged his back, shoulders, and hips. He purred as I rubbed away the pain. And I cooed over him and apologized as though he were a simple housecat instead of a magical familiar.

I looked up and gasped. Dori stood in the doorway to the bedroom. Just as she did in my dreams, she beckoned to me.

"Lucius," I whispered, not daring to speak louder. "Do you see that?"

I pointed to Dori. Lucius stared, his feline face covered in wonder.

"Yes, I do," he said. "But I can hardly believe it."

Dori beckoned to us again. I looked at Lucius and he at me. We exchanged a silent message. Following Dori seemed to be the only logical thing to do. So, I got out of bed gingerly, somewhat surprised that I wasn't bruised from Andrew's beating. Lucius hopped down to the floor, and the two of us followed Dori wordlessly out of the bedroom.

It wasn't hard to guess where she was taking us. Every time I had seen Dori, either waking or asleep, it had been in the library. So I was unsurprised as she led us to the stairway, down to the first floor, and along the narrow hallway until we at last reached the room I had spent so much time in the last several days.

Wordlessly, she raised her right arm and pointed to a bookcase. I recognized it immediately – it was the one Lucius had been staring at every time I had caught him in here, the one that held six of the seven volumes on conjuring.

"Find the missing book to read the answer," Dori said.

"Yeah, that's what we've been trying to do for half the week." I said.

Dori gave no reply. She simply stared at me with those bright, hazel eyes of hers as though I should understand exactly what she meant.

"Any ideas?" I asked, turning to Lucius.

"I'm afraid not," he replied, "Dori shouldn't be here in the first place. So this is either a visitation of some sort or a waking vision."

"Or I'm still dreaming."

"No, unless we're having the same dream, which I suppose is possible, I'm perceiving all of this, too. So it stands to reason that this is actually happening.

"There is magic at work here, Bethany. It's going to take magic for us to solve this puzzle."

Magic. If this was indeed a puzzle that could only be solved with sorcery, then I needed to rely on the power I knew how to use.

And that meant music. Indeed, it had been the song, "Magic," that had enabled me to wake Declan from his fifty-year torpor. Briefly, I considered singing the Olivia Newton-John song again. But somehow, that seemed off to me. The concept was right, but that was the wrong song.

Andrew had beaten me nearly to death in my dream. Grieving for him, I had sung "Race You to the Top of the Morning" the other day. Was Andrew's presence in tonight's dream related somehow to what was happening? Dori had been in the dream, too. Running on pure instinct, I started singing.

I stayed with *The Secret Garden*, but instead of "Race You to the Top of the Morning," I sang, "Show Me the Key." As soon as the notes issued from my mouth, I felt the *kundalini* energy nesting in my sacrum uncoil and begin to rise. I closed my eyes and gave myself over to the magic. The power rocketed up my central channel and came to rest in my Throat Chakra. And though my eyes were closed, I could see the entirety of the room. Dori, Lucius, the furniture, the books. And the music coming from my mouth was covered in beaming, blue light. I watched as the notes and words streamed forth, floating purposefully across the air, touching the bookshelf, and lighting its edges with bright, yellow energy.

"It's behind the bookshelf," I said.

"What's going on?"

I turned and saw Declan standing behind us.

"Declan, look over there," Lucius said. "Do you see Dori?"

He turned and stared in her direction. Those gorgeous, blue eyes of his went round.

"Yes," he said. "How is this possible?"

"How it's possible, I couldn't say," Lucius answered. "But her presence here has activated some sort of magic in the house."

The bookshelf continued to glow with soft, golden light. The missing book wasn't on the bookshelf; it was behind it.

I walked forward and examined the case. It looked like every other one in the library – tall, wide, and packed with books edge-to-edge on every shelf. But it was different somehow. In *The Secret Garden*, Mary searches for the key to the garden. She finds it, but then has no idea where the door is. I seemed to have the reverse problem. I was staring at the door, but I had no idea how to open it.

All right, well, we were in a wizard's library. So, in keeping with the *clichés*, there had to be a secret chamber beyond the walls. I started running my hands over the bookshelf, looking for a button or a catch or even a book that would trigger the door to open.

"What are you doing?" Declan asked.

"In a previous vision," I explained as I kept searching, "Dori told me to find the missing book to read the answer. She just repeated that instruction before you came in. Lucius and I have been searching for Volume III of a series on summoning spells. The other six volumes are right here on the shelf. I'm convinced there's a room or something behind this bookcase, but I can't figure out how to get it open."

"Have you tried simply moving it?" he asked.

I knew that wasn't right. Besides which, I didn't see how the shelf could be moved even if we unloaded all the books off it, it was an enormous and seemed to be attached to the ones next to it.

"It's built into the wall," I answered, uncertain how I knew this but confident that I was right. "There has to be some other way."

"Alexander Ellington was a magician," Lucius said. "It stands to reason that if he had a hidden chamber in the mansion he built, it would require magic to access it."

Memories crashed through my mind like runaway trucks.

"Come to me," I said in a voice not my own.

If I'd had even one second to think about it, I probably would've freaked out. But the response to my command was immediate. Summoned by the authority in my vocal cords, Alexander Ellington's cane flew from Evan Longfellow's grasp, tumbled across the intervening space, and landed perfectly in my lap.

"How did you—" he began. But once again, he didn't get to finish.

"Reggie," I ordered, gripping the cane tightly with both hands, "stop him."

As soon as I walked into the house with the cane, my vision washed over black. I couldn't see a thing, and my head started spinning.

Release me. Yes, you can hear me now.

Use your power – let the dead go free.

Unbind me!

The sheer force of the voice made me my head hurt. I put my free hand up to my forehead and squeezed my eyes tightly shut, trying to block out the sounds.

Holy shit! Was it that simple?

"Declan, give me the ring," I said, turning to face him.

"What?" he said, instinctively covering it with his other hand.

"I promise I'll give it back," I said. "I only need it for a moment."

"Why?" he asked.

"Because I need something of Alexander Ellington's to trigger the secret door," I snapped as though it should be obvious.

He stared at me in confused wonder. He knew I was onto something, but he couldn't follow the logic of it.

"Declan," Lucius said. "She's right. The entire manor is a large magical conduit – the house itself is an artifact. None of us has the sorcery to access the secret chamber. But Bethany may be able to get around that if she has some token of Ellington's power."

Declan frowned. I could see he was still worried about giving the ring up. It was the only leverage he had against Marcel Truffaut. But there was no way we were going to figure out the truth without it.

"Please," I said, covering the word with sugar and honey.

With a final look of worry, Declan removed the signet from his finger. He stepped forward and held it out to me. But when I put my hand on it, he refused to let it go.

"I'm trusting you, Bethany," he said. "Don't betray me."

I sighed heavily and shook my head.

"Do you really think that's the kind of woman I am?" I said. "I bent over backwards to save Sheriff Mueller. And I held up my end of a devil's bargain with Truffaut. I promise you, I'll give it back right after I get that door open."

He searched me with his blue-eyed gaze, trying to determine if I was telling the truth. I didn't know what other proof I could offer him.

"Very well," he said and let go.

"Thanks," I said.

Deciding to give him further assurance, I didn't put the ring on my finger. I just held it.

I turned and faced the bookshelf again. Closing my eyes, I focused on the image of the ring that I clutched tightly in my fist. I envisioned the bookshelf before me, still glowing, the borders of the door outlined in yellow light. Giving myself over to the power of the *kundalini* that remained present throughout me, I triggered the power of my Throat Chakra.

"Open," I commanded.

The response was immediate. The golden glow turned blue. And then, with a deep rumbling, the bookshelf slowly pivoted outward. It was indeed a secret door – just like in a classic movie. Beyond it, was a round room. At its center, was a large pentagram engraved in stone on the floor. A grandfather clock with a hole where the "3" should have been stood on one side of it, and a short, wooden stand was positioned opposite it. On the near side, stood a podium. A blue, leatherbound book lay on its surface. The title was clear from where I stood – *The Complete Encyclopedia of Summoning, Conjuring, and Binding, Volume III*.

"Jesus, Mary, and Joseph!"

I opened my eyes and saw Dorigen standing where Dori had been.

"What the hell have you done?"

Twelve

I blinked in stunned surprise. Dori had appeared without warning. And now it was Dorigen who stood before us. Some magic I didn't understand was at work here.

"Dorigen," I said, "if you don't mind my asking, how did you get here?"

"How the hell should I know that?" she snapped. "I was asleep and dreaming. And then, I woke up to find myself staring at you fools opening a secret door!"

She was dreaming? Had she sleepwalked? And if so, did that mean that Dori was present while Dorigen slept?

"What were you dreaming about?" Lucius asked.

"It doesn't matter!" she shouted. "You shouldn't have opened this door! You're going to doom us all! Can't you see that's what he wants? Are you so stupid that you don't know when not to kick a hornets' nest?"

"Dorigen, I don't understand," I said.

"Of course, you don't!" she replied. "You're a great bumbling fool, who's been stirring up trouble since you first arrived. Can't you feel the thing's influence on you?"

Her voice had risen to a screech. Dorigen was in full-on panic mode.

Her cheeks were flushed, her eyes burned with horror, and her breathing was rapid and shallow.

"Dorigen, what are you talking about?" Lucius asked.

"The darkness!" she screamed. "You've released the darkness! We are all going to die!"

Tears ran down her cheeks. She looked as though she might asphyxiate. I had no idea what to do. I didn't know what she meant, nor could I tell how to help her.

Declan stepped forward swiftly. He grabbed Dorigen by the shoulders and forced her to look at him.

"Dorigen," he said in a quiet-but-commanding voice. "Calm down."

For a moment, she stared at him as though he were crazy. But then, her expression changed. The panic left her eyes. Her shoulders relaxed. Her brow unfurrowed. Soon, she was placid, almost zombie-like. Revulsion roiled in my stomach. Declan may have solved the immediate problem of Dorigen going to pieces, but I was disgusted he had used his vampire charm on her.

"That's good," Declan soothed. "That's better. Come, let us all go to the kitchen and talk."

Dorigen nodded wordlessly. She turned and shambled towards the library door.

"What are you doing?" I asked.

"With the door open, exploring this chamber can wait," he answered. "For the moment, we need information. Dorigen knows something she hasn't shared with us. Whatever it is will certainly tell us what we've stumbled into."

I examined him carefully. He didn't seem to be hiding anything. Though he had been largely aloof and unknowable for the past few weeks, Declan's plan was sensible. I wished I knew what his motivations were, especially after he'd vamped out on me earlier in the evening. But for the moment, he seemed to be on my side.

"Okay, good idea," I said.

"You promised to return the ring when you had the door open," Declan said.

I raised an eyebrow in response to that. I'd had no intention of keeping the ring. I just wasn't thinking about the fact that I had it in my hand at the moment. Declan's insistence that I return it right now suggested he had a deep and perhaps unhealthy attachment to it. I needed to get to the bottom of that. But for now, we had a more important task.

I crossed the library and handed it to him. As soon as he had it in his hand, a look of relief washed over his face, and he slipped it back onto his finger.

"Thank you," he said.

"You don't need to thank me," I said. "I was never going to screw you over. In fact, it's me who should be thanking you – I couldn't have done it without the ring. So, thanks again."

He nodded once.

"Shall we?" he said, indicating the door with his hand.

I didn't answer. I followed Dorigen out of the library to the kitchen. Somehow, I knew this was going to be the most frightening conversation I'd had yet since moving to Enchantment.

♫

Five minutes later, we were all seated around the kitchen table. I had a steaming mug of tea. Darjeeling this time, not the chamomile shit. Dorigen had poured herself a double whiskey into a tumbler. She sipped it slowly, and her hand shook every time she lifted it from the table to her mouth. Declan had nothing. Lucius sat in the fourth chair like he was a person. If the circumstances hadn't been so alarming, it would've amused me.

"Sorry for the outburst, everyone," Dorigen said, her voice sounding far away. "I didn't mean to be so rude. I was just frightened."

"Frightened of what?" Lucius asked.

Dorigen didn't answer right away. She lifted the glass to her lips again and drained it. Then she set it down unsteadily on the table and poured herself another.

"He's been whispering in my dreams," she said, clearly afraid to even make mention of this. "He keeps ordering me to instruct Bethany to unbind him."

Unbind him? That was what the giant man-bat always said to me.

"Who's been telling you this, Dorigen?" I asked.

I was hoping that Dorigen could finally solve this mystery for me, that she could tell me who had been calling to me. She drank half her whiskey before she answered.

"The dark heart of the mansion," she replied, as though she were telling a ghost story. "When I was only eighteen, he called out to me to free him. I dreamed of him night after night. He promised if I came to him, I could escape my father's abuse. So, one night after he'd beaten both my mother and I in a drunken rage, I waited until he passed out. And then I left home, never to return."

A shiver went down my spine. I had known that Dorigen had fled her home life when she was young, but I hadn't realized it was because her father beat her. The brilliant scholar of British literature apparently had a mind poisoned by alcohol.

But that didn't disturb me nearly as much as the similarity to Dorigen's summoning and mine. After Jess had thrown me out, I'd heard a voice calling to me across the distance. It begged me to come to it. I hadn't realized I might've been answering its call when I left Lawrence. I'd been on my way to my parents', because I couldn't afford to live on my own. And Rhoda had talked me into staying in Enchantment after I'd stopped for breakfast.

Of course, I'd been lured to Enchantment by a billboard ad for Drogo's Diner that did not exist. Had that been the man-bat's doing? Rhoda had told me it was my Sight showing me what I needed to see to find the town. But had my brain conjured that on its own, or had whatever this dark presence was put it there for me?

"I followed the voice to Enchantment and Ellington Manor," Dorigen went on. "And every night in my sleep, it would whisper to me, begging me to help Mr. McGruder.

"I sometimes think that's why I was so attracted to him. I wasn't at all interested in sex or romance. But I felt an overpowering need to be with him every night."

My eyes opened wide at that. Maggie Cartwright had been convinced that Dorigen was moving in on Declan. She became insanely jealous of the time that her vampire lover and his housekeeper spent together. Now, it seemed that the attraction had nothing to do with Maggie's fears.

I felt terribly sorry for Dorigen in a way I had not before. If she was right, if indeed the manor and whatever spirit possessed it had been compelling her to spend time with Declan, then she was a doomed woman. She fled her father's abuse, only to be drawn into a supernatural spiderweb of jealousy. And then, she'd been cursed. It wasn't right. I was suddenly aware that I had rescued everyone *but* Dorigen. I'd saved Sheriff Mueller from Karl Markiewicz, and I'd broken the curse that kept Declan asleep for fifty years and Lucius confined to the house. But Dorigen's nightmare still wasn't over. She remained a prisoner of the dark force that had drawn her here five decades ago.

"When the crazed, witch enacted her curse," Dorigen continued, "she did me a blessing. For though I was trapped here in perpetuity, the terrifying voice fell silent.

"But once you broke the curse, Bethany, it started up again."

She might as well have shot me through the heart. No wonder she didn't act as grateful as it seemed like she should have. She wasn't as free as I'd supposed. Though Dorigen was now able to leave the grounds, she was still trapped in the darkness. I had a long sip of tea to avoid shedding tears.

"At first, I didn't recognize it," Dorigen said. "It had been so long since I'd heard it, I'd forgotten the soft sounds of its whisper, the cloying, sickly sweetness of its suggestions. I'd assumed it was my paranormal sensitivity, detecting an ill wind. Indeed, that's what I told you, if you'll recall."

I nodded. Yes, I remembered Dorigen telling me an ill wind was blowing, and after I'd given the cane to Marcel Truffaut, she scolded me again, saying it hadn't ceased. It was now obvious what she'd meant.

"But lately, I can feel its intentions, Bethany. It's been asking me to draw you to the library. It's been telling me to lead you to that door."

Understanding struck my brain like a bolt of lightning. That was why I had been seeing Dori in my dreams. Dori kept drawing me to the library and giving me clues. But those weren't the only visions. I had seen Dori while awake, and both times she'd become Dorigen afterwards.

"Oh my God," I said.

"What?" Lucius replied.

"We've seen Dori twice – once during the day in the library. Once tonight. After the first time, Dori left the library. When I tried to pursue her, I ran into Dorigen just outside the library door."

"And then tonight, we both saw her in your bedroom and followed her down to the library," Lucius said.

"And she turned back into Dorigen once we had the door open," I finished. I took a deep breath and stared deeply into her frightened, hazel eyes. "Dorigen, can this thing possess you?"

All the color drained from her skin. She didn't just look like she'd seen a ghost; she appeared to be one herself. She reached for her glass, brought it swiftly to her lips, and threw the entirety of its contents back. Then, she poured out another and drank it before answering me.

"I don't know," she said, her voice shaking. "Tonight, I was dreaming of you. I could feel myself instructing you what to do. When I woke up, the dream was real."

My flesh crawled. Raised in the mundane world and only recently awakened to the supernatural, I had no idea what a possession looked or felt like. But Dorigen's description of what had just happened sounded pretty close to what I'd always imagined.

"The first time, I don't remember what I was doing. When my consciousness returned, you came barreling out of the library and nearly ran me over."

I thought about that. I remembered the look of abject fear on Dorigen's face, when I'd told her what happened.

"You knew then, didn't you?" I said. "You knew the … voice, for lack of a better term, was manipulating you to get me to open the secret door."

Dorigen didn't say anything right away. But I could see the wheels of her mind turning as she considered my question.

"Yes and no," she replied. "I knew it was using me to get you to fulfill whatever sinister plans it has. But I didn't know that it wanted you to find and open that secret chamber. I didn't know what it intended for you, Bethany. I just realized that it was using me."

"Why didn't you say something?" I asked.

"Because I was scared!" she snapped. She immediately looked regretful. "Sorry. You didn't deserve the sharp end of my tongue for that. And I should've told you as soon as I suspected something."

I couldn't blame her. I'd acted in largely the same regard. When I knew something was wrong, I didn't want to ask anybody about it. I'd keep my suspicions to myself and try to work them out. That kind of behavior had cost me my marriage. I'd been unhappy for years, but I didn't say anything because I didn't want to upset Jess. Here was another lesson for me: I needed to be honest about the things I thought and felt. People got hurt if I didn't.

"I felt it too," Lucius said. "Like you, Dorigen, I couldn't tell what it was. I have detected its presence here ever since we first set foot in the manor. But after Bethany broke the curse, the sensation has intensified. All of this is leading to something."

"Wait a second," I said. "You've been feeling evil vibes coming from the walls of the house ever since I broke the curse, and you didn't think to say anything to me?"

"I apologize, Bethany. Like Dorigen, I didn't understand what I was perceiving. As a fey creature, I have a heightened sensitivity to magical forces. So, while I did perceive the manor's presence intensify once the curse was broken, it didn't occur to me that the two things were related."

I sighed heavily and shook my head. I had no way to be aware of these things to know what I should be doing. Despite having awakened to my abilities for the past couple months, I was still largely ignorant of the supernatural world. It would be great if people could tell me when I needed to know something.

"What about you?" I said, turning to Declan.

The vampire looked startled to be spoken to. He hadn't said a word since we'd come into the kitchen, and he looked as though he'd been lost in thought before I addressed him.

"I've felt nothing," he replied. "I never did. Lucius may have been able to detect this dark presence when the four of us first came to Ellington Manor, but I did not."

I studied him for several seconds. I couldn't tell if he was lying. It seemed strange to me that a vampire plotting to activate the mansion's powers would be unaware of a sinister presence within the house's walls. But Declan gave no clues, either verbal or facial, that he was being untruthful.

"It's possible that the ring has masked its presence from you," Lucius said. "Since the signet offers protection from supernatural forces, you might not be able to hear or detect its whispers."

A thought leaped out of the back of my brain, danced around my head, and then plunged back into oblivion before I could get a hold of it. Was it a memory? A clue? Whatever it was, it was connected to the artifacts somehow. I tried hard to recognize what my brain wanted to tell me, but the more I thought about it, the more elusive the idea became.

"But you didn't have the ring when you first came to the manor," I said, returning my attention to the conversation.

"True," Lucius said. "But Declan is not a fey creature. He's undead. He may not be as sensitive to magical forces as I am. And though both Dorigen and I have detected the increase in the voice's intensity, the ring may be keeping Declan proverbially deaf."

I nodded. That made sense to me, although I noticed that Declan neither confirmed nor denied how the ring was operating on him.

"Well, whatever this thing is, what does it want?" I asked.

"It wants out, Bethany," Dorigen said. "Whatever it is, it's bound here somehow. Perhaps it was Alexander Ellington himself who trapped it. But it doesn't matter. It wants to be free. It wants revenge."

Her last words were so ominous I forgot to breathe for several seconds. "Unbind me," the man-bat always said. And it wasn't a request – it was a demand, an order. Those malevolent red eyes haunted my dreams. Everything I'd ever feared swam in that scarlet gaze. I had no idea what this thing was, but I knew freeing it was an incredibly bad idea.

"Well, don't worry," I said. "There's no way in hell I'm letting that thing loose."

Dorigen shook her head. She met my gaze with a terrifying certainty.

"It's too late, Bethany," she said. "You have set in motion a chain of events that may be unstoppable. Maggie Cartwright's curse kept the thing at bay. But now, it's awake again. It's hungry, and it wants to feed."

I shuddered. Dorigen's tone and words made me feel like a Girl Scout again, sitting around a campfire while the adults told us dark stories of ghosts and goblins.

Only this time, they were real.

Thirteen

The next morning, I sat bleary-eyed across from Rhoda at Drogo's. Her usual cheery disposition was nowhere to be found. I couldn't blame her. I was still unnerved from the events of the previous night. Somehow, by the light of day. Andrew's vicious attack on me in my dream felt more real instead of less.

Between long sips of coffee, I related the night's events to Rhoda. For the most part, she showed no emotion. Her face remained wrapped in concern, but it didn't appear to be about anything I was telling her. She did look upon me with sympathy when I told her about the nightmare with Andrew, but otherwise her brain seemed to be a million miles away.

That is, until I told her about the secret chamber. Then, her eyes grew wide, and I had her full attention.

"There's a secret chamber in the mansion?" she said.

"Apparently so," I replied. "And it is spooky as shit. We took some time to explore it last night after Dorigen calmed down. There's a podium in it that looks as though it would hold a spell book or something. In front of that, there's a giant pentagram on the floor. And it's not just drawn on the floor with chalk, Rhoda. It's carved into the stone, a permanent part of the building. There's a ton of sigils on the outside of it that I don't understand. Lucius didn't recognize them, either."

"Dear God," Rhoda commented.

"Oh, that's not all. The roof in that part of the house is glass. It's not a skylight, exactly, but it's domed – like it was deliberately built to make it possible to summon something from the sky."

"Or to allow a celestial body to shine down on the circle," Rhoda said.

That thought hadn't occurred to me.

"What do you mean?" I asked.

"Ritual magic often is associated with seasons or with alignments of celestial bodies like stars and planets. Knowing that Ellington was a summoner magician and that he built the house for a specific purpose, it's entirely possible that he needed the sun or the moon or the planets or something similar to be able to cast their light onto the magic circle."

Jesus. I supposed I should have expected something like that. I'd seen enough scary movies to know all about ritual sacrifices and the planets being aligned at just the right time. But I'd always assumed – like I had with everything else magical – that it was just the imaginations of Hollywood writers, who were playing on old wives' tales. I should've known by now that if I'd read it in a book or seen it in a movie, it was based on truth.

"Last night, I felt a terrible disturbance in the spirit world," Rhoda said. "I was awakened from a dead sleep by the sound of lost souls crying out in horror."

My heart stopped. I didn't know what to make of Rhoda's confession, but it explained why she'd been distracted this morning. And it couldn't possibly be good.

"Do you think my discovering Ellington's secret chamber caused that?" I asked, making an unexpected leap of logic.

Rhoda didn't answer right away. She considered carefully, trying to piece together clues in her mind.

"I don't know," she admitted. "But Alexander Ellington built the house and enchanted the artifacts for the express purpose of opening a portal to the spirit world, and drawing the dead to him to make himself immortal. Your discovery solves a long-unsolved mystery. As you've no doubt observed, despite its early twentieth-century ostentation, Ellington Manor just looks like a normal mansion. No one ever knew where Ellington conducted his rituals. Now, we do. And it may be that the spirits were reacting to the possibility of his work resuming."

I frowned. Something about that didn't make sense.

"Well, I don't think 'no one' knew about the existence of the chamber," I said. "According to all the stories, Ellington's soul was sucked out into the spirit world, leaving his body behind. So, he wouldn't have had time or the ability to put away the artifacts. And since we know The Order scattered them to the four winds, his body would have to have been found.

"Assuming he was casting the spell when something went wrong, his body would've been in the chamber. The Order, therefore, must know about the secret room. It must have been there when they took the artifacts out of the house and shut the secret door so that the chamber could not be found.

"I was only able to open it with magic, and I needed the signet ring to trigger it. The general populace of the supernatural world may not have known about this room, Rhoda. But somebody does. It couldn't have been hidden if they didn't."

"Good point," Rhoda said.

I surprised myself. I wasn't certain how the answers had come to me. Maybe two months in Enchantment had taught me to think like a mage.

"You said Dorigen was summoned by the mansion?" Rhoda asked.

"That's what she told us. And frankly, that frightens me."

"Why?"

"Because that's exactly what happened to me, Rhoda. I dreamed of a voice calling out to me when I was still in Kansas. It begged me to come and find it. And since I've been here. It keeps asking me to free it."

"Yes, you've mentioned that. Didn't you say that's what Reggie told you in a dream?"

"Not exactly," I said. "I was speaking with Reggie, and then he transformed into this giant man-bat thing. It was that creature who cried out, 'Unbind me.'"

Rhoda's gaze drifted out of focus. I watched as she turned thoughts over in her mind.

"There's something else, Rhoda."

"What is it?"

"Bats."

"What about them?" Rhoda said, cocking her head.

"From the moment I started towards Enchantment, I've been seeing bats in my vision. I saw them when I first came to the house in my dreams. And I saw them in the visions about Sheriff Mueller."

"Yes, I remember," Rhoda said, thinking carefully about this new information. "They would get tangled in your hair and bedevil you while you were trying to save Rusty."

"Yep. And I saw them again when I had the vision with the cane. I walked into the house, and, in addition to hearing the voice of the creature, I saw hundreds of bats. And after Reggie transformed into the creature in that dream, I saw bats again.

"I don't know, Rhoda. I've never been able to figure out why there were bats in my visions. I sort of assumed it had something to do with Declan and/or Truffaut. I kind of figured they were metaphors for the vampires. Now, I'm not so sure."

Rhoda sipped some coffee and drummed her fingers on the table. A look of deep concern covered her face.

"Describe this creature to me again," she said at last, digging into her purse.

She pulled out a pen and a small notebook. After opening it to a blank page, she looked at me expectantly.

"It's like I told you," I said. "It's a giant man-bat. It stands, like, eight feet tall. It has a human body, but instead of proper arms, it's got these enormous bat wings. And its head is also a bat. And of course, it's got those hell-red eyes. They're the most terrifying thing I've ever seen. They make me fear I'm going to die and burn for all eternity."

I fell silent, and Rhoda continued to scribble notes. When she was finished, she looked up. "It sounds like some sort of a demon," she said. "But I'll have to do some research to figure out which one."

"I'm afraid to know," I said.

"I don't blame you," she said. "Demons are horrific creatures.

They're insanely powerful, and if Alexander Ellington bound one into the mansion to power it, it'll be desperate to be free.

"It wants out, Bethany," Dorigen said. "Whatever it is, it's bound here somehow. Perhaps it was Alexander Ellington himself who trapped it. But it doesn't matter. It wants to be free. It wants revenge."

Dear God. I'd thought many times since coming to Enchantment that I'd gotten in over my head. But this, this was so much worse than I'd ever imagined.

Fourteen

When I got back to the manor, I was determined that I was going to figure out this mystery. The more I discussed the strange bat-like creature with Rhoda, the more frightened I became.

And I was tired of being scared.

Fear had ruled my life for years, decades even. I'd made all kinds of stupid decisions because I was afraid of what I really wanted. It had cost me my second marriage and my children. And it was the reason I got into my first marriage. I was done with fear-based decision-making. For good or ill, I was going to confront this monster.

I reflected that realigning my Heart Chakra had been more beneficial than I'd realized. It gave me access to my higher chakras, but it also granted me courage that I had not known for many a year. Offhandedly, I wondered if it had been out of alignment forever. Maybe it had been blocked since I left college.

That didn't matter now, though. I couldn't go backwards. But I could definitely deal with the future by confronting problems in the present.

I went to the parlor and searched the LP's stacked under the record player. To my delight, they had *Phantom of the Opera*. I was a Lloyd

Webber girl through and through. *Cats* had helped me use my Third Eye to direct Declan and Truffaut to Sheriff Mueller to rescue him. So, "Phantom" could definitely help me figure out this mysterious monster.

I put the record on, and then walked over to my favorite chair by the fireplace. As the thunderous organ of the overture blasted through the speakers of the sound system, I seated myself, put my hands on the armrests, leaned back, and closed my eyes.

Okay, Bethany, I thought. *Let's do this.*

As the overture crashed towards its conclusion. I pictured the monster I'd seen in so many dreams. It seemed to leer at me from the shadows of my memories, daring me to be foolish enough to call it up. For a moment, my willpower faltered. I thought to myself that this was incredibly stupid, and I was just asking for trouble.

But then I remembered my newfound bravery. Steeling my resolve, I plunged forward.

By the time "Think of Me" was playing. I could feel the music flowing into my soul. It lifted me up and levitated me in the ether. Breathing deeply, I soon found myself completely entranced – I heard and felt the music, but I wasn't listening to it anymore. I used it instead as fuel for my magic. Gently coaxing the *kundalini* energy to rise from my sacrum up into my mind, I attempted to open my Third Eye and truly see.

But the only thing that appeared in my vision was the brick wall from my dreams.

That was strange. Was this what I was supposed to see? There were no clues written on the wall, no pattern in the bricks. I just stood before it in the blackness like I had in my visions. I knew better than to go left. Andrew waited to assault me there. And going right would only result in Dori leading me back to the library. I sensed that that was not the answer. I'd already cracked her riddle. We'd found the secret chamber. So if I couldn't go left or right, and the wall was too tall to climb over, then what was the answer here?

Perhaps listening to music wasn't enough. If I needed to knock down the wall or discover another clue, maybe I needed to be actively searching. Opening my eyes, I rose and shut off the record player. Then I left the parlor for the conservatory.

I strode purposefully into the room. I was a woman on a mission. This thing was not going to defeat me. Not after I'd discovered that my Heart Chakra was not just a source of courage but also of willpower. I hadn't felt this determined, this inspired, since high school, when I was certain that I would become a pop singer. Well, that hadn't worked out, but the tools I needed were born of that dream, and I was determined to put them to use to solve this mystery.

I sat at the piano and played a few warm-up exercises to get my fingers loose and open the channel between my mind and my hands. I had no idea what to play or even where to begin. What song might unlock this door?

It occurred to me that this whole thing had started with Andrew's email. He'd knocked my Heart Chakra out of alignment with his hateful remarks, with his misguided revenge. And when I'd walked to the left of the wall, he had been waiting for me. The memory of that violence sent a chill down my spine.

That had to be the key. My Heart Chakra was the source of this entire problem. It had gone out of alignment due to Andrew, and it had given me the courage to confront him again. All at once, the perfect song leaped into my mind.

I've been a huge fan of Indigo Girls since I first heard their breakout hit, "Closer to Fine" back in 1989. I'd bought every album they'd released for years. And each time, there was at least one plaintive love ballad written by Emily Saliers. It would rise like cream to the top of my playlist and was always my favorite song on the album.

Their third record, *Rites of Passage*, featured the song, "Ghost." And though it was written for guitar, I'd learned to play it on piano. My fingers tapped out the soft, arpeggiated intro.

"There's a letter on the desktop that I dug out of the drawer," I sang.

And within seconds I was plunged fully into the song. I had always loved the sense of regret in the lyrics, the confession to oneself that a broken love affair from the past still haunted the singer. And now, I realized I was in love with Andrew's ghost the same way Emily was with the unnamed subject of the song.

As I hit the bridge, I was singing directly to Andrew, telling him how much he meant to me, how much I adored my darling boy, despite the way he loathed me, despite the violence he did to me. The power of the music and the energy of my magic built in me, and I channeled it through my Throat Chakra as I sang to bring down the brick wall blocking access to my Third Eye.

Andrew materialized in front of me, once again wearing his Lawrence High School baseball uniform. He brought his bat chopping down onto my hands, smashing them against the keys, breaking my fingers and interrupting the song with discordant cacophony.

I cried out in alarm, and he swung the bat like he was tattooing a lazy breaking ball towards the centerfield fence. It connected with my forehead. Stars exploded in my vision, and I fell backwards off the piano bench, banging my knees on the underside of the keyboard, before landing roughly on my back on the floor. I screamed in agony.

Andrew stood over me and brought the bat down again and again and again. I went fetal and covered my head with my arms, just trying to ward off the blows by giving him no weak spots to hit. But it didn't matter. He kept raining blows down on top of me, and I cried out in agony, desperate for it to stop.

But he wouldn't. He continued to beat me.

"Bethany!" someone yelled. "Bethany, what's the matter!"

What was the matter? I had no idea who this was, but couldn't they see that my son was trying to beat me to death?"

"Bethany! Bethany, open your eyes! Look at me!"

There was a familiarity about the voice – something intimate and real and compelling. I snapped my eyes open and found myself face-to-face with Lucius.

"Bethany, what is happening? Tell me how to help you."

The pain stopped. Andrew ceased assaulting me. I turned my head in frightened anticipation to look on him.

But he was gone.

I wiggled my fingers. They were no longer broken. My skull was not cracked. The only bruises that remained were the ones forming just above my knees from my impact with the piano as I toppled over.

"Lucius?" I said, only barely aware of where I was.

"Yes, Bethany, it's me."

"Jesus, Mary, and Joseph!" Dorigen shouted as she barreled into the room. "What the hell is going on in here?"

I shifted my gaze back-and-forth between my housekeeper and my cat. Both of them showed great concern for me. What the hell had just happened?

Carefully, I sat up. To my relief, my head didn't hurt, my vision didn't swim.

"I was … I was trying to use my magic. To understand what the creature is that's haunting the house."

"Creature?" Dorigen said. "What do you mean a creature? It's a dark presence. It's evil incarnate."

I thought about that. Was it evil? No, it was something … else.

"That's not right," I said, shaking my head. "Just like it did to you, Dorigen, the manor called out to me while I was still in Kansas. It invited me here, drew me in. Ever since my visions began, I've been seeing bats. And their leader is a giant man-bat. And it's this creature that keeps begging me to unbind it."

Dorigen blanched. I could practically hear her heart racing.

"Whatever this thing is," I continued, "it's at the center of whatever's going on. Rhoda thinks it may be a demon bound into the mansion by Alexander Ellington. She's doing some research to figure out which one it might be.

"But I've been sharing a connection with it ever since I got here. And so, I attempted to use my Third-Eye Chakra to see what it was."

"For the love of God, Bethany," Dorigen said, her voice trembling. "You are messing with powers none of us can control. You're going to get us all killed if you keep it up."

I opened my mouth to retort. I understood Dorigen's fear, but I also knew that the only way out of this mess was through it. Before I could say anything, though, Lucius spoke.

"And did you see it?" he asked.

"No," I said, turning to him. "That's the thing: In my visions, I keep seeing this giant brick wall. There is no way around or over it. If I go left, I encounter Andrew, who tells me to turn back and beats me with a baseball bat if I don't. That's the nightmare I woke up from last night. If

I go right, Dori leads me into the library and gives me a clue about opening the secret door."

"Right," Lucius said. "So, what does that have to do with what happened just now?"

"First, I put on music and tried to open my Third Eye," I explained. "But it wouldn't work. I kept seeing the brick wall.

"So, I figured just listening to music wasn't going to be enough. I came in here to activate my powers by playing the piano."

"And did it work?" Lucius asked.

"Heh," Dorigen barked. "I'd say from the state of things it didn't."

"Correct," I said. "I activated my magic. The brick wall appeared in my vision. And as I was attempting to destroy it, Andrew suddenly materialized and began beating me with his baseball bat again."

Tears formed in my eyes. I had to swallow several times before I could continue.

"It seemed so real," I said. "I mean, he was actually here – attacking me, attempting to kill me. It wasn't until you came along, Lucius, and snapped me out of it, that he disappeared."

No one said anything for several seconds. I could see horror written all over Dorigen's face. Lucius's green eyes sparkled in thought.

"I don't think this brick wall and your stepson are mere visions, Bethany," Lucius said at last. "This is not the universe revealing itself to you. There is some deeper magic at work here."

"Oh, terrific," Dorigen said, her words covered in equal parts fear and sarcasm.

"What do you mean, 'deeper magic'?" I asked.

Lucius frowned.

"I don't know exactly, Bethany," he answered. "I'm completely out of my depth here. This is not the way mysticism works. You shouldn't be having visions that inflict physical harm in the waking world."

"But I'm not actually harmed," I interrupted.

"Yes, I know," he said. "But until you were snapped out of the … vision, for lack of a better word, you were being impacted in the physical world. It's as though the real world and the dreamscape merge while this is happening."

My eyes opened wide. Was it possible that I was somehow bringing dreams into the waking world? I'd seen Dori twice. God help me if Andrew could actually get out of my dreams and assault me for real.

"This brick wall mystifies me," Lucius said.

"You're not the only one," I commented.

"I suppose it is possible that you've somehow misaligned your Third-Eye Chakra," he said. "But did you ever have this brick wall imagery before?"

"No. That didn't start until after Andrew's email."

Lucius hopped up on the chair. He walked in circles for several seconds, clearly lost in thought. Then he sat down and faced me.

"Andrew's email knocked your Heart Chakra out of alignment," he said. "That blocked the ability to activate your Throat and Third-Eye Chakras. But once you realigned your heart, you should have had access to the other two that were in alignment. I don't think that Andrew's email is what's throwing up this brick wall, Bethany. It just feels like something else to me."

The implications of Lucius's theory frightened me. Something else seemed to be wrong. I couldn't access my Third Eye. Whenever I tried, a literal brick wall would be in the way. And if I tried to get around, over, or through it, Andrew would beat me nearly to death.

Deep in my heart, I knew he would eventually succeed. If I kept confronting him, he would kill me in my dream. I could only assume that would mean I died in real life, too. Or who knew? Maybe I'd just become brain-dead, a vegetable for the rest of my life.

Either way, I needed to figure out what this was. I needed to remove the threat of my estranged stepson from my mind. If I didn't, we were all doomed.

But I had no earthly idea where to begin.

Fifteen

Later that night, Dorigen, Declan, and I all sat at the kitchen table eating dinner. Well, Dorigen and I ate dinner – fried chicken and green beans. Declan sipped a mug of blood. I explained to him what had happened earlier in the day, Lucius had been unable to come up with any ideas on what to do next. And though I wasn't holding out much hope, I asked Declan if he had any insight.

"I'm afraid I don't, Bethany," he said. "Despite the research that I've done on the manor, I honestly know very little about sorcery. Or mysticism. If there is magic at work on you, I don't know what it would be or how to defeat it."

Yeah, I'd figured as much. It was a longshot at best. But as Declan had said, he'd been researching things like Ellington Manor and Blood Heirs of Dracula, so I had hoped he'd come across some little tidbit that could help me.

Especially since the nightmare beast hiding somewhere in the mansion seemed to be responsible for all of this. Dorigen had called it an evil presence, and though I knew that was not correct, it felt authentic. It might not be evil at work, but it *was* darkness, and it was taking its toll on everyone. Declan had become more reserved and defensive in the last several weeks. Dorigen was haunted. And me? I was at the center of this mess, and the only way out at the moment seemed to be my death. Frankly, I was hoping for a better scenario than that.

I had just put another bite of chicken into my mouth when the doorbell rang. I stopped chewing immediately. Dorigen and I both exchanged a glance. Who would be calling at this hour?

There was only one logical answer. We weren't expecting anyone, and it was after dark. Marcel Truffaut had returned.

"Dorigen," I said in a commanding voice, "get a cross and some holy water."

Her eyes opened wide for a moment. But she understood me clearly. With a nod, she dropped her napkin onto the table, rose, and left the kitchen.

"Holy water?" Declan said. "What's going on?"

"If I'm not too much mistaken," I said, a calm but dark note in my tone, "your friend, Marcel Truffaut, has returned at last."

With that, I stood up and turned to leave the kitchen. Declan looked mystified. I had no idea why. Marcel had twice tried to kill me. We may have been allies when we parted company, but I did not trust him even an inch.

I met Dorigen at the door. She had a full water pistol in one hand and a large, wooden cross in the other. Lucius sauntered in a moment later.

"Who is it?" he asked.

"If it's not Truffaut, I'll be stunned," I answered. I indicated Dorigen's water gun. "Nice."

"There's a super-soaker full of the same stuff in the parlor," she commented.

"I think we're all overreacting here," Declan said.

"Oh, are we?" I snapped. "You won't tell us a damned thing more than what we know, Truffaut has finally returned, and we're overreacting? Go down to the store and buy yourself some perspective, Declan."

My remark confused him. The doorbell rang again. I sighed heavily.

"You ready?" I asked Dorigen.

"When am I not, Sorority Girl?"

Okay, that was fair. Dorigen never ceased to be able to step in and save me when I really needed it. Swallowing hard, I opened the door.

To my utter surprise, Paul Hernandez was standing on the stoop.

"Well," he said with one of his signature smirks, "I wasn't expecting an entire welcome committee."

I scowled. Paul's condescending sense of humor was the last thing I needed right now.

"What are you doing here?" I said, a little more nastily than I'd intended.

His eyebrows raised. Despite the fact that I had told him off more than once, he still seemed surprised at how I spoke to him.

"I'm afraid I'm here on official Order business," he said. "May I come in?"

Every instinct told me to deny him. I couldn't say what it was, but somehow the idea of letting him in the house sounded like an extraordinarily bad one.

"What sort of business?" I asked.

Paul sighed. Steam issued from his mouth in the cold, night air. He gave me a reproachful look.

"I can see you've no interest in being sociable about this," he said.

"Quit screwing with us and come to the point," I said.

He fixed me with a hard stare. I could practically see the loathing behind his brown eyes, as though he were plotting some wicked revenge against me. Go ahead. Try it, you fool.

"Declan, I'm afraid I have bad news," he said, directing his attention to the vampire. "The Order has decided it wants all of Alexander Ellington's artifacts back under its control. I'm going to have to ask you to surrender the signet ring."

I had to admit, I hadn't seen that coming. I managed to keep from gaping in response, but I couldn't help but be surprised.

Immediately, my mind started racing. Had Truffaut sent Paul to strip Declan of his last protection? It seemed plausible. It would be a simple enough ruse to convince Declan to give up the ring because The Order wanted it. And then Truffaut could show up here with three or even all four of the artifacts and activate the manor, with little resistance.

"No," Declan said as Paul extended his hand.

Paul winced, clearly disappointed. He didn't drop his hand.

"I'm sorry, Declan," he said. "I understand how you feel. But these orders come from the top."

"I do not care from whence they come," Declan said. "I will not surrender the signet to you."

Shit. Declan was stirring up a war on my front doorstep. I couldn't really blame him, but I could also imagine The Order beating down the door and arresting us all. Desperately, I tried to distract Paul from his mission.

"What about Truffaut and the cigarette case?" I asked. "And what about you supposedly helping him get the pocket watch?"

"Well, that's just it," Paul said. An embarrassed look set up shop on his face. "Monsieur Truffaut's quest for Alexander Ellington's artifacts has been discovered by the authorities. To prevent him from activating the mansion's powers, I've been ordered to collect all known artifacts and return them to headquarters in Indianapolis."

His words rang false. I could only guess that it was my Sight at work, but I did not believe he was telling us the truth.

"That seems awfully convenient," I said.

"How so?" he asked.

"The Order has decided that all of the artifacts must be gathered into one place for safekeeping? And they've asked the very man who's been helping a vampire acquire them to get them back? Why would they do that, Paul? Why wouldn't they take you into custody and send one of their other agents?"

Paul shrugged. A look of false innocence passed across his face.

"Fortunately for me," he drawled," my involvement in Monsieur Truffaut's scheme has not been discovered."

"Really?" I said. "I wonder what they would think if someone were to provide them with that information."

Paul's face darkened. I could see the edge of a threat on his lips. But he evidently decided not to make it, because a few moments later, his face relaxed and he smiled again.

"Let's not be harsh with our words, Bethany. I'm sure we can come to an equitable arrangement that allows me to follow my orders and maintain my status in the community."

Holy shit. Was he offering me a bribe? He must be desperate!

"There will be no bargains," Declan said. "The ring is my only protection against Marcel Truffaut. When you can demonstrate you have him or the other artifacts in custody, I will consider surrendering it. Until then, it stays where it is."

Declan's voice had an edge to it I'd not heard before. Just as he'd turned on me the other day, he made it very clear now that he was a vampire and not to be trifled with.

"I won't ask again, Declan," Paul said, drawing himself up to his full height. "This is no casual request. As the official representative of The Order, I am telling you to hand that ring over right now. If you don't, there will be consequences."

"Consequences?" Declan said, stepping forward.

I could feel the malice pouring off him. He stepped straight to the threshold of the door, nudging me out of the way so that he could confront Paul directly.

"Let me explain consequences to you, little man," he growled. "You will not take what is mine. And if you choose to pursue this foolishness, I will teach you what it means to anger a vampire. I will kill you, drink your blood, and make you my thrall. And you will live out your days suffering any humiliation I choose to inflict on you.

"Those, Mr. Hernandez, are consequences. Do not provoke me."

Once again, the memory of his bloody fangs in my vision scared the hell out of me. Now, he'd threatened Paul with basically the same thing Truffaut had me. Any last echoes of desire for him drained from my heart. Dorigen was right – Declan McGruder may have been charming and polite, but he was a monster.

"I'm sorry you feel that way, Declan," Paul said, dropping his hand at last. "I had hoped you would be willing to do this the easy way."

"Go away," Declan said, every syllable drenched in murder. "While you still can."

Paul sighed. He flicked his eyes around the rest of us. Then he stepped back from the door.

"As you wish," he said. "Good night, all."

He backed slowly away, ensuring Declan wouldn't pursue him. Then he got into his car, started it up, and drove off. When his taillights had at last disappeared over the horizon, I shut the door and turned to face Declan.

"All right, God damn it," I said. "It's time to tell me what the hell is going on."

Declan had the gall to look surprised, as if he had no idea what I was talking about. I had no patience for it.

"I want to know what you stood to gain from Truffaut activating the mansion," I said.

Declan's expression turned from confusion to fury.

"I have already told you I will not share that information," he growled.

A clear threat set up shop on his face, as though he dared me to speak of this again. He was messing with the wrong woman. Since I'd gotten my Heart Chakra back into alignment, I was done with taking people's shit.

But before I could snap back at him, Dorigen spoke:

"I am sure you're thinking of turning your vampiric fury on her, Mr. McGruder. But I'm telling you right now: You so much as twitch, and I will douse you in holy water until there's nothing left of you but steam and bones."

Declan turned to her, a fierce expression locked on his face. She raised the water pistol and pointed it at his forehead.

"I mean it, sir," she said. "It's time for you to remember your manners."

"I agree," Lucius said, interposing himself between Declan and me. "We all like you, Declan. But none of us will hesitate to destroy you if you can't keep your temper in check."

Lucius's voice was deadly serious. I knew from the threats he'd made to Truffaut, that he meant every word of it. He was perfectly willing to kill Declan on my behalf. I wasn't sure if I should be flattered or frightened.

"My motivations in Marcel's quest do not matter," Declan said, forcing a placid look onto his face.

"Bullshit," I replied. "You've already told me you're afraid of Marcel Truffaut. And you told me that you had reasons for associating with him, even though you could have run at any time. Now, you've put everyone in this house in danger by refusing to cooperate with The Order. I'm happy to back you in that endeavor.

"But you are going to tell me why."

Maybe I'd used my Throat Chakra to beat him into submission the way he might've used his vampire charm. Or maybe he just ran out of excuses. But regardless, his shoulders sagged, and he sighed.

"Let's go sit in the parlor," he said. "We may as well be comfortable."

Part of me wanted to demand that he just come out with it now, here. But I suspected that if I let him do it his way, I would get a better answer. So, I relented.

"Lead the way," I said.

Sixteen

Declan stared into my eyes for a moment. I refused to meet his gaze. There was no way in hell I was going to let him charm me out of this.

He turned at last and walked down the hall towards the parlor. Dorigen went after him immediately, keeping her pistol leveled at his back. Lucius and I followed.

We all resumed our usual seats in the parlor. The only things missing were a glass of wine for me and a tumbler of whiskey for Dorigen. But otherwise, this was like every other big meeting I'd had at the house. The sense of familiarity boosted my confidence.

"All right," I said, "spill."

Declan grimaced. I watched as he twisted his mouth, trying, I supposed, to figure out where to begin.

"Vampires are poorly understood," he began. "There is very little research on them, because unlike other supernatural creatures, we don't have a society or culture of our own. We are, by our nature, loners."

"And yet, you had no problem working with Marcel Truffaut," Dorigen said.

Declan grimaced again. He spread his hands as if trying to welcome her into his understanding.

"Occasionally, two or three of us will form of cooperative. Sometimes you'll even see clusters of five or six. But that's rare. Particularly as civilization advanced, it became harder and harder for vampires to remain undetected. And as you can well imagine, people are afraid of us. Unless we're talking about a large metropolis, a human community cannot support more than one or two vampires without us risking discovery.

"Since vampires tend not to associate even with each other, little is known about our origins. The powers and weaknesses are well understood from centuries of casual observation. But otherwise, no one really knows what we are or how we came to be."

I could sense that Declan was coming at whatever he wanted to tell us in a roundabout way, and my patience for it was wearing thin. He'd dodged my question several times already, and once, he'd actively threatened to hurt me.

"Come to the point, Declan," I said.

He sighed as though I were stupid. That frosted me. I opened my mouth to snap back at him, but before I could form the first word, he resumed his story.

"The Blood Heir is a different case," he said. "They can do things that other vampires cannot. No one knows why this is. It's possible that Dracula himself doesn't know. But they have extraordinary powers, the rest of us do not – the most desirable of which is to be able to bear the touch of sunlight."

"Yes, I know," I said, growing testy. "You told me all this. Why were you involved with Marcel Truffaut? What were you hoping to get out of it?"

"Marcel was studying Blood Heirs in hopes of learning to emulate their abilities, so that he could make himself a vampire lord. But I was hoping that in our research we would discover a means to get around the curse."

"Which curse, Declan?" Lucius asked. "There are several associated with vampirism."

"I wanted to be able to die without being condemned to Hell."

He might've slapped me in the face. He wanted to die? He'd mentioned the curse to me earlier. I definitely recalled him fearing death because he would go to Hell. But I hadn't realized that it was only the Hell part that scared him. Declan McGruder had a death wish.

"Why would you want to die?" I asked.

I didn't know what he would tell me, but I could sense with every ounce of mystic surety I had that somewhere within this tale lay the key to all of this.

"I'm afraid I wasn't a very good person in life, Bethany," he answered. "I emigrated to this country in 1893 with my wife and son. We settled in upstate New York. I had a small sum of money – a modest inheritance. So, I brought my family here to make my fortune.

"I began a business with a partner, Henry Bozeman. He had already made a fortune in cattle farming, and he took a liking to me right away. He confessed that he was looking for a new venture, and he had a thought about shipping.

"By this time, the railroads dominated transportation in America. There was a vast call for goods out West, and Henry believed that he could make a second fortune by filling this void. The supply lines were already there in the form of the railroads. All we had to do was garner the product.

"But neither of us had goods that were in demand. As wealthy as Henry had become via cattle ranching, there were great wide spaces in Montana, Wyoming, Colorado, and elsewhere that provided the perfect opportunity for ranching.

"As you are likely aware, industrialization led to surplus product. I hit on the idea that since we couldn't very well break into the shipping business without becoming rail barons ourselves, and since we had no goods of our own that were in demand, we should create a business that would store things and move them to rail depots. So, Henry and I founded a warehouse business. We created hubs where manufacturers could store their products, and we would get them to the cities that would ship them out West."

"Heh," Dorigen said. "So you became America's first middleman."

"Perhaps not the first," Declan said. "But that was essentially the model. We made it possible for goods to get to the markets they were needed in."

"I'm still waiting for the point, Declan," I said. "I understand that you think you need to spin this elaborate tale so that we'll fully understand, but what I really want is to know why you wanted to die and how teaming up with Marcel Truffaut would accomplish that."

He nodded. But he didn't indulge me.

"As I've told you, I was not a good person. The business was successful to an extent. We were profitable, but I wanted more. I was very ambitious then, and I did not care what I needed to do to achieve my ends. So long as I could have the things I wanted, I was willing to act.

"After two years, we were not getting rich the way I had hoped. There simply weren't enough goods in the cow country of New York to ship elsewhere. And most of the big production companies had warehouses already located in the major shipping hubs. So, while we made money, we weren't getting wealthy.

"You may recall from your history books, that the 1890's and early 1900's were considered the Gilded Age. It was a time marked by a fabulously wealthy few and a great, unwashed mass of those struggling to get by. I didn't want to just be profitable. I wanted to be a millionaire, to be respected in society.

"Henry had invested considerable funds in the business. It was he who was the senior partner due to the size of his startup capital. And so, what profits there were, he gained the lion's share of.

"I decided that, since I was the one actually managing the business, that wasn't fair.

"So, I began taking more than my fair share. I fixed the ledgers to show the business making a smaller profit that it was, and I collected the rest for myself.

"Greed is a dangerous animal, and over time, I became less and less satisfied with what I was making. I began to take funds from the business's profits. And eventually, my fiduciary malfeasance caused the firm to start losing money. We couldn't provide all of the services that we promised, because I was stealing funds that we needed to pay for them."

I shook my head. I had felt sorry for Declan from the moment I first met him. But now he was confessing to be just another privileged man. Someone who felt life owed him a living, and so he was going to take it whether he deserved it or not, whether other people got hurt or not. I was disgusted.

"Of course, Henry was no fool. He was bound to discover my embezzlement eventually," Declan went on. "Soon, he began asking questions. He wanted to see the books, because he couldn't understand how we were losing money. I had no choice but to let him examine the ledgers. Eventually, he would discover the math didn't add up.

"There was only one thing to do: I needed to ensure that Henry Bozeman took the fall for the businesses debts."

"Yes, of course," Dorigen said. "Because the option of actually owning up to what you did and taking responsibility for it was unthinkable."

I smiled. Not only did I appreciate her sarcasm, but I was glad that she called Declan out for being the shitheel that he was.

"As I said," he continued, "greed is a dangerous animal, and I was not a very good person.

"I created a second set of books and planted evidence to show that it was Henry, not myself, who had been stealing from the business. But I knew that wouldn't be sufficient. I couldn't afford for him to be able to sue me or to counter my version of the books with the ones I had given him. I knew when he discovered the truth, he would come for me. So, I waited for him, preparing to shoot him and claim self-defense. He would be unable to testify against me if he were dead, and I would be able to sell off the company for the money. Indeed, I'd even be able to sue his estate for the money I was 'owed'."

"You're quite a piece of work, Mr. McGruder," Dorigen said, her tone covered in disgust. "A man helps you start a business, and you murder him so that you can get rich. A century later, Maggie Cartwright believes your promise that you'll help her become immortal, and as soon as Truffaut's out of the picture, you turn on her, too. You refused to give her what you promised. You haven't changed, and if it were up to me, I'd turn you out on the spot."

As much as I sympathized and agreed with Dorigen's position, I still didn't know what all this had to do with Ellington Manor. I loathed Declan's behavior as much as Dorigen did, but he was being painfully honest with us about his past. He didn't have to tell us all the bad things he had done in his life as a human. So for the moment, I gave him the benefit of the doubt.

"I didn't murder Henry Bozeman," he said. "My crime was far worse than that."

As much as I wanted to tell him to drop the whole dramatic storytelling routine, I was hooked by the fact that he'd done something worse than embezzle money from his business partner and murder him to cover it up.

"I waited for him in my office," Declan continued. "I knew he would be coming that evening. It was Wednesday, and we always met at four o'clock on Wednesday afternoon. So I was prepared for his arrival.

"At three o'clock, I heard a creak in the floorboards outside my office. Thinking he had come early, I drew my pistol and crept to the door. Then, I threw it open, took aim, and pulled the trigger.

"It was not Henry Bozeman who stood before me. It was my ten-year-old son who had come to surprise me with a visit. I shot him dead before his mother's eyes."

My heart stopped. Declan had murdered his own son? Oh, my God. I wanted to tell myself that I couldn't even imagine what that would be like. But I knew. I hadn't taken Andrew's life, but I had hurt him so badly that he said awful things to me. He could have just left me alone. I was gone. I didn't live in Lawrence anymore. They'd thrown a party to celebrate my leaving town. There was no need for him to follow up with an email months later.

But he had. He was so angry, so spiteful, that he felt the need to drive a stake into my heart like I was a vampire and needed to be vanquished. And whether he'd been a selfish brat, a *naïve* teenager, or a traumatized boy, he was so hurt and angry that he'd felt the need to lash back at me.

So I understood Declan's remorse perfectly. In a way, our stories were similar. Both of us had been blind to what was happening around us, and it had cost us everything.

"So you see, Declan," I said, leaning forward and meeting his gaze, "we're the same. We were betrayed by someone we trusted. They destroyed our worlds. And now, we have to figure out how to negotiate this brand-new environment that we don't understand."

Declan stared at me awestruck. I couldn't look at him anymore. I was too ashamed.

"Forgive me for making assumptions," he said. "As you say, I'm trying to figure out how to negotiate this brand-new environment I don't understand. I shouldn't have been presumptuous."

Dear God. I hadn't understood then how sincere his sympathy had been. He must have known it then, too – that we were the same.

"Horrified by what I'd done," Declan said, resuming his tale, "I fled. I leaped onto my horse, and I drove him away, galloping as fast as he could go. When the poor thing was at last spent, I abandoned him. I found a saloon not far from there, and I sought to drown my sins in drink.

"When I had consumed nearly three quarters of a bottle of whiskey and could barely stand, I realized that I was irredeemably corrupt. I had taken the life of an innocent child – and not just any child, my own. There could be no forgiveness, no redemption for what I had done.

With that understanding locked into my mind, I knew what I had to do. I staggered out of the saloon and found a quiet spot in the grass where no one would see me.

"But as I put the barrel of my pistol into my mouth, planning to take my own life with the same instrument with which I had murdered my son, I discovered I was not as alone as I'd thought. A gentle voice spoke behind me.

"'Pardon me, sir,' it said. 'But I believe you're aiming that Colt .45 in the wrong direction.'

"I never forgot those words. They announced the end of my life and the beginning of a new one far more terrible than the last.

"'No,' I told him. 'I have the weapon pointed towards its intended target.'

"'Now, why would you want to do a funny thing like that?' he asked me.

"I turned to face him at last. But it was dark. I couldn't see any features but for one – his eyes. He had terrible, scarlet eyes. Drunk, despondent, and unable to sense the danger this dark stranger represented, I confessed what I had done to him. I told him of my sin and that I meant to pay for it by claiming my own life.

"He laughed. I was so stupefied by that reaction, I actually put down my weapon.

"'Do you mock me?' I asked him.

"'Oh, yes,' he replied. 'I do mock you, sir. You want to die? You think that death redeems you? I'll show you how little death matters against the weight of your crimes.'

"He fell on me, knocked me to the ground, and sat across me so that I could not move. He leaned in closely, and for the first time, I saw the face of a vampire.

"'Here is the death you crave,' he said.

"'He tore out my throat and drank my blood. Despite my terror, I was glad of it. He gave me what I'd been seeking – the death I so richly deserved.

"But then, he gave back some of that blood and raised me from the grave to be his thrall."

Unbidden, tears rolled down my cheeks. I shouldn't feel sympathy for Declan. He'd been a horrible person, committed a terrible crime. The fact that he was now a vampire spoke to the truth that he had gotten what he deserved.

But he also tried to make amends, feeble though they were. I remembered lying in a shitty hotel room on the night of my fiftieth birthday after Jess had thrown me out. Unable to sleep, I just stared into the blackness of the dark room and wished I had some means to kill myself. I was ashamed of that now. Taking my own life would only have devastated my parents, to say nothing of the fact that Maggie Cartwright's curse would still be in operation and Declan Lucius and Dorigen would still be prisoners of it.

But I understood the thinking. Declan's urge to destroy himself was the same as my own. When I discovered the children hated me, that Jess hated me, that everyone blamed me for their failures, I had wanted to die – not because I felt sorry for myself. But because I had caused so much harm to the people I loved, and I could think of no better way to make it up to them.

I didn't know then the things that I knew now. I was clueless at how selfish they were, how traumatized all of us, myself included, had been by our respective personal tragedies. More importantly, I found that blood does not quench the fires of fury. Death does not bring justice to the executed or to the victim.

In that moment, though, it had seemed like such a perfect solution, like the thing that was most logical that any right-thinking individual would have done. Declan's suicidal misery was understandable. I hadn't been a bad person. He had. But the connection I felt to him only grew stronger as he confessed how he had been turned.

Even Dorigen, who had been every bit as judgmental as I had, looked on the vampire with compassion.

"For the next three years, we terrorized the Northeast. He made me commit all sorts of atrocities. If I tried to resist, he would simply dominate me into submission. A vampire cannot resist the will of its maker. And if I begged him to free me or to leave me out of his villainy, he would drain me nearly to death, and then bury me in the ground to starve until I could either dig my way out, or he elected to free me on his own."

Holy shit. I thought Marcel Truffaut was about as cruel a vampire as I could imagine. But this guy who vamped Declan sounded even worse. And it occurred to me that, if Declan had spent three years being terrorized by his master, it was no wonder he wanted leverage and protection against Truffaut. Whether or not Truffaut would have turned on him as he feared, the sheer possibility of it, the remembered horror of his early life as a vampire, had to invoke naked fear in Declan and a desire to ensure that never happened again. I recalled the night that I broke the curse, waking him from his fifty-year slumber. He had been insane with bloodlust. Dear God. Maggie Cartwright's revenge on him had been even more wicked than she had known.

"Fortunately, he was careless," Declan went on. "He reveled in the violence, in the terror he inflicted. Human beings don't take kindly to being threatened. Eventually, they took action against him. He was slain on New Year's Eve of the turn of the century.

"I escaped. And with the vampire who had made me dead, I was free at last."

"I knew very little of this about you, Declan," Lucius said. "And I understand why you wanted to die. But you still haven't answered Bethany's question. What is it you would get out of Monsieur Truffaut activating the mansion?"

"I should have thought that would be obvious to you, Lucius. Especially since you've been trapped in your own unending curse."

"My curse is over, Declan. Bethany freed me when Maggie Cartwright died. I'm afraid I don't see the connection."

"Tell me something, Lucius, is this your first life?"

Lucius didn't answer right away. His green eyes blazed with fury at Declan picking at his wounds.

"No," he answered, a frosty note in his words. "It is my third. The question still stands."

"My point," Declan replied, "is that you of all people should appreciate being unable to escape a long life.

"As to the question you and Bethany have asked, I still want to die. But I no longer believe that that will free me of the burden of my sin. I have spent nearly two hundred years suffering this curse as punishment for my deeds. I do not wish to spend all eternity in these chains. I want to see my son."

He might've stabbed me in the heart. Oh God, I understood that pain. The desperate desire to fall to your knees before your children and beg them for forgiveness.

"But you can't do that if you go to Hell," Dorigen said.

"Correct," Declan replied.

"So, you mean to tell me that you have spent all this time, first pursuing the mystery of the Blood Heir and then how to activate the mansion's power so that you can find a way to rid yourself of the curse of vampirism and then die?" Lucius said.

"Precisely, Lucius. If I go to Hell, I'll not see my son. He was an innocent and no doubt resides in Elysium. And since Alexander Ellington was working with magic to control all the dead and become immortal, I had hoped that somewhere in his research he had discovered a solution to my conundrum."

I folded my fingers crossed my chest and thought for a moment about Declan's words. I was no magical expert. I barely understood my own abilities. But I simply could not figure out how harnessing the spirits of the deceased to give oneself immortality could hold any clue to Declan's problem. And since Marcel Truffaut wanted to repeat Ellington's experiment, but correct his mistakes, it seemed even less likely Declan could benefit.

"I'm sorry, Declan," I said, "but you're an idiot."

His gorgeous blue eyes grew wide at that statement. I saw no fury in his face though. He was genuinely perplexed.

"How so?"

"Both Alexander Ellington and Marcel Truffaut only wanted power for themselves. Ellington desired immortality; Truffaut wants to rule the world, or at least the world of vampires. Both of them are only seeking to use the dead for their own ends. You're looking for redemption, possibly an escape. You're not going to find it with these methods, and I can't believe somebody as intelligent as you doesn't see it."

He smiled – not a big grin, just a small upturn of his lips. But I was certain the words about to come from his mouth would be mansplaining.

"Perhaps," he said. "But when you live with a curse like this, Bethany, hope is the only thing that keeps you going."

"Really? Because what I think is keeping you going is fear." Once again, Declan looked stunned. "You're afraid to die, because you're afraid of going to Hell. There's no hope or bravery in your continued existence. You just keep getting up each night because you fear the consequences. I imagine those fifty years you were unable to wake were the best of your undead existence – the closest you ever came to dodging the bullet with your name on it. In that respect, I'm sorry I woke you. I feel I owe you an apology, because I've brought you back to the world you were trying so hard to escape.

"But if I were you, Declan, I would abandon this hope you believe you're clinging to. If you want to undo the curse of vampirism, you're not going to find it in this house, walking the path that you are on."

If I hadn't been the one speaking, my jaw might've fallen open. I couldn't believe I had said all that. I sat for a moment absolutely marveling at my own wisdom. Maybe it was my Sight that was cluing me into the hard truths Declan wanted so badly not to see. But it seemed obvious to me that he was running away, and he had been since the day he pulled the trigger on his son. The problem with running from yourself is that you can never, ever get away. I knew that all too well.

I realized I was tired. We'd been up until nearly dawn the night before. First, my nightmare had shaken me awake, and then, after we'd discovered the secret chamber, we'd discussed the dark presence of the manor with Dorigen before exploring the hidden room. I wasn't sure I was ready for bed yet. We had just finished dinner perhaps an hour ago as a result of Paul's ultimatum.

But living through the emotional stress of Declan's horrifying tale and the threat that Paul made against him and by way of association, my household, I found myself suddenly disinterested in company. With a yawn, I stood.

"I think I'll retire for the night," I said. "Paul will be back, probably as early as tomorrow. I need time to think, and I need rest.

"Declan, I appreciate the fear you feel, especially since we don't know what's become of Marcel Truffaut. I'd like to tell you you should turn over the ring. But somehow, I don't trust Paul either. I need to decide what the best thing to do is.

"But let me make one thing perfectly plain to you: You will not endanger me or my friends. If you invoke the wrath of The Order, it's you against them. I'm not putting Dorigen or Lucius at risk. I won't throw you out, but you might think about leaving. Just something to consider."

Declan nodded thoughtfully, as if everything I had said made sense to him. He stood and faced me.

"Thank you for your candor, Bethany," he said. "I shall take all that you have said into consideration. But I wouldn't be here if I didn't know there was more to this than what you believe."

That unnerved me a bit. He was clearly holding something back. He had one more secret he hadn't divulged.

But I was too tired to wring it out of him. I needed rest. I needed to recharge my batteries and my brain.

Because I had a strong suspicion that tomorrow was going to be a big and difficult day.

Seventeen

I came once again to the brick wall. I sighed heavily. God, I was tired of seeing this damned thing. I had no idea what it meant, except that it had been blocking my Third Eye. Clearly, there was still some mystery to it, because here it was yet again in my dreams.

Dori approached me from the right and beckoned me. I shuddered, now that I knew who she was. But I hoped that maybe this time she had something different to tell me, something new that would at last crack the code of the strange vision.

Besides, I had no desire to let Andrew beat the hell out of me again.

Turning to my right, I followed Dori along the familiar path, keeping the wall to my left. As usual, she led me to the library, but this time, we continued into the secret chamber. Dori turned back to me.

"Observe," she said. "The hour approaches."

With a grand sweep of her hand, she indicated I should look all about me. Everywhere my gaze fell, there were clocks. They varied from standard, industrial wall clocks to ornate grandfather clocks and kitschy ones like Felix the Cat, whose tail was the pendulum. Not all of them told time. Some showed what I could only presume were moons and planets. Some had magical sigils on them I could not read. There was one that had no numbers at all, just hands. And there were several that were limp, as though they belonged in a Salvador Dali painting.

But the ones that told time, all showed the same moment – two fifty-nine. And I watched as the sweep hand rose to the top, clicking the minute hand to three.

There was a terrible cacophony of bells. Hundreds of clocks all chimed the hour, but they played different songs. And a cuckoo clock screeched louder than all the rest.

I turned back to Dori. Her pretty, hazel eyes turned hell-red, and she morphed into the giant man-bat who'd been haunting my dreams for months.

"Unbind me!" he roared.

♫

I opened my eyes and stared up at the ceiling. For the first time since having these frightening visions, I wasn't actually afraid. It all kind of felt so matter-of-fact – like watching a horror movie so many times that the jump-scares no longer affect you. Light poured in through the window, and I stared at it trying to get my bearings. The trees, still without leaves, looked bleak and barren, as though they were ready to die. The sky was slate-grey and gave all the indications of a storm headed our way. How wonderful. The outdoors was just as depressing as inside the house.

I reached down to stroke Lucius, and discovered he was gone. I rolled over and looked at the clock. My eyes popped open wide, bringing me fully awake. It may have been three AM in my dreams, but in the waking world, it was already ten after ten. I'd overslept. Must've been a side effect of all the late nights recently.

With a yawn, I dragged myself out of bed, shivering when my bare feet hit the hardwood floor. I really needed to get some slippers.

I went to the bathroom and tried to put myself together. Then I decided a shower was in order. I was weary, my fifty-year-old joints were sore, and I wanted to feel good. So I drew the curtain around the claw-foot bathtub, turned on the water, making sure it was hot and steamy, and then stepped inside.

I don't know how long I was in, but it must've been at least twenty minutes. I kind of just stood there, luxuriating in the hot water melting away the aches and pains in my muscles. The steam cleared my sinuses, and the threat of a headache that had been lurking behind my eyes vanished. My hands were pruned before I'd even washed my hair. But I decided not to skip that step. Something told me I wanted to be fresh and fully human today. And I had learned to listen to the universe when it gave me hints. After all, what good was being a mystic if you didn't do anything with the insights you received?

By the time I dried my hair and dressed in a cozy sweater and jeans and made it downstairs, it was nearly eleven o'clock. I figured I was going to have to make my own coffee this morning, since it already would've been drunk hours ago by Dorigen. But as I hit the bottom of the stairs and turned to head for the kitchen, the doorbell rang.

I froze in my tracks. Had Paul returned? Was he planning to force his way down the stairs and physically rip the ring from Declan's finger as he slept? It seemed plausible.

I scanned the foyer for anything I could use as a weapon. The best I could come up with was an umbrella. Probably not ideal, but I could imagine it hurting if I swung it like an axe.

"Lucius," I said, not raising my voice at all, simply confident in my power.

Half a second later, he appeared in the foyer. He took up a spot near the edge of the door and prepared to spring should it be necessary, wordlessly understanding my summons and command. Holding the umbrella behind my back, I took a deep breath and opened the door.

Sheriff Mueller stood on the stoop, looking troubled. He was alone.

"Morning, Sheriff," I said as Lucius relaxed from his crouch.

"Hi, Parker," he replied. "Do you mind if I come in for a moment?"

Something was wrong. I had no idea what it was, but the grim expression on the sheriff's face and the heavy tone of his words told me he had something gravely important to discuss.

"Of course," I said, stepping aside.

He removed his trooper hat and stepped into the house. I shut the door.

"What's up?" I asked.

"Sorry to disturb you at home," he said, holding his hat as though he were a military man coming to tell me my husband had been killed in action. "I looked for you at the diner first. But you weren't there, and Drogo said you hadn't been in this morning. So, I came out here."

"Yeah, I overslept. I was just on my way to get some coffee. Would you like some?"

"Not today," he said. "Parker, Paul has ordered me to get the ring from Declan."

My heart stopped. So, Paul hadn't come in person. He'd sent the sheriff as his errand boy. Figured.

"The Order insists that Declan return it," he went on. "If he won't give it up, I have instructions to take it by force."

My eyes popped open wide. By force? What did that mean?

"Sheriff, why are you doing this? You know this isn't right."

"I don't have a choice, Parker. The Order pays my salary the same as it does yours. I have to do what they say. And whether he wants to or not, so does Declan."

My mind worked at a frantic pace. I supposed I should have realized The Order was responsible for my stipend. After all, Rhoda had told me simply that the estate paid it from its trust. And given that Alexander Ellington and his terrifying mansion were *persona non grata* with The Order, it made sense that I was working for them by being its caretaker. Sheriff Mueller no doubt reminded me of that to apply leverage.

At the same time, this didn't sit right with me. It had been more than twelve hours since Paul had come here to demand the ring. Indianapolis was a two-hour drive from here. He could've had a dozen agents on the spot in no time, ready to seize Declan and potentially stake him if he resisted.

So why send the sheriff? Even if he did get his pay from The Order and was therefore technically bound to obey Paul, it didn't make any sense. Paul came last night asking for the ring. This morning he'd sent some muscle to get it, but it had been a local official instead of a more powerful unit. Why? If The Order wanted the artifacts back under their control so badly why use the locals to get them?

"Be that as it may, Sheriff," I replied, "do you have any sort of confirmation that The Order actually gave you those instructions?"

"What do you mean?" he asked, looking confused. "Paul is the one who told me to collect it. He's the Order representative in town. It doesn't need to be any more official than that."

"Doesn't it?"

"No," he insisted. "Why would it?"

"Sheriff, we know that Paul was working with Marcel Truffaut to collect the artifacts. Truffaut's been missing for two weeks. Doesn't it seem strange that suddenly The Order wants all the artifacts back under its control and that it sent Paul, Truffaut's collaborator, to collect them? This all feels highly suspicious to me."

For a moment, he seemed to consider what I said. I watched as he turned the ideas over in his mind. But then a look of frustration and irritation set up shop on his face, and he shook his head.

"You're seeing conspiracies where there aren't any, Parker. This is all perfectly by the book. Paul's the Order representative in town. If he gets an order from his superiors. He has to follow it. And he's totally within his rights to deputize me to execute it.

"I know you like Declan and that he is your friend. That's why I came out here. Out of respect for you and for Declan and what he did for me, I was hoping that you could talk some sense into him. Paul's got a bee in his bonnet about this. He's insistent that Declan turn the ring over tonight. And if he won't, I am supposed to get rough with him."

I imagined the fight between the sheriff and Declan. On the one hand, I gave Declan the edge – I'd seen how much vampire speed made a difference when he and Truffaut took down Karl's heavies. But I also knew Sheriff Mueller was a crafty opponent. He'd outwitted Karl brilliantly. And if he thought he was going to have to take on a vampire, he would come prepared.

Shit. This was no kind of good.

"Thanks for giving me a heads-up," I said.

He stared hard at me with those deep, brown eyes of his. His sheer masculinity, his alpha personality, threatened to overwhelm me. But Rusty Mueller was not the first man I'd ever stood up to. And I wasn't afraid of him.

"Seriously, Bethany, please try to talk to Declan. I'll be back after sundown. If he doesn't cooperate, things are going to get ugly."

I almost didn't hear the threat. I was so blown away by him actually using my first name for a change, I almost missed the intent of his words. And it occurred to me that that had been a point – he'd tried to be a little more intimate with me in the hopes that he could persuade me to avert violence. I wasn't sure whether to be complimented or insulted. But either way, it didn't change my response.

"I'll tell him Sheriff," I said. "I'll even try to reason with him as you suggest. But Declan McGruder is a dangerous vampire. And if he refuses, I don't want to think about what could happen to you if you try to take it by force."

He studied me for several seconds more, trying to see if I were sincere about telling Declan to give up the ring. He grimaced again and put his hat back on.

"Thanks, Parker," he said. "I'll see you tonight."

"I wish I could say I was looking forward to it," I replied.

He looked me up and down. Then he opened the door.

"Yeah," he said, "me, too."

And then he went out, shutting the door behind him.

"That complicates matters," Lucius said.

"Gee, you think?" I snarked. "Come on. We better figure out what to do, and I need coffee."

The two of us walked to the kitchen. I had no idea what to do next. But I knew I was going to need some help.

♪

Once I'd brewed some coffee and had a few sips, I called Rhoda. She was the only one I could think of who might have answers. I could feel some critical piece of this mystery just out of reach – as though there were one final clue that would make it all fall together for me. I could nearly see the picture, but it was still unclear.

"Hey, Bethany," Rhoda said after picking up. "I missed you at the diner this morning."

"Yeah, I'm sorry. I overslept."

"Well, I'm not surprised, given all the things that have been going on. You have to be exhausted."

She was right about that. I could feel the fatigue weighing on me like a heavy blanket. Deliberately, I sipped some more coffee to try to bring my brain fully to focus.

"Rhoda, have you figured out which demon I've been seeing in my dreams?"

"I'm afraid not," she replied. "There are a lot of demons with batwings, but I have yet to find one that seems to have some sort of association with bats themselves. And your physical description is similar enough to so many demonic forms that it's next to impossible to figure out which one it might be. So far, nothing I've read coincides with what you've seen."

Great. Somehow, I knew this was a wild goose chase. There was not enough information, or maybe Rhoda was looking in the wrong place. But though I'd hoped there might be some connection between her search into the issue at hand, the truth was I had more important things to worry about at the moment.

"Rhoda, we've got a problem."

"What's that?"

"Paul wants the signet ring," I replied. "He came to the manor last night and demanded Declan turn it over to him. He said that The Order wants all the artifacts back under their control. Declan refused to give it up."

"I'm not surprised," Rhoda said. "Did he say why he wouldn't turn it over?"

"He says he needs its magic for protection against Marcel Truffaut."

Rhoda didn't say anything for a few moments. If I hadn't been used to her sitting and thinking, I might've thought the line went dead.

"That's not the worst of it, though," I said.

"What else is there?"

"This morning, Sheriff Mueller came by the house."

"Yes, I saw him at the diner. He said he was looking for you."

"Yeah, well, he was looking for me, because he wanted to tell me that Paul had ordered him to take the ring from Declan."

"What!"

"I kid you not," I said. "He came by to talk to me. He wants me to try to talk some sense into Declan, so that things don't have to get ugly, as he put it. But he's coming back tonight after Declan's awake. And Paul has authorized him to take the ring by force if necessary."

"Oh, my God," Rhoda said.

"That's what I thought," I said. "Rhoda, this whole thing stinks. Why would Paul order the sheriff to get the ring for him? Why not just call in help from the regional office in Indianapolis?"

"Good question," Rhoda said.

"This just doesn't feel like how a super-secret, international organization dedicated to keeping knowledge of the supernatural away from normal people would act. Wouldn't they just come in with a bunch of men-in-black, take care of things, and hush it all up?"

"That is their usual *modus operandi*," Rhoda replied. "It's not necessarily unusual for the Order representative to give instructions to local law enforcement, especially in a supernatural community like this one. But for something this big, you would think that they would bring in a little more force."

"Especially since we are dealing with a vampire," I added. "Why send your wolf-shifter sheriff in to take down a vamp by himself?"

Rhoda didn't say anything. I could practically see her nodding and thinking through the phone.

"So, what are you suggesting?" she said at last.

"Rhoda, what if Paul doesn't have instructions from his superiors? What if he's leveraging his position as the Order representative in town to get the ring away from, Declan?"

"Why would he do that?"

"He keeps talking about The Order wanting all four artifacts under its control again," I answered. "Maybe he and Truffaut have the pocket watch. That would give them three of the four artifacts."

"And Declan has the fourth," she mused.

"Right. And the one Declan has gives him protection from the other three."

"So, they need to get it away from him, so that they can ensure his cooperation," she said, following my line of thinking.

"That's what I'm afraid of," I said. "I'm deeply worried that we haven't seen Truffaut, because he managed to finally wring the location of the pocket watch from Paul. Now he's got three of the artifacts, and he's trying to use Paul as leverage to get the fourth away from Declan."

"So he can betray him?"

"Maybe. Or maybe he just is tired of working with Declan and wants it all for himself."

"Damn," Rhoda swore. "That sounds like a pretty plausible scenario, Bethany."

"I was afraid you'd tell me that," I said.

"So, what do we do now?" Rhoda asked.

"Well, I'm not sure. But I've got a few hours before sundown. I figure we're safe until then, since Declan's asleep anyway, and Sheriff Mueller said he'd be back after dark, not before.

"I really need you to figure out which demon this is and what its powers are. If we know what we're dealing with, then we'll probably be able to anticipate what Truffaut will do and why. So you get cracking on that."

"I will," she said. "And maybe I'll bring you some wolfsbane before Rusty arrives."

I frowned. I really didn't want to go up against the sheriff. I liked him too much. But I knew better than to let him enable Marcel Truffaut to harness the power of Ellington Manor.

"That's probably a good idea," I said.

"All right," Rhoda said. "I'm hitting the books. I'll be over before the sun sets."

"Thanks, Rhoda."

"No need to thank me," she said. "I've got skin in this game, too."

Ah, yes. So far as we knew, Reggie was trapped in the manor somewhere. And I had promised Rhoda I would free him.

But as the pieces aligned on the board for Marcel Truffaut's endgame, I couldn't help but feel that I was overmatched.

Eighteen

By midafternoon, I was in full-blown panic. I'd been discussing ideas with Dorigen and Lucius for hours, but none of us knew what to do. It seemed certain that turning the ring over to Paul was a bad idea. But I was equally afraid of Declan. He'd always seemed so stoic and kind, but after learning he was corrupt and a killer, I simply could not look at him the same way. An aura of tragedy clung to him that generated sympathy in my heart for him. But he was as Dorigen had described him to me – a monster. And after my vision and the tarot reading, I'd feared he would betray us. Now, he and the sheriff were headed for a showdown on my front doorstep, and I could not figure out how to stop it.

"Well, you've got yourself in a fine pickle this time, Missy," Dorigen said.

I threw her a withering gaze.

"Dorigen, that doesn't help," I said. "I get it. Sarcasm is your defense mechanism. It covers your fear and gives you a false sense of confidence. I'm the same way. But right now, I need practical solutions, not recriminations."

Dorigen looked stunned for a moment. Then she nodded.

"Sorry, Bethany. A lifetime of habit."

"Don't worry about it," I replied. "Like I said, I get it.

"But what the hell are we going to do? I feel like we can't let Declan give the ring to Sheriff Mueller, and we can't let him keep it."

"Why the latter?" Lucius asked.

"I'm not sure," I replied. "It's like I know what the answer is, but it doesn't help because I have no idea what question I'm asking."

They both nodded. Dorigen toyed with the tea she'd poured herself. After making it ten minutes ago, she had yet to take a sip. I sympathized. There was a raging hunger in me I had no desire to sate. I'd barely eaten today. In fact, I'd only had coffee. My hands shook, and I couldn't be certain if it was because I was overcaffeinated, or if I had I was anxious about tonight. Probably both. But I had no appetite.

"Well, Bethany," Lucius said, "you're simply going to have to try to talk sense to them."

I laughed.

"Have you ever tried that with either of them?" I said.

"Not with the sheriff," he replied. "But I see your point.

"Still, you're very persuasive, Bethany. You still have access to your Throat Chakra. Use its power to talk one of them down."

My eyes opened in alarm at his suggestion. I studied him for a moment. He was absolutely serious.

"Isn't that unethical?" I asked. "That's the exact same thing I did to Reggie, and you and Rhoda laid into me about it."

"Declan and the sheriff have incompatible positions," he said. "They will come into conflict unless someone talks one of them down. If you want to resolve this situation amicably, you may have to employ your power."

"I don't know, Lucius," I said after a moment." That sounds like using my mysticism to force my will on the world. I don't think that's what I'm supposed to do. I don't think it's right."

Lucius gave me one of his cat shrugs. A look of casual, feline indifference washed across his face.

"Unless one of them relents, blood will be spilled, Bethany," he said. "It's up to you whether you want that to happen or not."

"I just don't understand why you keep insisting on this after you scolded me in Cincinnati."

"You'll recall that Rhoda went with you to acquire the cane," he said.

"Yes, Lucius, I was there."

"Rhoda knew stealing was wrong. She weighed the potential outcomes and the ethics involved. And then she elected to help you.

"When you used the cane to order Reggie to take action to free us, you did not contemplate the consequences. You did not consider whether it was right or wrong. You simply acted.

"This is different, Bethany. You have time to weigh the options and decide what the best thing to do is. If you feel it would be wrong to compel the sheriff and Declan to back down, then you shouldn't do it. If on the other hand, you decide that it's the only way to prevent a disaster, then you will have to content yourself that this is one of those times when the ends justify the means.

"I'll grant you. This is a sticky ethical question. But it is the one you are facing."

Great. So, I either had to let two of my friends tear each other to pieces, or I needed to use my powers unethically. This was bullshit. There had to be a third way. But what was it?

The grandfather clock in the parlor chimed three. I realized I was running out of time. Panic began to seize control of my heart again.

But then I heard a fourth ring. That shook me out of my depressive reverie. Was it later than I thought? I checked my phone. No, it was three o'clock.

"I'll answer it," Dorigen said. "Seems to be a dead end here anyway."

It took me a moment to realize what she was saying. It hadn't been a fourth chime from the clock. It was the doorbell. Damn, I was definitely overly focused on this problem. Maybe I needed a break.

Briefly, I worried it would be Paul, preparing to take the ring from Declan while he slept. But then I realized that if he had intended to do that, he wouldn't have ordered the sheriff to get it tonight after sundown.

A minute later, Dorigen returned to the kitchen escorting Drogo.

My eyes about fell out of my head at the sight of him. I'd never seen him outside the diner, let alone standing in my own kitchen. In his hands. He clutched a Drogo's to-go bag and a large, paper cup with a top and a straw stuck through it. As always, he wore a beaming grin across his gorgeous, Middle Eastern face.

"Greetings, Bethany Parker," he said, a delighted note in his tone.

"Hi, Drogo. What are you doing here?"

"I did not see you in the diner this morning. And I know that today is a very important day for you. I worried you wouldn't be eating well, so I brought you something."

Once again, I stared at him as though he were from outer space. He knew this was a big day? How did he know I hadn't eaten anything?

"I'm sorry, I don't know what you mean," I said, feeling stupid.

"The hour approaches, Bethany Parker," he replied. "Tonight, your destiny is at hand."

My heart stopped. The hour approaches? That was what Dori had told me in my dream last night. And the monster from my visions had told me on more than one occasion that I was here to fulfill my destiny.

I was suddenly wary of Drogo. His presence here was not coincidental.

"Perhaps, Dorigen and I should leave you to talk," Lucius said, as though he, too, could sense magical forces at work. He hopped down off the chair and walked towards the doorway. "Come on, Dorigen, I'm sure we can find diversion elsewhere."

Dorigen nodded. She stared hard at me for several seconds, as if she thought I was up to something and wished I would tell her what it was. Then, she turned and followed Lucius out of the kitchen.

Drogo crossed the room and set the bag down in front of me. He smiled broadly, and his silver eyes twinkled.

"I have just the thing you need, Bethany Parker," he said.

The smell of grease hit my nose, and the ravenous hunger I'd been suppressing all day returned with a vengeance. Without saying thanks, I pulled the bag to me and withdrew a wrapped sandwich.

"One of my famous quarter-pound hamburgers," Drogo said. "Cooked medium rare, just like you like, and topped with onions, blue cheese crumbles, and hot sauce. And of course, French fries to cut the spice."

"That's my favorite burger of all time," I said in wonder. "I've never ordered it at your restaurant. How did you know?"

"I keep telling you, Bethany Parker," he said looking pleased with himself, "I am an angel. I know many things. For instance, I know you love to wash that burger down with a strawberry milkshake."

He put the cup in front of me as well. I couldn't remember the last time I'd had a milkshake. I'd loved them as a child, but somewhere along the way as an adult, I'd abandoned them. I took hold of the cup and was stunned that it was still frosty cold, as though perhaps he had just removed it from the freezer. But as I pumped the straw to loosen up the ice cream, I discovered it was already well mixed and smooth. Tentatively, I put the straw to my lips and sucked.

An explosion of fresh strawberry ice cream hit my mouth. I was immediately cast back to childhood. There had been a Dairy Queen not far from our house. And though my dad would take us to get ice cream cones, I always wanted shakes instead. Suddenly, I was eight years old again and happy in a way I had not been in decades.

"Oh, my God," I said, as though I were having an orgasm. "This might be the most delicious milkshake I've ever had in my life."

"I am glad you enjoy it, Bethany Parker," the angel said.

"How do you do this?"

"Do what?" he asked.

"Make everything as perfect as it seemed to be when I was a little girl."

He smiled conspiratorially. For a moment, I was reminded of my father.

"You may as well ask the wind how it blows," he replied. "Or why it's always so still when it snows. It is the way of things, Bethany Parker. I am an angel, and I have chosen to lend my magic to food."

As empty as that answer was, I found it strangely satisfying. As a child, I'd often wondered how things were as they are. And when you're a kid, magic is a perfectly good explanation.

"Do you mind if I sit down?" he asked.

"Please," I said, indicating the chair across from me.

He beamed another of his spotlight smiles and seated himself. Then he laced his fingers together and rested his chin on his fists, his elbows on the table.

"Okay," I said. "Cards on the table. I very much appreciate the visit and the food. But why are you really here?"

"You're so suspicious, Bethany Parker. Why do you believe I would not simply check in on a friend and make sure she is eating?"

"Because you said the hour approaches. And I heard that very phrase in a vision while I was dreaming this morning. I've been in Enchantment long enough to know those sorts of things are not coincidences, Drogo. Tell me what's going on."

"I am not in the habit of explaining the workings of the universe, Bethany Parker. No angel is. But I sensed you needed my aid today, and so I came."

I chewed on a few of the French fries. God, they were delicious. He was right of course. I needed help. But I wasn't sure what kind he could offer me.

"And how do you propose to aid me?" I asked, with a smirk of my own.

"Food soothes the soul, Bethany Parker. A full stomach makes many things possible. And good food creates pleasure that opens the mind to possibility. You are stuck. You find yourself at a crossroads with no answer on which path to take. So, I have brought you some of your favorite foods to help clarify things."

When I was growing up and my mother insisted we go to church, I would always hear, "The Lord works in mysterious ways." Well, here was a bona fide angel, somehow summoned to my house in my hour of need. And his solution to my problems was a cheeseburger. Suddenly, Pastor Frank sounded very wise.

"I can't access my Third-Eye Chakra," I said. "No matter how I try, there's a wall in front of me that I cannot get over or around."

"This is indeed a problem for you," Drogo said. "Without the Third Eye, you cannot see things as they truly are. And this is critical to you at the moment, for there is much deception at work in your affairs. Not all are being truthful with you. And you cannot determine how to proceed without understanding what's happening."

"Exactly!" I agreed. "And it's frustrating, Drogo. I know my Third Eye is in alignment. But it's like someone ripped it out of me. I can't sense it, and I can't access it. Whenever I try, even if I use all of my power …"

Suddenly I couldn't go on. I didn't want to admit to this angel what it was that I saw when I pushed too hard.

"When you try?" Drogo prompted.

"Bad things happen to me," I said, trying to stay vague.

"You have been ensorcelled, Bethany Parker."

"What?"

"A blockade has been placed in your mind," he said, as though this were the most cheerful news I'd ever heard. "While it exists, you cannot use your higher chakras. You are cut off from them."

I stared at him, round-eyed. How did he know this? And how did I not?

"What do I do?" I asked.

"I will help you," he pronounced. "But first, eat your burger. The pleasure of the food will help relax you, and you will need fuel for what is to come."

The implications of that worried me. I could tell by the tone of his voice something ominous was before me. I had no idea what it was, but if an angel told me I needed to gather my strength, it couldn't possibly be good.

The burger was every bit as good as anything I'd ever eaten at Drogo's, which is to say it was the best I'd ever had in my life. Just as the milkshake had been cold, the burger remained impossibly hot, despite the fact that it was a ten-minute drive from the manor to the diner. Offhandedly, I wondered if Drogo had teleported here.

He had cooked it perfectly pink in the middle so that it was greasy and juicy, and the blazing heat of the hot sauce combined with the sweetness of the onions and the savory of the blue cheese created a taste sensation in my mouth that I could only think of as orgasmic. Despite the fact that I was practically starving from not having eaten today, I did not wolf the food down. I ate it slowly, savoring every bite, every flavor. I had never eaten with such concentration before in my life. The experience was a pleasure unequaled by any I had ever known. And between the burger and the strawberry shake, I'd never enjoyed a meal more than this. It took me back to the first time I'd eaten Drogo's food – the blueberry pancakes I'd seen advertised on a billboard that did not exist. It was everything.

As I put the last French fry into my mouth and wiped my hands and lips, I found myself perfectly at peace. Nothing could harm me, and I felt as connected to the universe as I ever had. Drogo had promised to help me defeat the spell blockading my mind. But I didn't care at the moment if he did or did not. He'd already done more than enough for me with the meal.

"That was absolutely amazing," I said. "Thank you so much. I hadn't eaten today, and this was exactly what I needed."

"I've told you, Bethany Parker," he said, with a shrug, "breakfast is the most important meal of the day. Without it, things do not go as well."

I smiled broadly.

"You sound like my mother," I said. "Only, you know, more … angelic."

He favored me with a chuckle. Then he leaned forward.

"Are you ready to begin?" he said.

Ordinarily, that might've broken the spell. Kicking me back to the problems at hand always seemed to ruin the placidity I had acquired from whatever relaxing activity I'd been involved in. But this time, I *was* ready. The magic of Drogo's cooking had me fully prepared to take on the world.

"Yes," I replied. "I'm ready."

He reached out across the table.

"Take my hands," he instructed.

I did. As soon as my fingers touched his, sparks of pleasure zapped up my arms and into my heart. I had no idea how many men I had touched in the course of my life, but holding hands with an angel was unlike anything else. When I was little and my father had held my hand, I had always felt safe. Drogo created a sensation of joy and security several magnitudes higher.

"Now," he said, "close your eyes."

Once again, I did as he instructed.

And then, we were standing in front of the brick wall. There was no transition. There was no warning. We were just there.

I turned in surprise to Drogo, but before I could say anything, my mouth fell open in shock. He was no longer a handsome, middle-aged, Middle Eastern man in a grease-stained T-shirt and jeans. Rather, he wore a shimmering, sheer shift. Enormous wings with golden feathers sprung from his back, and glory streamed from every pore of his skin. For a moment, I was overwhelmed by his celestial magnificence. And then I realized as a result of the thin material covering him that angels were not sexless like I had been taught in Sunday School.

Drogo was impressively equipped, and I felt the urges that often came to the surface whenever I looked on his silver eyes spring forth and magnify. Sudden heat rushed through my body, and I felt like a schoolgirl in his presence.

"Yes," he said. "This is definitely the work of someone else. It is not only blocking the path to your Third Eye, but it conceals certain memories behind it."

"What?" I said.

For a moment I had no idea what he was talking about. Then, I snapped out of my lusty reverie.

"Oh," I said. "So it's not just blocking my central channel?"

"Correct," he said. "Someone does not wish for you to remember certain things, Bethany Parker. I cannot tell if the wall's occlusion of your Third Eye is deliberate or coincidental. But regardless, your memory has been tampered with, and that is keeping you from seeing things as they truly are."

Holy shit. Someone had messed with my mind? Who the hell could've done that?

Declan was the first person who sprang to mind. He had his vampire charm. Perhaps he had done something in order to make me to forget.

If he had, he was going to pay for it.

"So how do we get rid of it?" I asked.

"This is a powerful spell, Bethany Parker. It cannot be easily defeated. It won't just disappear. But a spell such as this one always has a solution to it. All magic can be undone. You must piece together the clues to defeat it."

He might as well have asked me to write a doctoral dissertation on quantum physics and defend it before Nobel laureates.

"But I've been trying," I said. "I can't figure it out. I can't get over it,

and going left or right doesn't knock it down. There's no way to get around it."

"You have tried walking in both directions?"

"Yes."

"Tell me what you find each way."

I didn't want to answer that. Just the memory of what lay to the left scared the hell out of me. And I was ashamed to tell Drogo that my own son would attempt to beat me to death with a baseball bat.

"When I go right, I encounter Dorigen. But she's always Dori – the young version of herself. She leads me into the library. By doing that, by following her, I get clues. They enabled me to find Alexander Ellington's secret chamber, the one from which he presumably cast his ill-fated spell. Last night, she led me through the library and into the secret room. There, she told me that the hour approaches, and she transformed into a giant monster."

"Yes," Drogo said. "A giant half-man, half-bat creature, who desires you to release it from its bondage."

"Yes, how did you— Never mind."

"You have learned all you can from this direction, Bethany Parker, what happens when you go left?"

Terror exploded in my stomach. Even the calming divinity oozing from Drogo was unable to soothe me.

"I meet my stepson," I said, swallowing hard. "He orders me to go back. And if I don't, he attempts to beat me to death with a baseball bat."

"This spell has a very specific design to it, Bethany Parker. It wants you to go a particular way. It wants you to go to the right and entices you with a familiar and safe face to move in that direction. There, are the clues and the tasks whoever placed it here wants you to complete. It is to the left that the answer to defeating the spell lies."

I shuddered. Somehow, I'd known that was what he was going to say. But I did not want to believe it.

"A guardian has been placed at that gate, Bethany Parker. Its purpose is twofold – to encourage you to go in the direction the spellcaster wants and to prevent you from learning what they do not want you to know."

Dread burbled up from my heart and into my mind. Drogo's instruc-

tions were perfectly clear without him having to voice them: If I wanted around this wall, I would have to face Andrew.

My flesh crawling, my heart pounding, I turned to the left. I sucked in a deep breath.

"Okay, here we go," I said.

"I am right beside you, Bethany Parker. There is nothing to fear."

Ha! Easy for him to say. He was an angel. Nevertheless, I forced myself forward, measuring each step carefully and setting my face with grim determination.

Andrew sprang into being almost immediately. As usual, he wore his Lawrence High baseball uniform. A look of abject fury covered his face.

"I told you not to come back!" *he shouted.*

And then, before I could respond, he rushed me, the bat held over his shoulder like an axe.

"Andrew, wait!" *I said.*

He ignored me. Instead, he brought the bat down with all of his eighteen-year-old might. It connected between my neck and shoulder, splintering my collarbone and knocking me to the ground. I cried out in pain.

"I hate you!" *Andrew screamed.* "Never come back again!"

With each word he brought the bat down with another savage blow, bruising my muscles, breaking my bones. I screamed.

"Drogo! Help me!"

And then, we were back in the kitchen, sitting at the table. I started bawling immediately, the echoes of Andrew's attack still stinging my body.

"I can't do it," I sobbed. "I can't do it! He's too strong!"

"This is a sinister spell, Bethany Parker. It is terrifying and harmful. Whoever cast it is an accomplished magician.

"But you can defeat it. You are strong, Bethany Parker, so much stronger than anyone knows, even yourself."

"I'm not," I wept. "I'm not strong enough. I can't do this, Drogo. I'm so sorry."

"You have nothing to apologize for, Bethany Parker," he soothed. "Not to me, anyway. But if you do not face this demon, it will haunt you all your life. You are the only one who can exorcise it. I will stand at your side, so that you will know you are not alone. But I cannot defeat this monster for you. Only you can do that."

Fresh tears sprang from my eyes. He couldn't understand. It was just too awful. I was a failure. I had taken my loving boy, my sweet son, and turned him into a killer who lusted for my demise.

"I can't," I said. "I can't face what I did to Andrew."

Drogo smiled sympathetically. He reached across the table and softly, expertly brushed away my tears with his thumbs.

"The nature of this spell, Bethany Parker, is to face you with your greatest fear. This is not a monster that has been placed in your head, nor is it the consequences of any actions you have taken before. The spellcaster had no idea what form the guardian would take – only that it would take the shape of your greatest fear. And no matter who you are or what that is, it is a savage and terrifying enemy to fight.

"And that is why I say to you, only you can defeat this monster. You must confront it if you wish to go around the wall in your mind."

My greatest fear? Yeah, I supposed so. Andrew had ignited it with his email. The fires had burned down to embers. I'd been close to moving on. But then Andrew poured gasoline on them and fanned the flames until it once again become a roaring conflagration in my soul.

And now, he stood in my way, throwing log after log on that bonfire, hoping it would burn so hotly I would be vaporized.

I swallowed hard. Looking inside myself, I saw my Heart Chakra, glowing bright green. It remained in alignment. I realized I was indeed as strong as Drogo claimed. I had more courage than my mother or Jess or Mark or the children had ever given me credit for. And if I was being honest, I was braver than I'd ever given myself credit for. It was time to stand up, face my fears, and fix this.

Of course, I still shook with fear. I had no idea how I was going to defeat Andrew, but I knew it would be hard. I took a deep breath, and then I faced Drogo.

"Okay," I said, extending my arms, "let's try it again."

He smiled approvingly. It made me feel warm inside, like my mother or my father was immensely proud of me. Then, he took my hands.

"Close your eyes," he said.

. . .

Half a second later, we were standing before Andrew again. I hadn't even had to approach him. It was as though going back had summoned him into being.

"I will kill *you!*" he screamed.

And once again, he stepped forward and swung at me as though I were a fastball he could send deep into centerfield. I waited for the blow, willing myself to be stronger than it.

But to my surprise and disappointment, when the bat made contact with my body, pain rocketed through me just as before. I felt my arm shatter. Stunned, I fell to the ground, and Andrew rained down blows on me again and again.

"I hate you!" *he cried with each strike.* "I hate you! I hate you! I HATE YOU!"

I wailed in agony and fear and despondency. I could not defeat him. No matter how I tried, my grief, my guilt, was too strong.

"Drogo!" *I sobbed.* "Help me! I don't know what to do!"

"You are a mystic, Bethany Parker. You need to see the truth."

"What truth?"

Andrew was beating me to death. This time, he would succeed. That was all I knew. If there was an afterlife, hopefully Drogo would be kind enough to escort me to Heaven.

"That is not Andrew Metheny, Bethany Parker. You must open your eyes and look with your True Sight."

At first, I couldn't figure out what it was he wanted me to do. I couldn't look at Andrew. I was curled up in the fetal position, my hands over my head, vainly trying to protect myself from his fury. How could I see?

But if Andrew wasn't beating me to death, who was? Gambling that he wouldn't smash my face in when I tried to look, I rolled to my back and gazed up on my attacker.

Suddenly, I was standing next to Drogo. My body still lay on the ground, absorbing the deadly blows. But Drogo was right. It was not Andrew bludgeoning me.

It was me.

Nineteen

My mouth fell open. My eyes popped wide. What was happening here?

"I hate you!" I screamed with each strike. "I hate you! I hate you! I HATE YOU!"

Abject horror crawled across my heart like a spider. I blinked in amazement several times. I looked at Drogo as though the answer to this mystery were on his face. He smiled beatifically.

I turned my attention back to the assault in front of me. All this time, that was what it had been? I'd been beating myself up, drowning in self-loathing, so that I had rendered my own powers impotent? Dear God, Bethany. How could you have done this to yourself?

"Stop," I said to the version of me beating myself bloody.

She looked at me with a vicious, angry expression locked on her face. She was barely recognizable. Her blue eyes blazed with a fury I don't ever recall feeling. How long had I been repressing these emotions?

"That's enough," I said, more to myself than the apparition that stood before me.

And then, suddenly, they were gone – both the attacker and the victim. It was just Drogo and me and the brick wall. And I was the one holding the bat.

I shuddered in revulsion at the intimacy of holding the weapon in my hand that I had been using to try to destroy myself. Then, the tarot reading leaped into my mind.

"As a result of the actions you've taken," Rhoda explained, "you have been offered a gift."

"A gift?" I asked.

"Yes, a gift of entry into a new realm of understanding. As a result of the judgement, you have come to learn in new ways how the universe works."

My actions had brought about the need for justice. Andrew inflicted it on me with his email. But as a result, I was able at last to understand where I went wrong and why I needed to forgive myself. All of this misery I'd been suffering was self-inflicted.

I began weeping again. I threw myself into Drogo's embrace, and he wrapped his wings around me.

I don't know how long we stood like that, me soaking his shimmery shift with my tears and him rubbing my back with his hands. I felt safe and sheltered and cared for in ways I could not remember since childhood. I loved my parents deeply, but they had been hard to grow up with – my mother's strict standards for behavior and her ER-nurse fear that danger lurked around every corner; and my father's superiority, always certain he was the smartest person in the room. He was kind and loving, but he also had a curmudgeon's gift for making you feel stupid.

And even then, I couldn't blame my parents. They were products of the environments they were raised in. And like myself, they had done the best job they knew how to do to raise me. Perhaps one day, Ariel and Andrew would be able to realize that about me. For now, they dealt with their grief in their own way. I didn't believe it was healthy, but I no longer had any say in how they behaved. They had to make their own choices, and I had to accept that, just because I'd failed, didn't mean I hadn't done my best.

At last, I released Drogo. He unfolded his wings, and the two of us stood before the impenetrable brick wall. I'd defeated my demon, but the blockade remained.

"Now what?" I asked.

"The guardian has been removed, Bethany Parker. This wall was always a metaphor, an image in your mind. Without the guardian to defend it, it has no power over you."

I looked at it. It still seemed real and forbidding enough. It stretched to infinity to the left and right and remained too tall to climb over. Well, if there was no way around it, then the only path was through.

I looked down at the bat in my hand. Suddenly, I was a senior in high school again, playing for the conference championship. I assumed the stance that my father had taught me and that I had passed on to Andrew. Then, as though the pitcher had delivered the ball with all her effort, I stepped in and swung the bat.

When it made contact with the wall, bricks and mortar exploded, as though the thing had been made of graham crackers. The entire structure crumbled from that singular blow, and after a moment, the dust settled.

♫

I sat across from Paul Hernandez at Titania's Garden. At first, I couldn't figure out how I had gotten here. I'd thought I was at the manor, sitting across from Drogo.

"What time is it?" Paul said.

He reached into his pocket and pulled out a watch. He thumbed it open, and then pressed the button at the top.

There was a flash of golden light. A wave of magic broke from the watch and surged across my body. I sat frozen, unable to move.

Moving swiftly, Paul withdrew his cell phone from his pocket, he set it on the table and logged into it. I could hear the ticking of the pocket watch, as though there were some horrific countdown at work.

Paul tapped a few commands into his phone, and then he held it up so that I could see the face of it. A pink swirling pattern appeared on the display screen, and I could feel more magic seeping into my skin.

"Now, listen very closely, Bethany," he instructed. "Somewhere in Ellington Manor, there is a hidden chamber. I want you to find this for me. I want you to seek it out and get it open. Every night you will pursue this mystery until you have solved it."

Oh, shit. Paul was the one who had put up this brick wall?

He tapped a few more commands into the phone and then showed it to me again. Blue rays shot from the phone screen hit my eyes and burned. I felt as though he were firing lasers into my brain. What had he done to me?

"This spell will let me know that you have found it," he said. "When you have seen with your waking eyes that the chamber is open, it will tell me. I will know what you know."

That son of a bitch. Oh, I was going to make him pay for this.

He withdrew the phone, tapped commands into it one more time, and then showed it to me again.

"Now, Bethany, we're almost out of time here, so I have to work quickly. Please pay very close attention to this image."

The screen showed the image of a giant, brick wall. As though it were a 3D optical effect, the wall seemed to float out of the phone and hover in front of me.

"You will not remember that I have given you these instructions. You will not remember anything about this moment. The sixty seconds that this has taken will be locked away, never to be recalled."

And then the wall floated forward and through my eyes. I saw as it locked itself into place and Andrew took up guard at its left-most edge.

Paul hastily put the phone back in his pocket. He checked the watch, grabbed it from the table, and put it away. Merrylaugh emerged from the kitchen and flew towards our table. Paul tried to assume the same position he'd been in when he first triggered it. But I saw now the subtle differences.

♫

My eyes snapped open. I sat across from Drogo in the kitchen of Ellington Manor.

"Oh, my God," I said. "He's been manipulating me the whole time."

Drogo smiled. He let go of my hands and stood up.

"Well, Bethany Parker," he said. "Now that you have cleared things up in your mind and had your lunch, I had best get back to work. I'm sure you have many things to do."

"Yes," I said. "Yes, I have a great deal to do."

"Farewell, Bethany Parker. I hope to see you for breakfast tomorrow."

I opened my mouth to say thanks. But Drogo was gone as if he'd never been there. I really wanted to wonder about that, but I had much bigger things to consider. Before I could decide what to do, though, the doorbell rang again.

Oh, shit. What time was it? I checked my phone: a little after four. Okay, good. There was still time.

I rushed to the front door to answer it, but Dorigen was already there. She drew it aside, and Rhoda stood before me, a look of fear plastered to her face.

"Rhoda, just the person I wanted to see," I said. "We've got a big problem."

"We've got more than one," she replied. "Bethany, I figured out who the monster in your dreams is. Alexander Ellington didn't bind a demon into the house.

"He imprisoned a god."

Twenty

I stood in abject amazement. A god? Up to now, everything about the supernatural world had been fairly unbelievable. It flew in the face of everything I'd been raised to believe, and coming to accept it had been difficult. Cats didn't talk. Policeman didn't turn into wolves. Vampires did not exist. And I was just an ordinary woman. I'd been dragged kicking and screaming into these realities, and I'd only accepted them because there was irrefutable proof that they were true.

But a god? Which god? And how could a mortal have enough power to capture one? As much as I had learned to accept magic and monsters as real things, the idea of gods that could somehow be trapped by sorcerers was really straining my ability to believe.

"I'm sorry," I said. "What?"

"It was no demon that he summoned and trapped, Bethany," Rhoda said, stepping inside. I shut the door behind her. "It was Camazotz – the Mayan God of the Dead."

With access to my Third Eye, everything began falling into place. My ability to see things as they truly are brought so many moments from the recent past into focus.

. . .

"Have you seen Lucius?" I asked, as I started digging in the pantry for a snack.

"He was in the library a little while ago, while I was in there looking for something to read," Declan answered.

"What did you find?" I asked, emerging from the pantry with a can of cashews.

Declan closed the book and considered the title.

"*The Complete Codex of Mayan Mythology,*" he answered.

Not far away was a bookshelf with stacks of old tomes on it. There were manuals on architecture and theories of life after death. Even a book on Mayan culture, which surprised me. Why the hell would a guy building a ghost-battery house in Ohio be interested in Mesoamerican culture?

One of the pages was dog-eared. I flipped it open and read the story of Camazotz, the Death-bat. He was apparently a Mayan god of death – a giant bat that was encountered by the hero twins, Hunahpu and Xblanque during their trials in the underworld. They'd been challenged to spend a night in the terrifying House of Bats and squeezed themselves into their own blowguns to hide from the creatures. Xblanque convinced Hunahpu to stick his head out to see if it was daytime yet. When he did, Camazotz swooped down and tore his head off, carrying it to the home of the gods, so they could use it as a ball in their next game.

I shuddered and closed the book. Ancient peoples had grim imaginations. What kind of fruitcake had Ellington been to want to study this sort of thing?

"I followed the voice to Enchantment and Ellington Manor," Dorigen said. "And every night in my sleep, it would whisper to me, begging me to help Mr. McGruder. When the crazed witch enacted her curse, she did me a blessing. For though I was trapped here in perpetuity, the terrifying voice fell silent.

"But once you broke the curse, Bethany, it started up again."

. . .

"Jesus, Mary, and Joseph," Dorigen swore softly. "No wonder his voice is so strong."

Her face was chalk-white. Those hazel eyes paled. Dorigen looked as though she'd seen a ghost. But given what Rhoda had just revealed, it was something far worse.

"The ancient Mayans believed Camazotz took souls of the dead to the afterlife," Rhoda said. "Bats were seen—"

"—as his agents," I finished. "Yes, I know."

Rhoda cocked her head in surprise.

"How?" she asked.

"When I was searching for the key to the basement door," I answered, "I found a book in the attic. There was a dog-eared page describing Camazotz. He's not very nice."

"Show me a god of death, who is," Dorigen said, her voice faraway. "What do you say we go to the kitchen and have ourselves a drink?"

She wandered off before Rhoda or I could stop her. With a shrug, I followed. Rhoda hastily took off her coat, hung it on a hook, and fell in behind me.

When we reached the kitchen. Dorigen had already poured herself a double. She seated herself at the kitchen table and set the bottle next to the glass. She reached for the tumbler, but her hands shook. And though she curled her fingers around the glass, she did not lift it to her lips. She simply stared at the orange liquid as though there were some solution to be found in it.

Rhoda and I seated ourselves at the table. Dorigen didn't offer us anything, which was just as well. I was still full from the burger Drogo had brought me, and the last thing I needed was to get drunk before Declan even awoke.

"What's wrong?" Lucius said, trotting in and hopping up onto the available chair. "I can sense fear and evil."

Offhandedly, I wondered why he never mentioned being able to do that before. It might've come in handy somewhere along the line. Then again, he had kept insisting he was not a cat, that he was so much more. I should have asked what "more" actually meant.

"Rhoda was just explaining to us that Alexander Ellington bound the Mayan God of the Dead into the mansion to work his dark magic," Dorigen said.

"Camazotz is bound into the house?" Lucius said.

"I believe so," Rhoda said. "Based on Bethany's descriptions of the creature she's seen in her visions and given that Ellington was attempting to make himself immortal – to find some way to cheat death – I think that's exactly what we're looking at."

"What I find so fascinating," Paul said, "is that Alexander Ellington was a summoner. The entire manor is really a giant summoning circle, if you will. So the question is, if that's its purpose, who or what was it built to summon?"

Oh, shit. Paul had been right. The mansion was designed to summon Camazotz and bind him into the walls.

"Makes sense," Lucius commented, as though we were talking about some idle academic subject. "As a lord of the dead, Camazotz would have access to departed spirits, and chaining him here might have some benefit in terms of Ellington's quest for immortality."

I blinked several times. My freaking cat knew more about this than I did? Somehow, that didn't seem right to me.

"He wants me to release him," I said. "Every time I have seen him, he cries, 'Unbind me.'"

"You can't release him, Bethany," Dorigen said. "He's mad, a raving lunatic. He wants revenge, and it won't be a quiet, subtle one."

"Yes," Lucius said, nodding thoughtfully. "He's been bound here for more than a hundred years. That would make anyone insane, let alone a god."

"How the hell, did he get here?" I asked.

"What do you mean?" Rhoda said.

"Why is an ancient Mesoamerican god of death in Ohio?" I said. "Seriously, this is crazy."

"The gods are not confined to any geographic location," Lucius said. "They may have had certain peoples who worshiped them, but most of the ancient gods are weak now. The faith of mortals is what gives them their power. And with the vast majority of humans worshiping Yahweh and Allah, many of the old pantheons have lost their influence."

"But that doesn't make him impotent," Rhoda said. "No one may have worshiped Camazotz for hundreds of years, but he still a lord of the dead. He still has power in the afterworld."

"At least, he would if he were not imprisoned here," Lucius added.

Terrific. A power-hungry White man had decided he wanted to live forever during World War I, so he somehow summoned and bound a Mayan god. After a century of imprisonment Camazotz had gone bonkers. Seriously, Bethany, how the hell did you get yourself involved in all this?

"Bethany, when I first arrived, you said we had a problem," Rhoda said. "What is it?"

Oh, right! Rhoda had stripped all thought of what I discovered with her revelation that there was a god bound into the mansion.

"I almost forgot," I said. "Paul has the pocket watch."

"What?" Rhoda said, sounding profoundly disturbed.

"It seems our little dinner date was not as innocent as he let on."

"Save me from the shock of that to my poor, old heart," Dorigen said, sarcasm dripping like molasses off each word.

I ignored her.

"He wanted me alone so that he could use it on me," I said.

"Use it on you how?" Lucius asked.

"As you know, the watch can stop time for sixty seconds. With me isolated at a secluded table on another plane of existence, he triggered the watch to buy himself a minute to work his magic."

"What sort of magic?" Rhoda asked, alarm covering her face.

"He put a suggestion into my mind," I replied. "He compelled me to go searching for the secret chamber that we found the other night. And he cast a spell to prevent me from being able to remember that he had done that."

"If time was stopped, why would he need to do that?" Dorigen said.

"Despite the fact that the spell had been cast out of time, the memory would still be in Bethany's mind," Lucius said. "Paul clearly wanted to make certain Bethany would be unaware what she was doing."

"Yes," I said. "And that's why I haven't been able to access my Third Eye. Paul put up that brick wall I've been seeing in my dreams to force me to find the chamber for him. In so doing, he either deliberately or inadvertently cut off access to my higher chakras."

"So blocking your Heart Chakra didn't have an effect?" Rhoda asked. "I've never heard of that before."

"No, it did," I replied. "While my Heart Chakra was out of alignment, I had no ability to activate my Throat Chakra or Third Eye. But remember that I got the letter from Andrew that threw me out of alignment the same day I went to dinner with Paul. It was complete coincidence. But because those two things happened on the same day, I didn't realize that there were two blockades operating on me – one of my own making, one of Paul's."

Now that I thought about it, this also explained why I'd been vulnerable to Paul's attack. With my Heart Chakra out of alignment, I'd been out of touch with the universe. Andrew's email had stunted my ability to protect myself. I should've seen what Paul was doing, what he would do. But I hadn't, because I'd allowed myself to wallow in self-loathing. Suddenly, I felt ashamed – not for anything I did wrong with Jess and the kids, but with myself for allowing my overinflated sense of guilt to drag me down into a self-centered pit of misery.

"That explains the 'Ides of March' quote from your first vision," Rhoda said. "You saw Paul on the fifteenth. He ensorcelled you, making you unaware of how you had become his agent."

Disgust covered my heart like fungus. The fact that I'd been unknowingly working for Paul made me want to vomit. I may have discovered that fact an hour ago, but Rhoda phrasing it the way she had brought it home harder.

"So," Rhoda went on, "if Paul has the pocket watch, then all four artifacts have been found. Declan has the signet, Truffaut has the cane and the cigarette case."

"Which would mean the mansion could now be activated," Lucius said.

MYSTIC HARMONY

"Assuming Paul and Marcel Truffaut are still working together," Rhoda said.

Deep in my guts, a powerful understanding began to stir. All of this had been leading to this moment.

"We're going to see them tonight," I said.

"What do you mean?" Dorigen asked, icy fear in her voice.

"I don't know how I know," I said. "But I know this ends tonight."

"Bethany," Rhoda said, her eyes wide, "tonight is the new moon."

"What's that got to do with it?" I asked.

"Don't you remember?" Rhoda said. "When we were researching the artifacts, we learned that the mansion's powers can only be triggered on the night of the new moon."

"At three AM on the night of the new moon," Rhoda said, *"the pocket watch activates the cigarette case to open a door to the spirit world. With the gateway open, the cane commands spirits to pass through to our world, where the signet absorbs their essence."*

Oh, shit. Suddenly, all this made an even more terrible kind of sense.

"Paul knows the location or has possession of all four artifacts," Rhoda said. "He ensorcelled you to locate the secret chamber. Now, on the night of the new moon, he plans to take the signet from Declan."

"Paul Hernandez intends to activate the mansion tonight," Lucius finished.

"Or Marcel Truffaut does," Rhoda said.

"The hour approaches, Bethany Parker," Drogo said. *"Tonight, your destiny is at hand."*

"Oh, my God," I said. "It's *definitely* happening tonight."

"You mustn't let them succeed, Bethany," Dorigen said, her voice shaking. "If he gets out, he'll kill us all. He'll kill everyone he can."

I was reminded of the story of Hunahpu and Xblanque. If Camazotz had done that when he was of sound mind, what would he do now that he was insane?

"The sun will be down in about an hour," Lucius said. "We'd better have a plan by the time it does."

My heart sank. I knew he was right. I had no idea what to do to stop it.

But all hell was about to break loose at Ellington Manor tonight.

Twenty-One

By the time Declan awoke and came upstairs, we had the basics of a plan. I was fairly certain I could convince the sheriff to work with us. Knowing him as I did and that he trusted me in spite of his better judgment, I believed I could make him understand what the stakes were. Failing that, I could try using my Throat Chakra to get him to back down. I didn't want to. It still seemed grossly unethical to me. But Rhoda had lent her voice to Lucius's saying that, given the stakes, we had to do everything possible to keep the ring out of Paul's hands.

Once we had Sheriff Mueller on our side, I was hoping that the combined might of a wolf-shifter and a vampire would be enough to stop Paul from enacting his mad scheme. But there were a couple of wrinkles I worried about.

First, we still had no idea what had become of Marcel Truffaut. If Paul was indeed working with him, and if Truffaut was dead set on activating the mansion tonight, then he and Declan would surely come to blows. That would then leave the sheriff versus Paul, and I saw those odds as being even. It was entirely possible that if Truffaut and Paul were working together, they could overwhelm us.

And all of that supposed that Declan wasn't still working with Truffaut. If he was biding his time to complete his own goals, then two vampires and a techno-mage sounded to me like a formidable opponent.

There was also the matter of Paul having the pocket watch. He'd used it successfully against me at the restaurant. If he could stop time, could he simply use that minute to disable all of us? Could he freeze time and simply slip the ring off Declan's finger?

These thoughts made my heart race and my stomach burble with dread. I saw multiple ways for us to fail, and with my Third Eye in full operation, I could not discount any of the negative scenarios I imagined.

My mind returned to the tarot reading Rhoda had done for me. The cards representing the present, and the direction alarmed me to no end. The presence of the Three of Swords indicated sorrow caused by knowledge, and Rhoda had specifically said that I would likely be experiencing heartbreak, loss, and betrayal. I wanted to believe that those emotions were generated by Andrew's email. I'd even envisioned the Three of Swords when I was closing that wound.

But the purpose of the reading had been to determine what we needed to do in the absence of Truffaut's return. I could not help but believe that someone was going to betray me tonight. Indeed, the certainty of it settled deep in my bones. But whom?

And of course, the direction I was headed was the Five of Cups, representing grief and loss. That gave me no reasonable assurance that I was wrong about being stabbed in the back or that things would turn out right. According to the final card, my destiny, I had a decision to make and that two opposite things would come together and make my heart glad. I struggled to believe that the decision I would make tonight would save anyone.

Declan stopped cold when he entered the parlor and saw all of us sitting there, including Rhoda. We looked at him expectantly, and his soft, blue eyes darted around the room trying to ascertain what was going on.

"What is the matter?" he asked.

"Declan," I said, "Sheriff Mueller is coming tonight. I expect him any time. He has orders from Paul Hernandez to take the ring from you. If you refuse to give it up, he's authorized to use deadly force."

Declan smirked. A sinister light ignited in his expression.

"That would be a fatal error on his part," he said.

"Ah, yes," Dorigen spat. "I should have known we must begin the evening with a penis-measuring."

"Declan," Rhoda said, "we do not want you to give up the ring. Quite the opposite in fact."

That news seemed to confuse him. He studied us further.

"Then what is this about?" He asked.

"All four of Alexander Ellington's artifacts have been found," Rhoda said. "Tonight is the full moon. At three o'clock, the mansion's powers can be activated."

"We believe, Monsieur Truffaut and Mr. Hernandez are planning to recreate Alexander Ellington's spell tonight," Lucius said. "We cannot let that happen."

Declan came into the parlor. He appeared lost in thought as he shuffled to a chair and seated himself in it. At first, he said nothing. Then, after tapping his chin several times with his index finger, he looked at Lucius.

"Why?" he asked.

"What do you mean why?" Dorigen said. "Are you as mad as the rest of them?"

"Declan," I said, "Ellington didn't bind a demon into the mansion. He bound the god Camazotz."

"Yes, I know," he said.

My eyes opened wide. He knew?

Declan closed the book and considered the title.
"The Complete Codex of Mayan Mythology," *he answered.*

Oh, my God. Of course, he knew.

"How did you know that?" Rhoda asked.

"Because he's been researching Mayan mythology and related subjects," I said. "I should've known."

"It's not what you think," he said.

"Heh," Dorigen said. "What a typical man comment."

Once again, Declan seemed confused by Dorigen's insult. I didn't have time to explain it to him.

"Listen to me," I said, "we cannot allow the mansion to be activated. If it is, Camazotz may escape."

"But how?" Declan asked.

"He's been seeking freedom for more than a hundred years, Declan," Rhoda said. "He's been haunting Dorigen's dreams and sending messages to Bethany."

"What sort of messages?" Declan said, turning to me.

"He's been begging me to unbind him," I answered.

"Well, that seems easy enough," the vampire said. "If the mansion is activated, you don't free him."

"I don't think it's that simple, Declan," Lucius said. "We believe he has a plan."

"He hasn't just been demanding I release him," I said. "He called out to me while I was still in Kansas. He visited my dreams when I was staying in a hotel room overnight in Indianapolis. I believe he brought me here."

"And he did the same to me," Dorigen added. "I am no magical creature, Mr. McGruder. But I didn't come to Enchantment randomly. As you know, no one can find the town if they're not actively looking for it. But a mundane such as myself did. I am sensitive to the supernatural, and this Mayan death god reached out to me some fifty years ago, and drew me here.

"He's desperate, Mr. McGruder. He will say and do anything to gain his release."

"Declan, there were bats in the visions that led me to the cane. And when I first arrived here after retrieving it. I had a vision of Camazotz so overwhelming it caused me to faint."

"We believe the cane was the last missing artifact, Declan," Lucius said. "Paul Hernandez has the pocket watch, and he used it on Bethany the night she went to dinner with him."

That got the vampire's attention. He whipped his head in my direction, a look of alarm on his face.

"What did he do?" he asked.

"He stopped time, so he could ensorcel me to find the secret chamber and then stripped my memory of it happening. Declan, I've seen Dori both in the waking world and in my dreams. And she has both transformed into bats and into Camazotz. Maybe Paul was just greedily searching for the power himself. But I am convinced Camazotz had a hand in bringing this all about. If the mansion is activated, he will escape into the world."

"And if he does that, he'll kill thousands of people in his revenge," Dorigen said.

"And all the spirits that are trapped here already will be his revenant army," Rhoda added. "The spirit world has cried out to me again and again over the past several days. There's great turbulence in it, and it all surrounds the mansion, Declan."

"He cannot be allowed to be freed," Lucius said.

"Please, Declan," I said, "you have to believe us. You have to not only hold onto the ring, you must make certain the house doesn't fulfill its purpose and release an angry, insane god on the world."

Declan didn't say anything at first. His gaze drifted out of focus. Absently, he fingered Ellington's signet ring, as though it might tell him what to do.

"Paul Hernandez will not get the ring from me," he pronounced. "Not without a fight."

I nodded. His answer was frighteningly vague. He assured us he wouldn't turn the ring over, but he hadn't said he would join us. I tried to read him with my Sight, to predict his actions. But before I could arrive at any answers, the doorbell rang.

Shit. The sheriff was here.

"I'll get it," Dorigen said, rising. "Better have your story ready to go."

She went out with a grimace. I couldn't blame her. I was every bit as nervous as she was. Pulling this off depended upon the sheriff being reasonable.

I stood up, smoothed my pants, and faced the parlor entrance. Thirty seconds later, Dorigen returned with Sheriff Mueller in tow. He wore a hard expression, his jaw set, determination in those brown eyes.

"Evening," he said. He looked at Declan. "I assume you know why I am here."

"I do," Declan replied.

"Rusty, listen—" Rhoda began, but he cut her off without looking at her.

"Not now, Rhoda."

I stepped forward.

"You either, Parker."

"Sheriff," I said, "there's more to this than you know."

He turned and faced me at last. He put his hands on his hips, and an angry glare landed on his face.

"It doesn't, matter, Parker," he growled. "I have instructions from The Order. I have to carry them out."

"That's just it, Rusty," Rhoda said. "Your instructions don't come from The Order."

A shadow of doubt crept into his eyes. I could see he worried about the implication of Rhoda's statement. But he still showed a healthy skepticism. Crossing his arms, he faced Rhoda.

"What does that mean?" he asked.

"Paul told you to get the ring," Rhoda answered. "But he isn't following commands from The Order."

Now, Sheriff Mueller looked confused. He cast his gaze around the room before letting it fall on me like a hammer.

"All right, Parker," he said. "I know you're at the center of this. I'm sure Rhoda and maybe some of your cohorts helped talk you into it, but I smell your scent all over this. Fess up. What the hell is going on?"

I smiled, putting as pleasant a look on my face as I could. I was going to need all of my persuasive powers to make this work.

"Paul has gone rogue on The Order," I said. "I suspect they don't know this yet. But he has Alexander Ellington's pocket watch. He used it on me the night we went out to dinner."

The sheriff's eyes opened wide at that remark, and I thought I saw a flash of jealousy run across his face before retreating back into his mind.

"To do what?" he asked.

I explained to him the same thing I had to Declan and the others. As I told him what Paul had done, jealousy reasserted itself in his expression, before turning first to concern and then to anger.

"And he knows you've opened this secret chamber?" Sheriff Mueller asked.

"I'm certain of it," I said. "In addition to compelling me to look for it, the spell he cast was designed to alert him the moment I found it."

"Why?" he asked.

Unable to stop myself, I sighed. We really didn't have time for the whole police-interrogation act, and I just wanted him to trust me for once.

"Because the very next day, he showed up here and demanded Declan give him the ring. And when that didn't work, he sent you."

"God damn it," he swore. "I told you going on a date with him was a bad idea. That explains why you looked off when you came out of the restaurant."

I bit my cheeks to avoid unloading on him. I'd known before I went on that the dinner date was a bad idea. I didn't need the sheriff's I-told-you-so attitude.

"Rusty," Rhoda said, in her gentlest, most persuasive voice, "tonight is the new moon. At three o'clock, a person in possession of all four artifacts can activate the manor's power. Not only will that likely cause the same disaster that happened in 1918, it will probably be worse. Camazotz, the god bound here, has been manipulating events to make this happen, so he can escape and take his revenge."

"Paul Hernandez has the pocket watch," Lucius said. "Marcel Truffaut has the cane and the cigarette case."

"And Declan has the signet ring," the sheriff mused.

"Exactly," I said. "All four of the artifacts have been found. And we know that Paul was working with Marcel Truffaut, so three of them are in the possession of one party. If Declan surrenders the ring, they will have all four. And they will activate the mansion tonight."

In which case," Dorigen added, "if you haven't figured it out for yourself yet, we're all doomed. And so maybe is the world."

Sheriff Mueller hung his head. Then he shook it, and I watched as tension built in his shoulders.

"God damn it, Parker," he said. "I don't even want to know how you made this mess."

"She didn't make it, Sheriff," Lucius said. "Like the rest of us, she's been manipulated by Camazotz to bring all this about."

I couldn't decide if I were angry or grateful. Once again, the sheriff had accused me of making trouble, which infuriated me. But I wasn't certain I wanted Lucius defending me by saying that I'd been a tool.

"He's right, Rusty," Rhoda said. "This isn't Bethany's fault. Camazotz has been plotting this for years. He drew Bethany here, so that she could break the curse on the manor. He needed Declan free so that the ring would be accessible. And he needed Marcel Truffaut to complete his quest. Bethany didn't make this problem, but she did help discover it, and she can help solve it."

"The hell she didn't make it," the sheriff said. "If she'd listened in the first place and not broken the curse—"

I'd had enough.

"Stop talking about me as if I'm not here," I snapped. "And stop treating me as though I'm stupid. You think Camazotz wouldn't have just found someone else? He's been working this problem for fifty years. He drew Dorigen here before me. He's whispered to every single caretaker before me. My most recent predecessor committed suicide because living here drove her insane. That was Camazotz whispering in her mind, speaking to her in dreams. I'm just the person he finally got through to. This was inevitable, Sheriff.

"Good news, though! You're here to help make sure this doesn't go down badly. So are Declan, Dorigen, and Lucius. We have a capable group of people here motivated to ensure Camazotz does not get free.

"But for us to succeed, you've got to come to your senses. You're going to have to stop being a jackass, alpha wolf and let someone guide you. You need to listen – really listen – not just hear and then tell people what you want them to do or what you think."

The sheriff's eyes bugged out of his head at my outburst. I surprised myself a little with the sternness of my words and the temerity I'd shown to lay into him. But I don't know what else he expected. I was through being pushed around. I'd been treated like shit by my family for eight years, and it was time for Bethany Parker to draw a line in the sand and say, "No more."

"Damn it, Parker," he said. "You're going to cost me my badge."

"Better than costing thousands of people their lives," I said.

Sheriff Mueller nodded. I had him in a logic trap, and he knew it.

"True," he conceded. "So what you want me to do.?"

"I need you to stop Paul from taking the ring," I said.

"That will be easier said than done," a new voice said.

I turned and saw Paul Hernandez standing in the entryway to the parlor.

Twenty-Two

The first thing I noticed was that Paul was gripping Alexander Ellington's cane. He was also alone. Deep in my gut, I knew that meant something was terribly wrong.

"Where is Marcel Truffaut?" I asked.

Paul smiled thinly. He walked casually into the room, an air of smug satisfaction hanging around his head like a cloud of cigarette smoke.

"In Hell," he answered. "Where he belongs."

"You killed him?" Declan asked.

"Yes," he replied.

I blinked in stunned surprise. Maybe I should have assumed that Truffaut's absence meant Paul had lethally betrayed him. But Marcel Truffaut had been an extremely capable vampire. Just the thought of him scared the shit out of me. And I just couldn't imagine a weasely bastard like Paul Hernandez being able to get the upper hand on him.

"How?" I said.

"The same way I ensorcelled you, Bethany," he said, as though it should be obvious. "He came to the library and threatened my life. He showed me that he had the cane, which I might add, he informed me he got from you. Of course, I already knew he had the cigarette case, and since I had the pocket watch, that meant all the artifacts were now accounted for.

"So, I concluded it would be best if I terminated my partnership with him. Naturally, he would've objected. Violently. I therefore used the pocket watch to stop time, and while he stood powerless before me, I used his own cigarette lighter to send him to oblivion."

"You burned him alive?" I said, gasping.

"Vampires have superspeed, Bethany," he said. "And there are only a limited number of methods for killing them. I didn't have a wooden stake handy, and it was after dark. So, I used the means that he gave me. Had I not, you'd be speaking with him now instead of me."

My jaw dropped. I'd hated Marcel Truffaut, but Paul was so casual, so callous in his description of the vampire's demise that a shiver ran down my spine. With access to my Third Eye this time, I saw him for who he truly was – a sociopath.

"You son of a bitch," Declan growled, standing.

"Now, now, Mr. McGruder," Paul said. "Marcel Truffaut was no friend of yours. You know this as well as I. I have freed you from him. Don't make me send you to Hell to join him."

"Take it easy, Hernandez," the sheriff said.

"Ah, Sheriff Mueller," Paul replied, "it's so good to see you here. But I note that Declan McGruder still wears Alexander Ellington's ring. I believe you have a duty to execute."

"Don't be ridiculous, Paul," I said. "That's Alexander Ellington's cane you're holding in your hand there. The watch and the cigarette case are surely in your pockets. You're not acting on The Order's authority. You're here for yourself."

"I don't care what you think," he growled. "I am an official of The Order, and I command Declan to turn over Alexander Ellington's signet. It is Order property, and I have the authority to take it."

"I'm not giving you anything," Declan said.

Paul sighed. He shook his head sadly.

"Sheriff?" he prompted.

"I'm going to need to confirm your instructions with The Order," Sheriff Mueller replied. "I'm sorry, Paul, but unless you can prove your commands are genuine, I'm forced to believe that Parker here is right about your motivations."

Paul scowled. His face turned red, and I could practically see steam coming from his ears. Sheriff Mueller had hit him in his weak spot. Paul did not like being told what to do. He wanted his authority acknowledged. He pointed the cane in Declan's direction.

"Give me the ring, Declan," he said, power in his voice.

Declan simply smiled at him. He took two steps forward and folded his arms in a threatening stance.

"I am wearing the signet," he said. "The cane cannot affect me."

"Damn," Paul said, a slightly sad note in his tone. "I was afraid of that."

"Listen, Hernandez," the sheriff said. "You helped me out of a jam with Karl Markiewicz. I appreciate what you did, so I'm going to cut you a break. Put the cane down and leave immediately. I'll give you a few hours to make a run for it. Then I'm calling The Order, and they will be here by morning."

Paul sighed again. He reached into his pocket. Rusty drew his gun.

"Don't even think about it," the sheriff said. "Pull your hand out of your pants slowly. If I see a watch, I will shoot."

Paul withdrew his hand. He held a cell phone.

"I'm afraid that's not going to happen, Sheriff," he said.

The memory of him using his cell phone to ensorcel me leaped into my mind. And then the vision I'd had before the tarot reading raced to my heart – Paul Hernandez leering at me smugly across from the table; Sheriff Mueller shaking violently from electrocution.

"Oh, shit!" I said. "Sheriff, look out!"

But it was too late. Paul tapped a button on the phone, and a bolt of lightning shot from it, and electrified the sheriff's pistol. The power arced between the phone and gun for several seconds. Sheriff Mueller shook as though he'd stuck a fork in an outlet.

"Rusty!" Rhoda screamed.

At last, Paul ended the spell. The sheriff collapsed to the floor, unconscious. I couldn't tell if he were alive or dead. Horrified, I went to his body.

"Get away from him, Bethany, or you'll suffer the same fate," Paul threatened.

Lucius sprang from his chair. Fury burned in his green eyes, and he had a savage look plastered across his face – like he was a black panther, instead of a housecat.

But Paul simply turned, spun the cane, and cracked Lucius across the head with the metal handle. Lucius yelped once, fell to the ground, and didn't move.

I screamed. Dorigen's face went white.

"Lucius!" Rhoda cried.

"Declan!" I shouted, tears streaming down my face. "Do something!"

He hesitated for only a second. Then he raced to me, his superspeed making it appear as though he'd practically teleported. He gripped me by the shoulders and looked into my eyes.

"Bethany, go to sleep."

What? I thought.

But then the charm took hold. As though I'd been sprayed with chloroform, my eyes rolled up into my head, and I passed out before I hit the ground.

♫

When I regained awareness of my surroundings, I was lying on the floor of the parlor at the foot of my favorite chair. The fire had gone out, and the room was cold. A chill originating from the flue washed over me like icy water and sent fear and dread deep into my bones. I flicked my eyes around the room to assess the situation and discovered everyone was gone.

I sat up in confusion and looked around. Somehow, everything looked wrong. I was in the parlor, but the furniture seemed to have been rearranged or replaced or reupholstered. Nothing was as I remembered it. I strained my ears, trying to detect any sound. But I heard no voices, detected no movement. Indeed, I heard nothing at all. It was as though the volume of the world had been switched completely off.

Getting to my feet, I tried to figure out what to do next. There was an archway not far from me. It should lead to the kitchen, but it was not in the right spot on the wall, so I had no idea where it would take me. Curious, I decided to explore.

It led me down a long hallway – one I had never seen in the manor – before emptying out into the kitchen. This room was wrong as well. Instead of the early-twentieth-century, wood-burning stove and antiquated sink and cabinetry, I stood in one that looked as though it had been designed in the Sixties. There was an electric stove, a refrigerator with a rounded top, a Formica table with metal chairs and plastic padded seats. The floor was covered in linoleum. And everything was decorated that sickly avocado green that was so popular at the time.

Where the hell was I?

I still heard nothing, and spooked by the redecorated kitchen, I left, hoping to find my companions. The exit led to yet another long hallway I was certain was not in the house. It was decorated with the tackiest wallpaper imaginable – some sort of garish plaid pattern that hurt my eyes to look at.

When I came out of it. I found myself in the foyer. It was as abandoned as every other room I had visited. And like them, things were different. The staircase that led to the second floor did not exist here. Rather than a series of hooks by the door, there was a tall coatrack with everyone's jackets hung on it and topped by Sheriff Mueller's trooper hat. The door was wrong, too. Instead of being simple wood, it was dominated by an enormous stained-glass window that depicted Camazotz surrounded by bats. I shuddered. I knew I was dreaming now, and I feared what I might discover.

But it seemed to be the only way out of my predicament. Though I clearly stood in the foyer of the manor, there was no other exit, including the one I had just come through to get here. Taking a deep breath, I opened the door and stepped outside.

The world seemed to be black-and-white – as though I were looking at it on a television from the Fifties. Like the old episodes of *Gilligan's Island* and *The Beverly Hillbillies* that I used to watch after school.

The grounds looked absolutely haunted. In the trees, I could see hundreds of eyes lit up and staring back at me. It reminded me of my first night in Enchantment, when I had impetuously run out into the dark and nearly been torn to shreds by the ghouls bound to the grounds.

A new understanding dawned on me. They were here. They were all here.

The eyes that I saw were attached to faces that came forth from the trees. But they did not walk or even float towards me as they had in my previous encounters. Instead, they bobbed up and down at the whims of the breeze, and I realized that they were all tethered to the mansion like balloons, only with chains instead of strings.

A deep sense of horror crept into my heart, and though I didn't want to, I scanned my surroundings, turning slowly in a circle. Everywhere I looked there were chained spirits reaching towards me, silently begging me for release. And when I turned completely around so that I was facing the house, my jaw fell open. There were hundreds, no, thousands of lost souls chained to the house. The sky was blotted out, there were so many of them. All I could see were sad, frightened eyes, hands and feet stretched out to me, and mouths silently begging me to release them. The only sound was the rattling of the chains. And there were so many, it threatened to deafen me.

Trying not to panic, I went back into the house. When I pulled the door shut behind me the awful noise was gone. The mansion had returned to its usual appearance. Everything was back where it belonged.

But there were ghosts everywhere.

Chained to tables and sofas and chairs and lamps and anything else that could secure them, they bobbed up and down as though filled with helium, and all of them begged me to free them as those outside had done.

Dear God. Was this Camazotz's work? How many souls had he trapped here in the century of his imprisonment?

Remembering my promise to Rhoda, I went in search of Reggie.

I found him in the conservatory, which made a certain amount of sense. It was the center of my magic. As though I were one of Shakespeare's witches and the Steinway my cauldron, this was the seat of my power. So, I was unsurprised to find the spirit I sought chained to that very instrument. Reggie floated above it, a sorrowful look on his face. But he managed a smile of sorts when he saw me.

"Ah, Bethany," he said. "I knew you would come."

"Tell me how to free you," I replied, rushing to him.

He looked at me as though the answer were simple.

"You are dreaming, Bethany," he said. "You cannot free me here. You must awaken."

Yeah, no, shit. But what did I do when I woke up?

I opened my mouth to ask him, when a thought occurred to me. I realized this was exactly the same scenario as when I'd confronted Maggie Cartwright. I had inadvertently knocked myself out when I ran into her protection circle. While I was dreaming, I'd seen Reggie, and he had told me how to beat Maggie. Well, not exactly. He'd given me a clue, which had enabled me to figure it out on my own.

But still, I needed his advice.

"I understand, Reggie. Tell me what to do in the waking world."

"I do not know, Bethany," he said. "Bound by Camazotz, my Sight is closed off to me. I cannot see how this ends. But I do know that if you do not stop this, Camazotz will unleash apocalyptic harm on the world."

Oh, for God's sake. Everyone was depressed and on a doomsday rant. I got that the situation was dire, but there had to be a way out of it. Someone needed to help me.

"Reggie," I said, putting as much patience into my tone as I could, which frankly wasn't much, "I don't know what to do. I'm stuck asleep. Even if I were awake, Paul has the artifacts. I've got my chakras aligned, and they're not helping."

"No, Bethany," he replied, "you have one left to unblock – the Crown Chakra."

The Crown Chakra? Okay, yeah, Rhoda had told me there were seven chakras, and by my count I'd only aligned six of them. What the hell was this Crown Chakra about? Did it make me a ruler?

"It is the one that enables contact with the divine and true wisdom," Reggie said, as though he heard my thoughts. "If there is a solution to this puzzle, your Crown Chakra is the key to learning it. You must align your seventh chakra, Bethany. It is the only tool you have left to defeat a god."

I blinked in shock. Yes, defeat a god. Who the hell was I kidding? How could a mortal raised in the mundane world like me have any chance against an ancient Mesoamerican nightmare?

"I do not know the answer to that, Bethany," Reggie said. "But if you align your Crown Chakra, you may."

"Bethany Parker," Camazotz called.

I knew his voice as soon as I heard it. It had echoed so many times in my head over the last several months that I knew beyond any doubt to whom it belonged.

"Bethany Parker, come to me," he commanded.

"Hold tight, Reggie," I said. "I don't know how, but I will get us out of this."

"I have complete faith in you, Bethany. Make sure you have the same faith in yourself."

I nodded. Then I left the conservatory. I had no need to wonder where Camazotz waited. He was in the secret chamber behind the library. I went directly there, doing my best to ignore the frightened, floating corpses begging for salvation.

When I got to the library, the secret door stood open, and hellish, red light streamed through it. I had to swallow hard and force myself to keep walking. The sheer terror of this upcoming confrontation shook me to my core.

As I approached the opening, I realized there were tens of chains on the floor all leading into the chamber. And when I entered, I saw hundreds more lost souls, all of their chains tethered to Camazotz. Just as he had been bound to the mansion, he had imprisoned all of the people who had died anywhere near him or who had had the misfortune to chance near the mansion in their otherworldly travels.

"The time has come to fulfill your destiny, Bethany Parker. You hold the key to releasing all the spirits trapped here. You simply need unbind me."

The clock in the secret chamber struck three quarters to the hour. I looked at the face and saw it was two forty-five.

All the spirits wailed in terror, as the pendulum of the clock swung back and forth with its perfect, rhythmic ticking. They stared at it as though watching the final countdown for all of existence.

"The hour approaches, Bethany Parker," Camazotz roared. "Fulfill your destiny. Unbind me!"

My eyes snapped open. I sat in the library tied to a chair. Paul and Declan conferred with each other, making final plans. I checked the clock. It was, indeed, two forty-five.

Oh, shit. I only had fifteen minutes left to save the world.

Twenty-Three

Briefly, I struggled against the ropes. I hadn't been bound around my chest and arms, like I had in Cincinnati. Instead, they seemed to have just tied my hands behind my back. For a moment, I hoped that it been done hastily so that I might be able to easily escape. But there was no such luck. The bonds may have been crude, but they were tight and secure.

I scanned the room to assess the situation and hope perhaps someone might be able to help me. Rhoda was tied to the chair next to mine, asleep. Declan must have charmed her as well.

The sheriff lay on the floor not far away from us, his own handcuffs used to restrain his arms behind his back. He snored softly, which, frankly, was a relief. When Paul had cast his electrical spell, I'd worried he'd killed Sheriff Mueller.

Lucius lay at an odd angle on a table. I couldn't tell if he was breathing or not. But that had been a vicious blow Paul had struck to the back of his head, and I worried he hadn't survived it. I tried to reassure myself that if he'd been dead, they'd have left him in the parlor.

Dorigen shuffled past me with a tray of drinks. There was a bottle of water, and a steaming mug of blood on it. And as she approached Paul and Declan, I saw that she once again was Dori.

Oh, my God. What had they done to her?

As Declan took the mug from the tray, I fixed him with my sternest mommy glare.

"So, you decided to join the forces of darkness, eh?"

He turned back to me with an indifferent expression on his face. Though he looked at me, his blue eyes seemed to be focused elsewhere.

"It's not what you think," he said, like he was a husband caught by his wife with a secretary half his age.

"Really?" I said. "Because unless you're not actually working with Paul to activate the mansion, it's exactly what I think."

"Declan, perhaps you should put her to sleep again," Paul offered.

He thumbed through pages in the tome that had been missing, the book Dori had told me to seek out.

"We'll need her awake anyway," Declan said.

I laughed sarcastically.

"There is no way in hell I am cooperating with or helping you," I spat.

This time, Paul laughed. Without looking at me, he continued to leaf through the book on the podium.

"I don't need your cooperation, Bethany," he said. "Alexander Ellington made a critical error when he cast his spell to gain immortality. As the story goes, 'something went wrong,' and Camazotz sucked his soul into the spirit world instead of Ellington pulling the supernatural life through to himself.

"Well, I know what went wrong."

If my hands been hadn't been tied behind my back, I'd have flipped him a double bird. God, how I hated his condescending lecture tone.

"Do you want to know what it is?" he asked.

"No," I said. "But you're going to tell me anyway, so that you can feel smart."

He scowled. I was pleased to see that my insult hit the mark. But a moment later, a leering smile slid up his face like he was the Grinch.

"The Mayans were fond of human sacrifice, believing their gods required the nourishment of blood," he said. "High-profile prisoners such as an enemy king were their preferred victims. The usual method of sacrifice was decapitation, though they also enjoyed removing a still-beating heart."

I tried not to show any fear. I knew Paul was trying to bait me, and I didn't want to give in. But my flesh was crawling at his casual indifference to spilling blood and his implication that he would turn the savage ancient practice on me.

"Throughout human history, there is a fine tradition of sacrifice," he went on. "Even God demanded them. His Chosen People would lead their lambs or their goats into the temple, place them on the altar, and then slit their throats before tossing the bodies into the fire. And the Lord expected the best of their flock."

"So Camazotz wants a sacrifice," I said, deliberately stealing his thunder.

"Precisely," Paul replied. "Ellington thought that by binding Camazotz into the manor, he could simply give him orders. But even a bound god must be appeased, and when Ellington had nothing to offer, Camazotz took his soul in payment."

I could see where this was heading, and I tried very hard not to panic. But it was difficult. I had no desire to die, let alone as a blood sacrifice to a crazed god. Despondently, I realized that my mother might be proven right after all – by staying in this strange, rural town, I would indeed be found dead in a ditch somewhere. Or, more likely, I would just never be heard from again.

Rhoda's tarot reading had suggested someone would betray me. I was disappointed it had indeed turned out to be Declan. As much as he scared me, I was also deeply attracted to him. At least, I had been before he'd revealed he'd murdered his own child and then turned on me to help Paul activate the mansion – Paul who had heavily intimated he intended to sacrifice me to Camazotz.

My destiny was supposed to be The Lovers – me bringing two disparate things together that would make my heart glad. At the moment, I saw no way for that play out. My heart was not going to be glad if Paul cut it out and offered it to the Mayan God of the Dead.

"Why are you doing this?" I asked him, stalling for time and hoping for a bolt of inspiration.

"What do you mean?" Paul said.

"You work for The Order," I replied. "You're supposed to be against this ever being attempted again. It was a disaster last time, and The Order absolutely does not want the mansion powered. That's why they scattered the artifacts to the four winds in the first place. So why are you trying to do the very thing your employer doesn't want done?"

Paul didn't answer right away. He gave me a malicious smile – the kind that promised violence. For the first time, I saw the light of insanity behind those dark brown eyes of his. He may have been patient, obsequious, and smug, but Paul Hernandez was not mentally well. And I suspected he hadn't been for some time.

"My mother was an accomplished mage," he said. "My father ran off when I was only three. I can barely remember him being with us, and the only reason I know what he looks like at all is because my mother kept a picture of him.

"She worked for The Order. She was a very good magician, and she doted on me. So, I wanted to be just like her – a powerful wizard, who commanded the respect of his peers.

"Unfortunately, I did not have the same natural aptitude for magic my mother had. Though I tried with all my might to master the simplest of spells, I could not work sorcery.

"This mattered not to my mother. She told me I was special and sweet, and there were vast opportunities for smart little boys who worked hard.

"But I wanted to be a mage."

Dear God, he dripped with entitlement. Here was another man whose mommy had told him he was special, so he expected the world owed him whatever he wanted. God, I was so sick of them.

"Well, because my mother worked for The Order, she had access to a lot of information that a mundane such as myself would not normally be able to see," he went on. "It took some cleverness on my part, but I eventually figured out her passwords. And with that information I was able to do all sorts of research.

"That is how I discovered the modern art of technomancy.

"It was the most fascinating thing I'd ever seen – there were actually magicians who cast spells through technology. Unable to summon magical energy themselves, they could still work sorcery by using electronic machines to summon the eldritch power."

I could see where this was going.

"Skip ahead, Paul," I said. "I know you're a techno-mage. But if you don't get to the part where you actually answer my questions soon, you're going to monologue yourself right past the moment of truth."

Part of me thought I should've just let him talk. But I worried that he could actually get the whole story out before it was too late, and I didn't want to have to listen to it.

"Disrespectful as always," he commented.

"Respect is earned," I said.

"Oh, I've earned it," he replied, "I have more than earned it."

"And yet, here we are," I shot back. "You, a weaselly, little man, sneaking around behind his superiors' backs to harness magic no one should. Marcel Truffaut didn't respect you. I can tell you that for free."

"Marcel Truffaut is dead," Paul said, stepping forward.

His whole expression was screwed up in an angry sneer. I could tell my constant poking at his ego and sense of accomplishment was the key to undoing him.

"He paid the ultimate price for his lack of vision," Paul said. "Just as you will."

I set my face in a hard stare so that he would not think that I was frightened of him. But I was.

"Well, magic in general is a difficult discipline to master, and technomancy is no different. If anything, it's harder."

The look on his face suggested that I should be more impressed because he'd managed to learn to work sorcery without the natural aptitude for it. I wasn't buying it.

"Every magician makes mistakes, has accidents while they're learning," he continued. "Well, I made a doozy. In my attempt to open a gate from my house to school, so that I would no longer have to endure the forty-minute bus ride packed with bullies and bitches, I inadvertently summoned too much energy and destroyed an entire power grid."

My jaw fell open at that. I had no idea how big a power grid really was or how many households and businesses it supplied with electricity, but I knew that if Paul had screwed up that badly, a lot of people were affected.

"I'm sure The Order took a dim view of that," I quipped.

Paul smiled sarcastically, as though he appreciated my joke.

"Quite. The Order exists for the purpose of hiding the supernatural from the mundane world. So when a city of a hundred thousand people loses power on a clear night with no storms, they have to act. First, of course, they came up with a plausible explanation for the power failure. They made certain that all the uninitiated believed it.

"Then, they set to tracing the source of the disturbance. It wasn't difficult to follow the trail to our house.

"My mother had figured out what happened first, of course, and she knew that if The Order discovered her fifteen-year-old son had been experimenting with technomancy without proper supervision or authorization, that I would be taken from her. And who knew how I would be punished? So, when the company agents arrived at our front door to make inquiries, my mother confessed to the crime. She told them she'd been working on her latest assignment, but a spell had gotten away from her and zapped the power grid. She shielded me from The Order's wrath, expecting that they would show leniency towards her since she was working for them.

"They did not."

Oh, shit. This was a revenge plot? I couldn't figure out what Paul planned to do with the mansion's power, but I could now see the source of the quiet, seething anger that rested just beneath the surface in his heart.

"My mother was stripped of her rank and imprisoned. Unaware that I had any talent of my own, The Order sent me to mundane foster care. There, I experienced one humiliation after another. Everyone saw me as a geeky boy who was into the occult. And you may recall, Bethany, how well that was tolerated in the Nineteen-Eighties."

I didn't really. I was too busy focusing on music and softball when I was in high school to notice what was happening to the nerds. When I wasn't obsessed with training or learning lines, I had just enough time to realize a lot of people thought I was a lesbian for being a jock and musician, even though I'd dated a number of boys.

"Once I was eighteen and graduated," Paul droned on, "I sought out The Order and applied to study technomancy with them. I had already shown an aptitude for it, of course, and though they knew who I was, the fools did not realize that my mother had lied to them about who was responsible for that blackout. And so, after they took me in, and I had access to the full knowledge and tools of a technomage, I excelled. I eventually got a job with The Order, and I began biding my time looking for a way to at last prove I deserved their accolades."

"And then one day, you met Marcel Truffaut, and he made all your dreams come true," I said. "You still haven't told me why you're doing this."

"Marcel did not make my dreams come true," Paul countered. "But he did put me in a position to do it."

"So what, Paul? By teaming up with Truffaut you were able to acquire three of the four artifacts. Declan has the fourth. Why do you want to activate the mansion?"

He looked at me as though I were stupid. I wanted to spit in his face, but he was out of range.

"You haven't been paying very close attention, Bethany," he said. "Ellington sought immortality. Truffaut wanted power. I will have both.

"After I have appeased Camazotz with my sacrifice, I will summon the spirits to me, and I will use their essence to become immortal. And then, I will turn my army of the dead on The Order itself. I will prove to them beyond any doubt that I am smarter and stronger and better than them. They will do what I want if they don't want me to destroy whole populations.

"And that's the beautiful part, you see. With power over the dead, I can use them to kill mass quantities of people, who will then swell the ranks of my army. I'm going to rule, Bethany. I'm going to have what I deserve."

I sat there, stunned for a moment. This was his whole motivation?

"So, let me get this straight," I said. "You're going to crown yourself King of the Dead, and destroy hundreds of innocent lives, because no one respects you?

"Damn, Paul, you must have the tiniest penis on Earth. I mean, I've never seen or heard of such an outlandish, phallic-compensation scheme. You think this will make you a real man? Think again."

Paul turned red. Fury masked his face.

"You don't understand," he said.

"Yes, I do," I retorted. "You're angry because you didn't get to learn magic. You're angry because when you figured out how to do it yourself, instead of being hailed as brilliant, they took your mother away. You're angry because you had to sneak into their organization so that you could learn how to do the things you really wanted to do and never got recognized for them. So now, you're going to have your revenge. Like some pathetic comic-book villain, you're going to show the world that they should have respected you.

"And the worst part is, you're angry at The Order for punishing your mother when she took the fall for you. You blamed them for doing the right thing, while you cowardly kept the truth to yourself.

"You don't get to murder and enslave people just because you didn't get what you wanted when you were a kid, Paul. You're just a selfish asshole with unearned entitlement. No one will ever respect you. Nor should they."

White-hot rage poured off Paul. He stood there, quaking with indignation. I held him with my most unforgiving death-glare. He was a child. And he planned to throw a temper tantrum that would hurt thousands of people both living and dead.

"Declan!" he barked. "Move her into the circle."

Declan glanced at me ruefully before he approached. I turned my disapproving gaze on him.

"And you," I snapped. "You're working with this lunatic? Last night, you told him you'd give up the ring over your dead body. You told him if he tried to take it from you, he would die. But now you're all buddy-buddy with him."

"Last night, I was unaware he had the other three artifacts," Declan replied. "We can activate the manor now."

"A few hours ago, you swore to me he wouldn't get the ring from you without a fight."

Declan held up his hand. The signet still adorned his ring finger.

"Paul and I have formed a partnership," Declan said. "I have retained possession of the ring, and I will control the cigarette case during the ritual."

In the back of my head, that alarmed me. I couldn't imagine what would encourage Paul to give up one of the artifacts to even the assets, but Declan had apparently made him an offer he couldn't refuse.

"I thought you had a soul, that there was something redeemable about you," I said. "But Dorigen was right. You're nothing more than a monster."

He grimaced at me. Then he grabbed the chairback and lifted me into the air as though he were picking up a toy. He carried me into the secret chamber and set me down inside the circle so that I was facing the podium. The grandfather clock stood to my right. I checked the time. It was two fifty-seven.

Shit. I was almost out of time.

"All right, Declan," Paul said, "let's prepare the spell."

Declan approached him and held out a hand. Paul reached into a pocket, withdrew the cigarette case, and handed it to him.

"What?" I said. "You're not going to decapitate me or cut out my heart?"

"I'm not a barbarian, Bethany. And besides, time is of the essence here."

"Declan, for God's sake, you can't do this," I protested. "You owe me! I freed you from the curse! You can't kill thousands, maybe millions of people."

He ignored me. He simply walked to the small stand, opened the cigarette case, and set it in place, tipping the lid back so that the stars shining through the glass dome on the roof were reflected in the mirror inside it.

Paul, meanwhile, walked to the grandfather clock. He opened its face, and then withdrew the watch from his other pocket. He flipped it open, checked the two timepieces to ensure they were synchronized, and then he fitted the watch into the hole where the "3" should have been.

I watched in horror as he walked casually back to the podium. Dori stood silently awaiting further instructions from him.

Two fifty-eight. I only had two minutes to live.

"Dori," I begged. "You need to hear me. You need to hear my voice."

She simply stared blankly at me. Paul chuckled

"Damn it, Dorigen I know you're in there!" I shouted. "Wake your curmudgeonly ass up and help me!"

"You can scream all you like, Bethany," Paul said without looking at me. "But no one is coming to help you. If I were you, I'd spend the remaining ninety-five seconds of your life making your peace."

"You vicious bastard," I snapped. "I don't deserve this! I don't deserve to die."

Tears spilled over my cheeks. It just couldn't end like this. I hadn't gotten a chance to say goodbye to my parents. I couldn't stand for Jess and the kids to find out that I'd been murdered as a result of them throwing me out. It wasn't fair.

"No one wants to die, Bethany," Paul said. "But we all do. Some of us are lucky and die in old age; many of us are not and are cut down in our prime. Sadly for you, you will be one of the latter.

"But if it makes any difference to you at all, I am grateful to you. Someone had to break the curse so that I would have access to the ring. And then you delightfully betrayed Marcel Truffaut by searching for the cane, acquired it, and traded it to him for Rusty Mueller's life. I already had possession of the pocket watch. When Marcel came to demand it, it was a simple matter to kill him and get the artifacts he possessed.

"So, Bethany, you were instrumental in this whole thing. Without you, I'd still be missing two of the artifacts. I'm very grateful to you."

"Then show me some gratitude and untie me, asshole," I said.

I may have been begging for my life, but I'd be damned if I was going to grovel before the son of a bitch.

"But don't you see?" he replied. "You granted me one more favor. Someone has to be sacrificed for Camazotz to be appeased. And in true Mayan fashion, I am offering my enemy to him. How perfect for it to be a powerful mystic, the very person who made it all possible. It's poetic. Don't you think?"

"I think you can take your poetry and your tiny-penis plan and shove them both up your ass," I said.

"Interesting choice for final words," he said.

"Go to Hell," I replied.

He smiled as Declan joined him at the podium. Then he drew Sheriff Mueller's gun from his belt and raised it.

"You first," he said.

He pointed the gun at my chest and squeezed one eye shut as he sighted down the barrel. Oh, God, this was it. No one had ever pointed a gun at me before, but this first time was going to be deadly.

I'm so sorry, Mom, I thought. *I love you, Dad.*

And then, I sent out a desperate, silent prayer to the universe, begging it to save me, pleading for someone to appear like a white knight and rescue me from certain doom.

Paul pulled the trigger. I saw smoke and heard a loud bang.

Death rushed toward me in the form of a speeding, silver bullet.

Twenty-Four

I had about half a second to prepare myself for the pain. Somehow, that was time enough to wonder if it would hurt much, or if I would die instantly. Was Paul a good shot? Or would he have to try to kill me multiple times?

I was about to squeeze my eyes shut and wait for death, when a streak of black flashed in front of me. At first, I thought it might be Death himself.

But then I realized it was Lucius.

The bullet caught him full in the chest. He spun backwards in a spray of blood, impacted with my chest, and then tumbled off my lap onto the floor. His tiny body was ruined. His bright green eyes went dark, and his tongue lolled out of his mouth.

"Nooooo!" I screamed. "Luciuuuuuus!"

Where had he come from? What had he been thinking? Why had he done this?

Shock and horror gripped my soul. This was the last piece of my vision. I'd seen Andrew beat me half to death. I'd seen Declan turn on me. And now tonight, Sheriff Mueller had been electrocuted. How could I have let this happen? I could have warned Lucius. I should have done something.

No. He couldn't be dead! He just couldn't! He was my best friend, my confidante. How could he be dead?

"Oh, damn," Paul said, sounding irritated.

All my grief and sorrow turned immediately to rage.

"You son of a bitch!" I shouted. "I'll kill you!"

"Now, that would be a neat trick, what with you tied up and at my mercy," he said.

I raged against my bonds, trying to free myself. All I could envision was closing my fingers around Paul's throat and squeezing the life out of him. How could he have done this? He deserved to pay.

But as I struggled, the only thing I succeeded in doing was tipping the chair over backwards. I landed roughly, and sharp pain shot up my wrists to my elbows. Offhandedly, I wondered if I'd broken any bones. But I didn't have time to consider that because my head hit the floor next. Stars swam in my vision. I didn't lose consciousness, but otherwise, I was living in a world of misery.

"Do you want me to reset the chair?" Declan asked.

I wanted to hate him. I wanted to curse him straight to Hell. But my head hurt too much, and it was all I could do to string two coherent thoughts together. For the moment, I was only concerned with Lucius's death.

"Actually, no," Paul said. "Lucius was a familiar. His fey blood will be more valuable to Camazotz than a mere mortal's."

Once again, I wanted to cuss at him. Instead, I kept working at my bonds. My hands hurt like hell from the impact, and I struggled find the knot to begin untying it.

I could see everyone in the library from my vantage point. The gunshot had awakened the sheriff and Rhoda. Sheriff Mueller tried to sit up and then realized he was handcuffed.

"What the hell is going on?" he asked.

But the only answer he received was the grandfather clock striking three.

As the last chime faded away, Paul and Declan joined hands. Paul raised the cane over his head like a wizard's staff. Declan curled his free hand into a fist and aimed the ring at the summoning circle. Black light streamed down through the skylight. Its purplish glow made it look like a beam from some sort of dark ray-gun. It struck the mirror of the cigarette case, and the artifact glowed with unholy light as the stars reflected in the glass.

Oh, shit. Things were about to get real.

Though I remained tied to the chair, I made certain to scoot my body outside of the circle. I wanted no part of my flesh in that ring when a death god materialized in it.

"Camazotz, God of the Dead," Declan and Paul chanted in unison, "you are lawfully bound here by the rules of magic. We command you to open the gates of the spirit world and send your prisoners to us."

Desperately, I tried to figure out how to stop this. Was there some way for me to ruin the spell while I was still alive? I needed a plan. I reached out to the universe with my Third Eye, but the pain in my head and the horror at what I was witnessing seemed to cut me off from anything else. I was about to panic, when I felt someone behind me.

Looking up, I saw Dorigen. She knelt beside me and put a finger to her lips, telling me to keep quiet. Then she drew a knife from somewhere under her skirt and began sawing at the ropes that kept me tied to the chair. A moment later, I was free.

She leaned in close and spoke to me in hushed tones, like the sound of a soft wind.

"You're the only one who can stop this, Bethany," she said. "Use whatever magic you have to do it. We're all counting on you, Sorority Girl."

"Camazotz, Lord of Bats," Declan and Paul chanted. "Your servants fly on the night sky, bringing their charges to you. By the laws of magic, command them to deliver these lost souls to us."

"You free the others," I whispered. "I'll see what I can do about this."

Dorigen nodded once, and then began creeping back around the circle towards the door to the library.

I sat up and tried to figure out what to do. Smoke seemed to issue from the center of the summoning circle. It swirled before coalescing into a familiar shape – that of a giant man with batwings for arms and a bat's head. Though he was transparent, not fully here, the sight of him in the waking world rather than my dreams sent rivers of terror streaming down my spine.

"Yes!" Paul said. "Come before us!"

"Grant us your power that we may rule the dead," Declan joined in. "And ourselves become immortal."

While the two of them were occupied casting their spell, I got to my feet and moved swiftly to the other side of the room, taking care not to step in the circle. If either of the men took notice of me, they gave no indication. Both of them stared in awe at what they had brought forth.

"Who dares invoke my name and power?" Camazotz rumbled.

The sound of his voice here in reality froze the blood in my veins. Now that I had made it to the other side of the chamber and could see his face, his hell-red eyes lit up the room like a pair of crimson stars. I felt like a mouse gazing upon a snake. Raw fear rooted me to the spot and made it impossible to think.

"I do," Paul declared. "Paul Hernandez."

"And I, Declan McGruder."

Camazotz leered at the pair of them, a look of disgust covering his alien face.

"A mortal magician and a vampire seek to command a god?" Camazotz roared.

"I do," Paul said in a confident tone that seemed totally inappropriate for the situation. "I have summoned you before me with the laws of magic. And I have made a sacrifice of fairy blood to appease and compel you."

The mention of Lucius's death returned me to myself. My anger with Paul for callously murdering my familiar and then speaking so casually of it focused my attention back to the matter at hand. These two madmen wanted to unleash this god upon the world to make themselves omnipotent. I was not having it.

"I see no offering, mortal," Camazotz said.

"What?" Paul said.

A look of complete shock set up shop on his face. Confusion mixed with fear gripped his shoulders.

"I sacrificed a familiar," he protested. "I spilled fey blood in your name."

"Then where is it?" Camazotz demanded. "You summoned me to your circle, mortal. But there is no blood and carcass for me to consume."

Paul stared at the floor in bewilderment. I joined him. As much as I was vengefully gleeful at the fact that he had made some critical mistake, I was just as mystified as he was. I'd seen Lucius die. I'd seen his blood spatter the floor and the walls. There was still some of it on my sweater. And his body had lain not far from where I'd been tied.

But it was gone now. I had no idea what Paul had done wrong or what would happen as a result.

"Ahem," a voice said.

I gazed in its direction. Impossibly, Lucius sat at Paul's feet. When Paul looked down, his eyes opened wide in surprise.

"I still have *five* lives left, asshole," Lucius said.

Like a bolt of black lightning, he sprang into the air and sank his fangs into Paul's crotch.

The obsequious techno-mage squealed like a pig. His hands went to his groin, as he tried to remove Lucius from his nether regions. But the feisty cat dug his claws into Paul's upper thighs and held on for dear life with his teeth.

I couldn't help but wince in sympathy as Paul wailed in agony, stumbling about trying to free himself from Lucius's death grip. Whatever revenge I'd thought I might take on Paul for killing my cat, this was so much worse.

At last, Paul managed to dislodge him, and he flung Lucius across the room.

He reached for the gun tucked into his belt, but before he could free it, Sheriff Mueller rushed him like a linebacker and tackled him to the ground. The pistol slid out of his reach.

"I don't think so, Hernandez," the sheriff growled.

And then he punched him in the face, breaking his glasses. That made me smile.

My satisfaction didn't last, though. As Sheriff Mueller recovered his gun, the Mayan God of the Dead roared in a terrible combination of fury and triumph. When I turned to look at him, an expression of total madness and joy seized his face.

"There is no sacrifice," he shouted. "No offering to appease and compel me.

"All lives here are forfeit!"

Twenty-Five

What did he just say? All souls are forfeited? What the hell?

"Wait just a damned minute here," I said. "I didn't summon you. Neither did Dorigen nor Rhoda nor Sheriff Mueller nor Lucius. It's these two fools who activated the mansion."

"I have been summoned," Camazotz said. "I have not been appeased. According to the laws of magic, I may therefore exact what punishment I choose."

"Well, that's bullshit," I said.

"Sadly, it's not," Lucius replied, "if you summon a celestial or infernal being, you have to follow the laws of magic exactly. Any infraction can be treated as a breach of the contract and therefore allow the summoned individual to do as they please."

"Yeah. Like I said, bullshit. All right, listen, God of the Dead—"

"You will all die and serve me in eternity," Camazotz went on. "Unless Bethany Parker unbinds me."

That stopped me cold. I wasn't expecting to be threatened with death because Paul had effed up the summoning. But I was even more stunned to be chosen as the linchpin to fix it. Especially since I knew I couldn't grant his request.

"I don't even know how to free you," I said.

"It is simple," Camazotz said. He leaned forward and leered at me with those sinister, red eyes. "Take the cane, step into the circle, and declare me free."

"No!" Dorigen shouted. "He'll destroy us all!"

"I'm afraid I agree, Bethany," Rhoda said. "He'll only imprison more souls and enslave the ones he has to wreak terror on the populace. He doesn't want freedom; he only wants revenge."

"He's a mad god," Lucius said. "He may be insane, but he is also cunning. Giving him what he wants can only end badly."

Shit. What the hell could I do here? Everything my friends said was true. I didn't dare release Camazotz, even though he'd been begging me to since Jess threw me out of the house. I had to do something, though. I couldn't just let him kill us all. So what then?

"I don't know what to do," I said.

"There is nothing you *can* do, Parker," the sheriff said. "Rhoda's right. You can't let this monster free."

"If you do not, I will kill everyone," Camazotz retorted. "I will kill them one by one in front of your eyes, Bethany Parker. And then I will send their souls to rip you to pieces."

Jesus Christ. I thought my ex-husband was an asshole. Camazotz put Jess to shame.

Desperately, I pleaded with the universe to hand me an answer. Everything had seemed so obvious in Cincinnati and when I was trying to rescue Sheriff Mueller. But this was too much. The scale was simply too large. What the hell did I do?

"If there is a solution to this puzzle," Reggie said, "your Crown Chakra is the key to learning it. You must align your seventh chakra, Bethany. It is the only tool you have left to defeat a god."

"You're the only one who can stop this, Bethany," Dorigen said. "Use whatever magic you have to do it. We're all counting on you, Sorority Girl."

. . .

Okay, yes. Reggie said I needed my Crown Chakra on this one, and I didn't doubt it for even a second. But how did I bring it into alignment?

The same way you have every other one, Bethany, I thought. *Music is your key. It's your magic wand. Use it.*

I opened my mouth and without thought, a song – the perfect song – came to mind.

"I came here to let you know," I sang, "the letting go has taken place."

Without the piano to accompany me, my voice sounded weak and scared and lonely. But I forced myself to keep at it. And as I continued to sing, my voice gathered strength, and confidence formed in my heart. Feeling the vibrations of my vocal cords, I deliberately and consciously activated my Throat Chakra.

Soon, the words of the song were coming from my mouth with deep conviction and plaintive emotion. I watched as everyone, even Camazotz, was entranced by my performance. I took two steps forward slowly, closed my eyes, and surrendered myself to the power of music.

As the words formed on my tongue and left my lips, the lesser-known tune by Melissa Etheridge that was so filled with grief and acceptance brought me to all the darkest moments of my past.

I sat curled up on the sofa, my knees tucked up under my chin and my arms embracing my shins tightly. The dull throbbing in my abdomen refused to go away, reminding me of what I had lost. I'd tried so hard to get pregnant, wanted so badly to have a child. And now, it was gone. Vanished from my womb as though it had never existed. But it had. And I had no idea how I would go on, how I would ever fill this emptiness inside me.

I sat at the kitchen table as Mark told me he wanted a divorce. He was going on and on about all the logical reasons, about everything he'd tried to do. He made it all about himself, absolving himself of any guilt. And yet, he refused to look at me, would not meet my gaze.

"It's not that I'm mad at you, Bethany," he said. "It's just that ... it's not fair to me. I want children of my own, ones that share my genetic code.

"So, you see, you have to do the right thing, Bethany. You have to let me go. There's no reason both of us should have to suffer for this loss. You love me, right?"

"Sure," I said with no emotion whatsoever.

"So then you see that there's only one thing to do. You have to give me my freedom, Bethany. You have to let me pursue the destiny I want."

"Okay," I heard myself say from somewhere far away.

There was no pain, no feeling at all. Just numbness.

Jess and I used to talk for hours. Before we started living together, we would see each other every Friday and Saturday night. Sometimes, he would get a babysitter, and we'd go out to dinner or maybe a movie. Sometimes, I went over to the house to visit with him and the kids. Or all four of us would go out to eat somewhere.

We talked so much. We laughed so much. We shared all the same opinions. What happened?

After we got married, we would still have date nights, but the older the kids got, the more "date night" meant ordering a pizza and watching a movie on Netflix. We stopped talking. We just sat in silence, sharing our space. I don't remember when we stopped talking, but I'm pretty sure that we stopped listening first. And I suppose that once we figured out the other person wasn't listening to us, there was no need to say anything.

I remembered when he landed his dream job at Kansas. He'd been over the moon. It paid so much better, and he would get to work at his *alma mater*. We all went out to dinner that night, and Jess took us to a steakhouse. We ended up spending almost three hundred dollars celebrating. I could remember being uncomfortable at the size of the check, but Jess said we didn't have to worry about that anymore.

The joy had been short-lived. Within six months, he was struggling to meet expectations. A little over a year after he started, they put him on a performance improvement plan. And at the end of three months, they fired him.

My heart broke for him. I was terrified at the loss of income, but I knew what to do about that. I could always go get a job or two to tide us over until he found something new. But my poor husband, the man of my dreams, had lost everything. I'd never felt worse on behalf of another human being than I did when Jess was fired.

Ariel sang at the top of her lungs, belting out "Tomorrow" from Annie. She was such a confident performer, and she was only eleven. Tears formed in the corners of my eyes as I played the accompaniment. With a voice like that and the courage to match it, she could do anything she wanted. The world could be hers.

I stood in the backyard playing catch with Andrew, marveling at how strong and accurate his arm had become, rejoicing in the sound of the ball landing with a satisfying smack in my mitt. After I tossed the ball back to him, he zipped another throw to me. I heard the hiss of the air around it as it rocketed to my chest, perfectly on-target. He could be great. If he stayed disciplined, he had the makings of a big-league ballplayer.

All this grief and joy and more gathered in my heart, and as I hit the crescendo of the song, I imagined all of these dark moments smashed together in a sphere – a dirty, scuffed softball resting in my hand. I tossed it up into the air and waited for it to fall. When it was at chest level, I swung my mental bat as hard as I could. With a loud *ping!* that softball of grief went soaring towards the outfield and over the fence.

As I watched it recede, I felt the *kundalini* uncoil in the base of my spine. As though it were starved for air and could find it at the surface of my head, it shot up through my central channel. I felt it activate and fully align each of my chakras as it went.

My Root Chakra glowed red, and I felt power and sureness under my feet. It hit my Sacral Chakra, and I was bathed in orange light as confidence resonated through my soul. When it reached my chest and my Solar-Plexus Chakra, the light turned yellow and courage gathered in my spine until it hit my Heart Chakra, turned green, and I was overwhelmed with love – for Lucius and Rhoda and Dorigen and Sheriff Mueller, but also for Andrew and Ariel and my parents and all the people who had ever given me anything.

The green light turned to blue as I felt all of that strength and power flow from my mouth in the words and notes of the song. Then, with a wash of indigo, my Third Eye opened fully and looked on the world with delight and hope and love.

All of this sprang to the top of my head, and like a geyser blowing at its appointed hour, the *kundalini* reached my crown, lit up my vision in purple light, and showed me the universe. I felt more connected than I had ever been to anything. All of my sorrow, all of my joy, every little disappointment and micro-success filled me with such a wonder for all things. It was like an orgasm of the mind, or perhaps of the soul. Tears ran down my cheeks. I was so overwhelmed with this knowledge and wisdom.

Suddenly, I understood everything. I saw that my whole life had been leading to this moment – not because I was destined to arrive at Ellington Manor in my fiftieth year to break the curse and free a god, but because all of the choices I had ever made had lined up along this path, building it one flagstone at a time. And the winds of chance and circumstance helped shape the pattern in which I laid them down and walked along them, until at last, I was where I needed to be.

The memory of the tarot reading returned to the fore of my mind.

"Note that three of the cups are overturned," Rhoda said. "These are the ones that are in front of the figure on the card. His head may be bowed in sorrow, but we could also view this as him being focused solely on what has been spilled. He only sees the loss. Behind him, though, there are two upright cups. If he would but turn and look, he would be able to see them. This indicates that all is not actually lost. There is still hope for the future."

. . .

This whole time, I'd been focused on the three cups in front of me – Jess's betrayal, Andrew's vicious attack, my own broken dreams. It was time to turn around and start looking at the full cups.

Quietly, softly, I sang the song's final line:

"I came here to let you know the letting go has taken place."

For a moment, no one spoke. They all looked on me with wonder, even Paul. But Camazotz at last broke the silence with a demand:

"Enough," the Mayan god said. "Make your choice."

A single tear escaped my eye. I pitied this poor creature. He hadn't asked to be trapped here by a selfish human who only wanted power that didn't belong to him. But that did not change what I had to do.

"I'm sorry, Camazotz," I said. "I cannot free you. There are too many lives at stake."

"Then I will kill your friends as you watch before they rend your own soul to pieces!"

I had to admit, even in my enlightened state, that sounded terrifying. I did not want him doing that. But before I could speak again, Declan snatched up the cane from where Paul had dropped it and rushed between Camazotz and me.

"No!" he shouted. "Take me!"

"What?" I said.

I hadn't seen this coming. Perhaps I should have, but I'd been so focused on trying to figure out what to do about Camazotz, I'd completely forgotten about Declan and his betrayal.

"Take me as your sacrifice," Declan said.

"What are you doing, McGruder?" Sheriff Mueller asked, giving voice to everyone's thoughts.

"Why would you offer your life, vampire?" Camazotz asked. "You are immortal, and if you die, your soul is condemned to Hell. Why would you sacrifice yourself to save these others?"

"You took Alexander Ellington's soul," Declan said, spreading his arms and walking forward. "You left his body to rot. Do the same to me. Take my soul; leave the body."

Understanding sprang into my mind. Dear God, this was what Declan had intended all along. This was his final solution.

"Declan," I said, "it won't work."

"It will," he said, whirling on me. "If my body dies with my soul in it, I'll be condemned. If Camazotz takes my soul and leaves the body, I'll be free."

"No, Declan," Rhoda said. "You'll be a slave. Camazotz is holding all of these souls prisoner. Yours won't be any different."

"Your purpose is to conduct the dead to their final destination," he said, turning back to Camazotz. "So you can take me wherever you want."

"I can take you nowhere while I am bound to this house," the god replied.

"I know," Declan said. "Swear you will take me to my son, and I'll free you."

"Declan," I said, "no, that won't work."

"I agree to your terms," Camazotz said, as though to drown out any sense of reason. "Enter the circle with the cane and unbind me."

Shit. I was just about out of time here. Declan was too blinded by his own grief to understand what was going on. Now, who did that sound like?

"Declan, listen to me," I said. "Camazotz has no intention of honoring his end of the bargain and—"

"Wrong!" Declan shouted, cutting me off. He fixed me with the most terrifying gaze I had seen from him since the night he had first emerged from the basement. "He is lawfully bound by magic. He must keep his word to me."

I shook my head sadly.

"Even if he does, he cannot give you what you want," I said. "Your son has been dead for over a century, Declan. He has moved on. You can't be reunited in the afterlife. He cannot pardon you for what you've done, and even if he could, Declan, you would gain no relief from it. It still happened. It cannot be undone, nor can the harm and suffering that befell you and your wife.

"I know what you are feeling. Trust me, Declan, I do. I've lived these very same regrets. But you have to make your own peace with what you've done. No one can do it for you, and no one can grant you absolution."

Declan stared at me. His soft, blue eyes were practically drowning in self-loathing and pain. I felt so very bad for him. I knew the guilt he was carrying around. Though I had not murdered my family, I may as well have. They all hated me for what I had done. And even if I could bring them before me, they would not forgive me. I had to live with that. I had to accept it. It was the same for Declan.

"She is wrong," Camazotz said. "All that you seek is within your grasp, you need only act."

I shook my head, wordlessly telling the distraught vampire that Camazotz was lying to him, manipulating him.

It did no good.

"My apologies, Bethany," he said. "When you have lived with your grief for one hundred twenty-seven years, you may tell me I am wrong. Until then, you haven't the perspective necessary to convince me."

He didn't give me the opportunity to refute him. He didn't wait for me to tell him that I had opened and aligned my Crown Chakra, that I was connected to the wisdom of the universe, and therefore, the things that I told him were accurate and true. Instead, he stepped into the ring and raised the cane above his head.

"Camazotz, Lord of Bats, God of the Dead, I free—"

"Come to me!" I shouted in a commanding voice.

Just as it had in Cincinnati, Alexander Ellington's cane flew from Declan's grasp, tumbled through the air, and landed in my hand.

"What have you done?" Declan said.

Camazotz roared in fury at being denied his release. He threw his fists up in the air and his head back and screamed for all he was worth.

"Your soul is forfeit!" he shouted.

He reached out a hand, and I saw Declan's eyes open wide. With my Crown Chakra open and my Third Eye looking on the world as it truly was, I saw Declan's soul yanked from his body. His ethereal hands grasped desperately, vainly at the body as it was drawn away.

As soon as it was free, Declan's mouth opened and uttered one terrible cry of anguish. And then I watched as his body rapidly decomposed. His skin rotted. His eyes sank into his skull. His bones turned to sand. It took nearly twenty seconds for Declan's body to disintegrate. And my jaw hung open in disgust and anger as my heart exploded in loss.

"Declan!" I screamed. "No!"

Then, he was gone, as if he had never existed. Camazotz set his face with a triumphant grin. I staggered back unable to express anything I was feeling.

"Now," the god growled, "who's next?"

Twenty-Six

My hands went to my chest. Tears streamed down my face. Oh, God, I'd gotten Declan killed.

No, the wisdom of the universe said to me. *He is dead by his own choice. You did what you had to to preserve the lives of thousands.*

Maybe. But I still felt like shit.

"Look upon your friends, Bethany Parker," Camazotz roared. "Do you want them to suffer the same fate? Unbind me!"

"Bethany," Rhoda said, her voice choked with tears of her own. "Don't listen to him. He can't escape without one of us freeing him. If we do that, we'll kill thousands upon thousands of people."

"I have your husband, Rhoda Matheson," Camazotz countered. "Release me, and I'll return him to you. Don't, and I shall have him kill you.

Rhoda blanched. I was sure she could well imagine the thought of Reggie as a ghoul tearing her to pieces.

"Stop it!" I snapped.

"For God's sake, Bethany," Paul cried. "Give him what he wants! He'll kill us all."

The sheriff backhanded Paul, knocking him to the floor.

"You shut your mouth," Sheriff Mueller said. "You brought that thing here; you of all people deserve to have him kill you."

"Parker, if you've got some way out of this. I'd surely love for you to do it. But if you don't, we're all ready to die. I'd rather not, all things being equal. But you can't let this monster free."

As grim as they were, Sheriff Mueller's words heartened me. My friends were here, and this was the choice we faced. Regardless of the cost, we were in agreement about what to do.

"There is no way out, Bethany Parker," Camazotz said. "If you do not give me what I want, I will kill you all. And I will torture you for decades, until eventually someone who does value their life comes along and unbinds me."

I sighed heavily and weighed all of the possible options before me. The only way to prevent him from killing everyone here was to give him what he wanted. But if I did that, the carnage on the unsuspecting mundane world would be unthinkable.

Still, perhaps I could at least minimize the impact of my decision. Remembering that I had used the signet ring to get into the library, into the secret room, I gambled that I could close the door the same way, even though I was holding a different artifact than I had to find the place.

I raised the cane over my head. A look of hope flashed onto Camazotz's face. Now, I felt even worse for him. He'd believed that my invoking my magic meant he was about to get his freedom. He was mistaken.

"Close!" I shouted, pushing magic from my Throat Chakra into my voice. The secret door to the chamber slammed shut with a boom, cutting us off from Rhoda and Dorigen, who remained outside the chamber in the library.

"What are you doing?" Paul demanded.

"Reducing the number of casualties," I said. "Rhoda and Dorigen are safe now. And they'll be able to tell The Order what happened here."

"Smart thinking, Parker," the sheriff said.

"You think I cannot harm them?" Camazotz said with a chuckle.

"Yes," I answered, knowing I was right. "This chamber is a large summoning circle. You're bound within it. It took me awhile to understand, but this is your actual prison, Camazotz. Alexander Ellington bound you into this room, and you cannot leave without being released. With the chamber sealed, there is no escape for you – even if I granted your freedom.

I let my words sink in. I watched as understanding dawned on Camazotz's face. His eyes grew darker red when he realized how I'd tricked him.

"Oh, my God, you've killed us all!" Paul wailed.

"No," I said offhandedly. "Lucius has five lives left. If Camazotz kills him here, he'll just escape and have four more to live.

"But, yeah, Paul. You, me, and the sheriff are dead."

Paul gurgled in raw terror. I had to admit, I was getting a certain pleasure out of making him squirm. He walked into the manor tonight acting so smug and confident, as though nothing could go wrong. Now, there was no escape for him.

"So be it, Bethany Parker," Camazotz growled. "Prepare yourself for an eternity of torture!"

I held up a finger, as though to say, "Wait." It was overall a weak gesture, but it nevertheless arrested the Mayan god.

"Now, hold on there, Camazotz," I said. "A thought has just occurred to me."

That was a lie. It hadn't just occurred to me; I'd thought of it the moment I aligned my Crown Chakra.

"What thought?" he asked.

"Well," I said, "it seems to me that killing us does you no good."

"It grants me revenge," he retorted.

"Sure," I conceded. "But then what?"

I saw the confusion on his face as clearly as if he'd written it there with a magic marker. He'd been scheming his revenge for so long, it was the only thought that he had. If he didn't take vengeance for what had been done to him, what good was he? And since I had not been the one to imprison him here, what good was having a revenge upon me?

"You'll still be stuck here," I continued. "There will be no one in here to release you. We'll all be dead. And I've made sure Dorigen, Rhoda, and Lucius will survive to tell what happened. So, you'll never get out."

"The sniveling magician will release me," Camazotz countered. "He's already begging for his life."

I let my eyes slide over to where Paul knelt on the floor next to Sheriff Mueller. His eyes were lit with hope. I smirked.

"No," I said, "I'll have the sheriff kill him first."

"What?" Paul cried. He looked at Sheriff Mueller. "You wouldn't!"

The sheriff took one step away from Paul and then aimed his gun straight between Paul's eyes.

"Wanna bet?" Sheriff Mueller said.

All the color drained from Paul's face. I thought he might wet himself from the look in his eyes.

"What do you propose, Bethany Parker?"

"Well, we're all equally screwed here. Unless...."

I let my words trail away. Camazotz waited impatiently for me to finish. When I didn't, he finally spoke again.

"Unless what?" he demanded.

"Unless we were to come to some sort of mutual agreement," I said, as though it should be obvious.

"Parker?" the sheriff said, worry in his tone.

"Bethany, what are you doing?" Lucius asked.

"Negotiating," I said. "Camazotz, what if I offered to unbind you from the mansion?"

"Bethany, no!" Lucius shouted. "You can't!"

"If you release me, I will spare your life and those of your friends."

"No, no, no, Camazotz," I said. "That's not enough. We've all already said we would trade our lives to keep you here."

"I didn't!" Paul protested.

"Yes," I replied, "but you're a spineless coward with a microscopic penis. I'll sacrifice you with no second thought to prevent an apocalypse.

"No, Camazotz, you'll have to offer something more than our lives."

Those hellish, red eyes narrowed. I could see him desperately trying to figure out what I was up to. I only offered a pleasant smile in return.

"What do you desire, Bethany Parker?" he asked.

"You forfeit your revenge," I said. "I know you want to inflict your pain and outrage on the mortal world. I know you want to slaughter as many humans as you can and enslave them. But none of those people is Alexander Ellington. You've already avenged yourself on the man who imprisoned you.

"So, if you want me to unbind you from the manor, you'll swear to forgo your revenge."

"Bethany, you cannot do this!" Lucius said. "He is a mad god. He has no sense of honor or law. If you free him, he will betray you."

"The cat's right, Bethany," Sheriff Mueller said. "You can't trust this monster to keep his word."

"I. Am not. A *cat*!" Lucius snapped.

Fury drenched his black face and green eyes. I had to bite my tongue to keep from laughing at him.

"What's it going to be, Camazotz?" I said, ignoring my friends. "Are you going to be bound here forever? Or will you forsake the carnage you yearn to wreak?"

"You dare bargain with a god?" Camazotz said.

Now, I knew I had him. He had no problem bargaining before. But I'd put something on the table he did not want to agree to. And he also saw there was no way out of this predicament.

"Please, Camazotz," I said, each word dripping sarcasm. "We're not standing in your temple. I didn't summon you here. You're a prisoner. You have no leverage. Agree to my terms or be bound here for another one hundred and four years."

Dead silence fell on the room. I could see out of the corner of my eye that Lucius and Sheriff Mueller desperately hoped Camazotz wouldn't take the deal. Paul, on the other hand, seemed to be praying, although I couldn't have said to which god.

I studied, Camazotz carefully. I watched as he worked out all the possibilities in his mind.

"Very well, Bethany Parker," he said, a smile on his lips and a sinister light in his eyes. "I will spare your friends and forsake my revenge."

Now, it was my turn to smile. I knew exactly what he was up to.

"Swear it, Camazotz," I said. "Without an oath, your word isn't binding."

"You question my word?" he roared.

"Sorry, Camazotz," I said. "But my familiar and the sheriff are right. Without an oath, you could be lying to me."

Like he had when I'd stopped Declan from freeing him, he threw back his head and screamed at the ceiling. For a moment I wondered if he wouldn't just kill us in a rage. But then, he got his fury under control.

"Very well, Bethany Parker, I swear on my heart, there shall be no revenge," he said.

"And?" I prompted.

"You and your friends shall be spared," he grumbled.

"You swear to that, too?" I said.

"I do."

"Very well then," I said with as much sugar and honey in my tone as I could manage. "We have a deal."

"Are you insane, Parker?" the sheriff said. "There is no way this fiend will keep his promise."

I did my best not to roll my eyes at Sheriff Mueller. I knew he would be skeptical. But I couldn't exactly tell him why I knew I was right.

"Sheriff, I know you are afraid I'm *naïve* and making a huge mistake. But I know what I am doing. Camazotz has sworn an oath. It cannot be broken, and he knows that."

"You honestly think you can bargain with a death god?" the sheriff retorted. "If that were possible, we'd be hip deep in immortals who were willing to make deals."

I sighed. I knew I was right, and I knew no one would believe me. But I had to play this game, so that no one would stop me. Still, it was tedious.

"Sheriff, despite my general ignorance of the supernatural world, I have made the right decision at every turn. I need you to trust me now."

He threw me a look that suggested I must be crazy to think that I had made the right decision at every turn. But I had, and he knew it.

Gripping the cane tightly, I started towards the circle. Lucius darted in front of me. He slid to a stop with a snarl on his face, his green eyes flashing, and his tail puffed out. He looked like he just seen a rat.

"Bethany," he said, "I cannot allow this."

I raised my eyebrow. He could not allow it? Who the hell did he think he was?

"Rhoda, Sheriff Mueller, and Dorigen are all correct," he said, an authoritative tone covering each word.

"Camazotz cannot be trusted. If you release him, he will kill thousands of people. You wanted the sheriff to trust you? I need you to trust me. My fey magic has seen it."

I wanted to be angry with him. He was speaking to me like I was a naughty child, and I did not care for that tone from anyone, most especially my cat. But I knew that losing my cool would only make things worse, and frankly, I understood his concerns. The nice thing about having all seven chakras in alignment was that I could truly see for real. Lucius meant no insult. He was just trying to prevent what he was sure was a disaster.

"Lucius, my dear friend," I said, speaking as sweetly as I knew how. "All seven of my chakras are in alignment. I have achieved harmony within myself and with all things. I know what I am doing, and I know what will happen. This is the right thing."

A shadow of doubt crossed his face, but he did not back down. He still looked like a cat about to scratch the face off its enemy.

So, like I had when I communicated my plan to him against Maggie Cartwright, I reached out to Lucius's mind and showed him my trump card. His eyes grew wide in surprise.

Are you sure that will work? he thought to me.

It will, I replied telepathically, nodding my head as I did so.

He lowered his hackles and stepped out of my way.

"I hope you are right," he said aloud.

I smiled. The sheriff looked like both of us had taken leave of our senses.

"I thought you had more intelligence than that, Lucius," he commented.

"I tire of waiting, Bethany Parker," Camazotz rumbled before Lucius could retort. "Unbind me."

I smiled at him. Then, I stepped into the circle. Swallowing hard and summoning the last of my courage, I looked the Mayan god in the face, gripped the cane, and spoke:

"Camazotz, Lord of Bats, God of the Dead, I unbind you from Ellington Manor."

White smoke swirled all around him. His transparent form became solid – his body black as midnight, his batwings blood-red, matching the feral light in his eyes. He stretched as though he'd been chained to a chair and could at last flex his muscles.

"At last!" he roared, his voice like a thunderbolt. "I am free! Free now to punish humanity for daring to command the gods!"

"Oh, great," Sheriff Mueller grumbled. "Way to go, Parker."

"Camazotz," I said, with no fear in my voice, "have you forgotten your oath so soon?"

He laughed the most sinister and diabolical laugh I had ever heard in my life. He was filled with genuine mirth at my comment, and I waited patiently for him to play his masterstroke.

"I have not forgotten the oath I swore, Bethany Parker," he said. "Unfortunately for you, it has no power over me. I swore on my heart to renounce my revenge. But I am the God of the Dead, and death is heartless."

"Oh, shit," the sheriff swore.

I smiled and shook my head sadly. Then I met Camazotz's leer.

"Oh, Camazotz, you disappoint me," I said in my sad-mommy voice. "I was really hoping you would keep your word."

"You should have listened to your smarter friends, mortal."

"No," I replied, "I did the right thing. It's you who's been had. I only unbound you from the house. I did not free you."

Camazotz laughed again. He spread his wings in an attempt to frighten me. But I had never felt more confident and courageous in my life. I knew I was going to win, and he didn't scare me.

"You are wrong, foolish mortal," he said. "The manor was all that held me in check. Now I am free to go where I please and do as I desire."

"No, Camazotz, the manor is what held you here. But you are still a prisoner."

I knelt down and scooped up Alexander Ellington's signet from where it had fallen in the ash heap of Declan's remains.

"By the power of these artifacts," I said, standing, "in the circle that confines you, I banish you forever to the Land of the Dead."

For a third time, Camazotz laughed uproariously. I thought this time, he might actually double over from guffawing.

"Those trinkets only have power over the dead, Bethany Parker," he shouted triumphantly. "And Alexander Ellington's ring cannot protect you from me. Witness your friend, the vampire."

The smug side of me, the part that shared my father's enjoyment of proving someone wrong, lit up like a Christmas tree. I wanted to be so serious about this. But I just couldn't manage it. A bemused grin broke over my face, and I threw the Lord of Bats my best I-told-you-so look.

"You *are* dead, Camazotz," I said. "No one has worshiped you for thousands and thousands of years. The culture you served is extinct. You are remembered only by a handful of scholars and Mesoamerican enthusiasts. That is the very definition of death for a god. I have all the power over you I require.

"Release the chains of the spirits you enslaved, and go to the Land of the Dead, never to return. I banish you from this Earth, Camazotz, forever."

This time, he didn't mock me. His red eyes turned round in horror as his bat ears heard the authority of my command.

"No," he whimpered like a child who'd had his favorite toy taken away.

Then he burst into flame. The fire was hot and scorched my skin. I thought for a moment it might consume me, too. But though it seared my very soul, I remained unharmed.

Camazotz, on the other hand was quickly consumed. His enormous body burned like dry twigs, and he screamed less in agony than in defeat. As though I'd opened an airlock, his immolating form was sucked backwards towards the mirror of the cigarette case and into the glass. The Mayan Death-bat reached for me with a huge flaming fist, hoping to drag me to Hell with him. But his fingers closed around nothing. They were immaterial and unable to harm me.

Then, he was gone.

I raised the cane like a scepter.

"Hear me, all you spirits chained here by the mad god, Camazotz," I cried. "Your ultimate destiny has come at last. No more shall you haunt this realm. Go now to where you belong."

No sooner had I uttered the words, than hundreds of spirits appeared before me. Their chains fell away, clattering to the floor before turning to dust. They rushed towards me and swirled all about me, forming a vortex of souls with me at its center. Ether brushed against my flesh, blew my hair in every direction, kissed my cheeks. All of them thanked me, some with smiles, some with tears, and some with simple words.

I was overwhelmed with such a sense of joy, the feeling of true freedom, of rest after a long, weary road magnified thousands of times. I quickly began crying from happiness. Never in my life had I ever been so overjoyed. I'd had some amazing moments – winning the role of "Fiona" in *Brigadoon* while I was at KU, being accepted into the College of Music, hitting my first homerun in Little League – but none of it compared to this. I, Bethany Parker, had performed an act of such goodness that it had impacted thousands upon thousands of souls. And I did not feel this happiness from conceit, but rather from a sense of having made the world a better place.

I had been right: I had achieved harmony with all things – most importantly, with myself.

Still, my work was not quite done. I walked over to the cigarette case, closed it, and slid it into my pocket. Then I crossed the circle to the grandfather clock. I opened its face and withdrew the pocket watch. The pendulum began to swing again. For a moment I soothed myself with its rhythmic ticking.

Then, I dropped the watch on the floor and stomped on it with my heel. The metal bent, the glass shattered, and the cogs spilled out onto the tile.

"Oh, no!" Paul wailed. "No, you've destroyed it!"

"Yes," I said. "That was the idea. Ellington Manor will never serve as a prison again."

Twisting the knife, I smiled at him as I snapped the cane across my thigh. Paul blubbered something unintelligible. The sheriff let out a long whistle.

"Damn, Parker," he said. "When did you become such a badass?"

"She always was," Lucius replied. "She just needed to awaken to that truth."

Twenty-Seven

I breathed a huge sigh of relief. At last, it was over. I could finally begin something approximating a normal life here in Enchantment. Not that a magical town populated by supernatural creatures had anything to do with normal. But still, my divorce was finalized, the manor was rid of its ghosts, and it was time to start thinking about new beginnings.

"You will pay for this," Paul swore.

I arched an eyebrow. Pay for this? What the hell could he possibly be talking about now?

"Are you joking?" I said. "I undid the curse of Ellington Manor once and for all. Who is going to punish me for that? And why would they?"

"You took power you had no right to," Paul spat. Every word was covered with venom. "You nearly killed us all with your bumbling *naïveté*. And you denied me my destiny!

"I swear, I will not rest until I have ruined your entire life."

For half a second, fear gripped my heart. I was supposed to get to start over. Now, I had to deal with Paul's petty-ass revenge?

But then, Sheriff Mueller smacked him upside the head.

"Shut your mouth, Hernandez," he said. "You're going to jail."

Grabbing a pair of handcuffs from his utility belt, the sheriff spun Paul around and quickly handcuffed him.

"Of course, that's just temporary," he continued. "I'll have The Order here by tomorrow night at the latest. That'll be the last anyone sees or hears from you. I'm sure they're going to have a very long conversation with their agent about how he teamed with a rogue vampire to activate Ellington Manor. Unless, of course, they just throw you in a dark hole without questioning you. But it won't matter. You're done."

As much as I wanted to gloat over Paul's demise, since he had absolutely infuriated me over the past few months, I had more important things to take care of.

"Open!" I shouted.

The secret door swung to, allowing the light from the library to spill in. Dorigen stood before us with a look of wonder on her face.

"Jesus, Mary, and Joseph!" she cried. "Somehow, they're all still alive!"

"Your confidence is inspiring," Sheriff Mueller said as he shoved Paul through the door.

I laughed.

"Look who's talking," I snarked.

He threw me a scowl before leading Paul out.

Rhoda and Reggie faced each other, talking quietly and smiling. Rhoda flashed me a look of gratitude when she saw me emerge from the secret room. It made me want to weep. I sighed heavily, and then started towards them with a grim expression on my face.

Before I got there, though, Dorigen intercepted me. She threw her arms around me and hugged me tightly. I allowed myself to succumb to the joy of it. After a moment, she stepped back with tears in her eyes and took my hands.

"You done well, Sorority Girl," she said. "My thanks to you."

I smiled.

"You're very welcome," I said. "You're free now. He's gone for good."

She drew me into another tight hug. I could only imagine what it must have been like for her after having been haunted by that voice for fifty years and held prisoner here by magic she wanted nothing to do with. I was saddened by the fact that at sixty-eight, she'd missed most of her life. But at least she had the freedom now to do as she pleased.

I disengaged from her and patted her arm. I gave her one more smile. Lucius wound between her legs. In an act of affection I had never seen from her, she bent down, scooped him up, and began stroking his ears. He tried to look offended, but I could hear him purring. With a smirk, I headed over to Rhoda and Reggie.

They both turned to face me. Joy and gratitude poured off Rhoda. I felt terrible about what I had to do.

"Reggie," I said softly, "it's time."

He frowned, marring his handsome expression. But he nodded. He knew I was right.

"What are you talking about?" Rhoda asked.

"I banished, Camazotz to the Land of the Dead," I explained. "Then, I freed all the trapped spirits and sent them to their final destinations."

Rhoda stared at me uncomprehendingly. I grimaced.

"That includes Reggie," I said.

"What?" Rhoda said, her eyes opening wide in alarm. "No! Spirits aren't required to move on! They can haunt for as long as they like!"

"Rhoda," I said in a sad but firm voice, "you need to let go. By clinging to him this way, you're not just denying him his final peace. You're making yourself a prisoner, too. It is time to grieve and move forward."

I hated everything I was saying. It was wise and sage and absolutely correct. I was an enlightened mystic, and I understood that Rhoda had clung too long to Reggie's ghost.

But I hated myself for being the person to separate them. I knew inconsolable grief all too well. And having put this off for so long, Rhoda would not overcome it easily.

"I'm afraid she's right, Rhoda," Reggie said. "It's my fault, really. I didn't want to let go. I wanted to know I had mattered, so I led you here to Enchantment. I helped you begin a new life, and I directed you to attract and mentor Bethany, so the curse could be broken. I wanted to have a hand in that, because I'd had my own visions that it could be done. It was for the greater good.

"But it was also selfish."

"No," Rhoda protested.

"Yes, it was," Reggie insisted. "I didn't want to leave you behind, didn't want your life to go on without me. By doing that, I made prisoners of us both. It's time for me to break those chains. It's time for me to move on the way I'm supposed to."

Tears were already running down Rhoda's face like Niagara Falls. She could barely speak. And my heart broke as she wailed in defiance.

"But I don't want to live without you," she sobbed.

"I know," Reggie said. "No one wants to let their deceased loved ones go. But it is the way of things."

Rhoda was crying hard enough now that everyone stared at her. I felt terrible. I suspected I was the only one who could see Reggie, probably the only one who could hear him. All they could experience was Rhoda's anguish, not any of his reassurances that this was the right thing to do.

"I can't even hug or kiss you goodbye!" she shouted before breaking into a fresh round of sobs.

"But you already have in your heart," Reggie said. "We cannot touch, but our hearts are connected forever."

Rhoda nodded vigorously. She put her hand on her heart as though she could feel him there. Perhaps she could. For if lost loved ones live anywhere, it is definitely in our memories and feelings for them.

"You be good to the other spirits," Rhoda said, putting on a brave face and blinking away tears. "Make sure you build me a nice house in Heaven. When I'm done here, I'll be looking for you. Don't you make yourself hard to find."

"When it's your time," Reggie said with a broad smile, "I'll be waiting to escort you."

They looked deeply into each other's eyes. I sensed this was my moment.

"Are you ready?" I asked.

"Yes," Reggie said with a sigh. "You take care of my girl now."

"I will," I assured him.

He faced Rhoda one more time.

"Goodbye, my love."

"Rest well, my husband," she replied.

I withdrew the cigarette case from my pocket. Carefully I opened the lid. Reggie winked at Rhoda. And then, his ethereal form became smoke and drifted into the glass of the case's mirror before vanishing altogether. Wordlessly, I closed the lid.

"Rhoda, I am destroying the artifacts," I said. "I can't let the manor be used like this ever again. Would you like to be the one to break the cigarette case? Maybe it would give you some sense of closure."

Rhoda stared at the metal case for several seconds, her eyes wet with tears. Then she nodded and took it from me. She opened the case and gazed into its mirror. A sad smile crept up her cheeks.

"You'll recall that the mirror shows the truth," she said.

"Yes," I replied.

"It's telling me I need to grieve."

Then she turned so that we stood shoulder-to-shoulder and held it out. I gazed on the two of us in the glass.

"And you," she continued, "are a fully ascended mystic."

She smiled at my reflection. Then she threw the case to the floor with all her might. The glass shattered instantly, and one of the hinges of the lid snapped. Then Rhoda threw herself into my embrace and sobbed into my shoulders. I wrapped my arms around her and gently stroked her back.

"I'm so sorry for your loss, Rhoda," I said. "Nothing I can say will ease your pain. But I will be right here to help you through every moment of it."

"You are a true friend, Bethany," she sobbed.

"It takes one to know one," I said, turning a childhood insult into the highest compliment I could imagine.

Twenty-Eight

The Order arrived at noon the next day, banging on my door while I was still in my PJ's and sipping coffee. When I went to answer it, there were three men in black suits, sunglasses, and carrying silver briefcases. They looked like some sort of cross between the Mafia and the FBI.

They asked me a lot of questions and stared at me as though I were some sort of traitor, selling nuclear secrets to the Soviets during the height of the Cold War. They wanted to know why I had freed Camazotz. They wanted to know what the state of the manor was now that he was gone. And perhaps most importantly, they wanted to know how I got ahold of the artifacts in the first place.

For the most part, I told them the truth. I didn't see any sense in lying, because I hadn't really done anything wrong.

But I didn't tell them about going to Cincinnati to acquire the cane. I left that part out, saying I had no idea how Paul had gotten it. But I told them he had been working with Marcel Truffaut to acquire the cigarette case and the pocket watch, and implied that that was probably how he found it, which was sort of true. I wasn't so much afraid for myself. I was a little bit worried they might lock me up if they knew that I had led the quest to get one of the four artifacts. But mainly, I didn't want to create any trouble for Rhoda or Lucius since they had been involved, too.

They demanded that I turn the artifacts over to them. I shrugged and complied. Of course, the lead agent, whose name I never got, looked perturbed when I handed him the broken cane, shattered cigarette case, and smashed pocket watch. I hadn't had the means to destroy the signet, since I couldn't build a fire hot enough on my own. But I figured without the other three, it was largely harmless.

I made sure to let them know that Paul had murdered Marcel Truffaut and conspired with Declan to activate the manor. They assured me Paul would be prosecuted for using the house's magic, but they figured the world was better off with two fewer vampires in it. That seemed kind of callous to me. I didn't have a lot of sympathy for Marcel Truffaut, but I knew that he had been abused and exploited as a young man. And Declan was definitely remorseful for what he'd done to his son. They deserved better epitaphs than that. Still, I didn't know what I could do about it.

When they finally left two days later, they put Sheriff Mueller temporarily in charge as The Order's official agent. And they allowed me to continue serving as caretaker for Ellington Manor. So at least I still had a place to live and, in theory, a salary.

♫

Once The Order was through interrogating me, I realized that I had one bit of closure left to make with my old life. I wasn't looking forward to it. In fact, I was dreading having to deal with Andrew's email. But I knew if I didn't, it would continue to haunt me. And we all needed to move forward.

So, I sat down at the computer with a glass of wine next to me in the study. And I endured rereading his hateful letter. It was easier this time, partly because I already knew the contents. But it helped that I had aligned all seven of my chakras, and I could now fully view his attack on me as the hurt ravings of a wounded child. With a heavy sigh, I typed out a reply.

. . .

My dearest Andrew,

I apologize for not responding to your email sooner. It took me a few days to be able to formulate a response. Yes, it was devastating to read. You achieved all your objectives with it. If you take nothing else from this letter, you can at least know you hurt me just as you intended to.

But I'm not writing to refute your claims or attack you back to get some sort of revenge. I have only one message for you: I'm sorry.

I can only imagine how much pain you must have been in to write and send such an angry message. I felt your fury intimately, and I am devastated that you were that miserable.

Much of it is my fault. While you and your sister were grieving the death of your mother, I was grieving over the loss of my first marriage and the child I miscarried. I was so blinded by my own unhappiness, I failed to notice that you and Ariel needed something different than what I was giving you. You trusted me to help you, and I failed. I'm so sorry for that.

With the benefit of hindsight, I see now that I should never have married your father, never attempted to mother you. There were warning signs I ignored that suggested it would never work. But I wouldn't have traded the past eight years with the three of you for anything. I would do things differently now that I know more. But I would still want to be your stepmom.

Perhaps I shouldn't have pushed you and Ariel as hard as I did. Clearly it had the opposite effect I had intended. Rather than enabling you to pursue your dreams, it made you both hate them instead. I apologize for that, too. It's how I was raised by my parents, so that's what I did for you.

I want you to understand something very important, though. Ariel making it on Broadway and you having a shot at playing Major League Baseball were not my dreams. Yes, I once wanted to be a pop singer. Yes, I played college softball. But I didn't force those ambitions on either of you. Both of you chose them for yourselves. I never told Ariel to audition for a show. I never suggested you play Little League. Both of you came to me asking for those things.

Ariel heard about auditions for Annie *at Theatre Lawrence. She asked me if she could try out and to help her prepare. I cried on opening night of* The Secret Garden *not because I was proud of her for stepping into my shoes, but because her dreams were coming true. She was getting what she wanted, and she'd triumphed. I was only happy for her.*

Likewise, I still remember your first base hit. I remember you standing on first, your whole face beaming. You weren't happy because you'd done what I taught you, Andrew. You were reveling in your accomplishment. And I was overjoyed for you.

If you don't want to play baseball anymore, I one-hundred-percent support you in that decision. I don't want you to be unhappy. Just make sure that choice is fueled by what you *want, not by spite to hurt me.*

It makes no difference to me if you play baseball or not. I don't care if Ariel never sings again. I only want for the both of you to make choices that will lead to a happy and fulfilling life. Whatever that looks like for you, I will be proud of you.

Perhaps one day, if you have children of your own, this will make more sense to you. Good parents take pride in their children's accomplishments not because they reflect well on the parent, but because the kids are getting what they want.

That is and always has been my wish for you and Ariel – that you get everything you want. And if that means me being out of the picture, then I gladly accept that. Because I only want all your dreams to come true.

I love you, Andrew. I will always love you and your sister. I will never not consider you my children, and if you ever decide you do want a relationship, I will welcome you with open arms.

Regardless of what you choose, I wish you all the luck, success, and happiness in the world. You are a good person, Andrew. So is Ariel. Both of you can accomplish anything you desire. Be good to yourselves and to each other.

All my love,
  Bethany

. . .

Tears streamed down my face as I wrote it. I realized deep in my heart that this was likely the last time we would ever communicate. For all I knew, he had my email address blocked. But I was pleased with the overall message, and I hit "send" before draining my wineglass. Hopefully, he would read it and be able to come to some sort of peace of his own.

🎵

A few days later, I met Rhoda for breakfast at Drogo's. I was relieved to see that Mona was at last back at work. And the rest of Enchantment seemed to share my sentiment, because the diner was packed for the first time in weeks.

"What can I get for you today, Bethany?" Mona said after pouring us coffee.

"I think it's definitely a blueberry pancake day," I said.

"How about you, Rhoda?" she asked, as she made a note of my order.

"Just an apple-cinnamon muffin for me, thanks," Rhoda said.

"Coming right up," Mona said before moving to the next booth.

I looked at Rhoda. Her eyes remained haunted from the loss of Reggie. She toyed with her coffee cup without drinking.

"How are you holding up?" I asked.

"I don't know, Bethany," she said with a shrug. "In a lot of ways, nothing has changed. I've been living alone for ten years, after all. I get up, and I go through my regular routine.

"But it's different, too. He's not there in a different way. I can feel his absence, especially when I'm at the store. Before, he was gone, but he wasn't. Now, he's just gone."

I nodded. I could relate. I was reminded yet again how, after the separation, it'd felt like Jess and the kids had died. I couldn't see them, and I couldn't speak to them. But they weren't dead. They were still out there, but they were totally inaccessible.

It occurred to me that maybe that was why I had replied to Andrew's email. I'd wanted to feel that connection once more.

"The thing I miss most is being able to talk to him," Rhoda went on. "He wasn't really there, but we could still converse. Now, it's just silent all the time."

"I'm so sorry, Rhoda. I would like to tell you, I understand. I miss my kids so badly – I miss hearing about their days. But it isn't the same. Reggie was the love of your life. Neither of you wanted to say goodbye. I can only sort of imagine what you're going through."

Rhoda sipped her coffee for a moment. Then she met my gaze.

"I don't know, Bethany," she said. "Loss is loss. Grief is grief. The circumstances don't really make it hurt more or less."

I supposed that was true. Just because Jess and the kids didn't miss me didn't mean I wasn't hurting. And just because I knew I was better off now did not make it hurt any less that my children were gone.

"You were both right about one thing, though," Rhoda said. "I've been avoiding the reality of his death. Because I'm a medium, I could always contact him. So it wasn't like he was really gone. I've been running away from that for a decade. It's time I did something about it.

"That's why I'm thinking about leaving Enchantment."

I nearly choked on my coffee.

"You're leaving?" I said.

"I'm not sure yet," she answered. "But probably."

"Why?"

"I came here because Reggie told me to. Everywhere I look, I see memories of him. The town is haunted for me – metaphorically, at least.

"In fact," she said, growing thoughtful, "I've been doing what Reggie told me to my entire adult life. I don't hate him for that. I enjoyed it. And I listened to him because I wanted to. And I was in love.

"But I'm fifty-three years old. I think it's time I did something of my own choosing."

Once again, I could relate. I'd moved to Kansas solely to get away from my parents. I married Mark, because I'd given up on myself. And I'd acted as Jess and the kids' servant, because I wanted to feel like I mattered to someone. I was free of all that now. I too could make my own choices.

"Any thoughts on where you'll go?" I asked.

"I've no idea," Rhoda said with a sheepish smile. "Maybe I'll buy an RV and drive around the country."

"Ooh! That sounds fun!"

The two of us chuckled as we could imagine driving around the country, getting into adventures, and causing trouble for the Rusty Muellers of every town we went to.

The bell on the door rang, and as though I'd summoned him, Sheriff Mueller breezed in, went straight to the counter, and ordered a coffee to go. I watched as Mona quickly poured it into a cup, put a top on it, and went to the register to ring him up. Ordinarily, the sheriff would look around, see us sitting at the booth, and come over. But today, he simply paid and left.

I frowned. I had one more piece of business I hadn't attended to yet.

"Would you excuse me for a moment?" I said.

"Sure," Rhoda said, a curious look on her face.

I got up and went out into the parking lot.

"Sheriff," I called as he got to his SUV.

He turned around. When he saw it was me, a look of mild exasperation lit up his brown eyes.

"Yeah, Parker, what is it?" he said.

"Can I talk to you for a minute?" I asked.

"I'm really busy today, Parker. Marty Jenkins's imp escaped again, Mrs. Holloway is convinced fairies are eating her roses, and Taylor Albany says there's a ghost in the attic."

"Please?" I said. "It'll only take a minute."

"Fine, Parker," he said with a sigh. "What is it?"

I suddenly felt my courage faltering. I had to swallow hard to be able to tell him what I wanted to.

"I know why you won't call me, 'Bethany'," I said. "Once I aligned my Crown Chakra, it all became clear."

He suddenly looked uncomfortable. I watched as he shifted from foot to foot.

"Yeah, well, good for you," he said. "I've got to go."

He turned away, put his free hand on the door handle, and opened it.

"Rusty, wait!" I snapped.

Calling him by his first name got his attention. He turned and looked at me with raised eyebrows.

"I like you," I said. "I really do."

I tried to figure out what to say next. For an enlightened mystic, it was suddenly difficult to talk about anything.

"But?" he said.

I sighed. Why was this so hard?

"But I've just gotten out of my second bad marriage," I explained. "I don't know when or if I'll want to get into another relationship. I need to take some time to heal. One of the benefits of awakening to my mystic powers has been acquiring a certain wisdom about myself. And it's telling me to get my head – as well as my heart – right before trying this again."

He searched me with his policeman's gaze, trying to see if I was sincere or if I would say more.

"Well, that's great, Parker," he said at last. "Congratulations. I need to get to work."

Once again, he turned back to the vehicle.

"Damn it, Rusty, wait a second!"

"No," he shot back. "What am I supposed to do with this information, Parker? Your mystic Sight finally told you how I feel. But you're telling me it's not going to happen. So, fine! You delivered your message. I gotta go."

"That's not what I said!"

God, how this man could piss me off!

"Well, what then?" he said.

For a moment I pleaded with him with my eyes, begging him to calm down and listen. But his face remained a mask of frustration and hurt feelings.

"I thought ..." I began. But I had to swallow to continue. "I thought maybe we could start spending time together. Maybe ... see what happens, find out if we are compatible."

Now his eyes were open wide. He looked back at me, uncertain what to make of my proposal. I watched as he analyzed every syllable of what I'd just said.

"What are you saying, Parker?" he asked.

"I'm saying, I'd like to get to know you," I answered. "Right now, all I know is a gruff stoic, trying to hide a tragic loss from the world. And you only see a bumbling novice, who causes more trouble than she solves."

"That's not what I think of you," he said, sounding chagrined.

"Well, maybe we could have dinner sometime, and you could tell me what you *do* think."

I thought his face might fall off. Whatever he'd been expecting, asking him on a date had been about as far away from it as possible. He looked me up and down, as though he were looking for some sort of deception, another trick.

"Yeah," he finally said. "Maybe sometime we could do that."

"How about tomorrow night?" I proposed.

He studied me again. His pale skin flushed a bit. I suddenly realized he felt both nervous and embarrassed. It was cute.

"Yeah, that might work," he said. "Listen, Bethany, I've really got to go. I'm running late. I'll call you, okay?"

"I'm looking forward to it," I said with a smile.

We stared at each other for several seconds. I could see he was really nervous and wasn't certain how to break off the discussion. But I hadn't missed that he called me "Bethany" instead of "Parker."

Finally, he nodded once, climbed up into his cruiser, and drove away. I watched until his taillights were out of sight.

Unwanted, the image of The Lovers popped into my mind. Rhoda had insisted it didn't necessarily mean romantic love. But I wasn't clear on how I'd brought two disparate ideas together to make my heart glad. And in the spread, the card had revealed it was my destiny.

Dear God, what had I just gotten myself into?

Slightly satisfied and incredibly nervous, I walked back to the diner. When I got to the booth, my food was waiting for me.

"What was that all about?" Rhoda said.

"I might've just asked the sheriff out on a date," I said.

Rhoda's eyes went wide. Then she smiled.

"Well," she said, "I'm definitely not leaving town before I hear how *that* turns out."

I smiled. I was pretty sure I was blushing like a schoolgirl. It didn't matter. As scared as I was about being alone with Rusty Mueller, I was happy that I'd made the move.

That night, I sat in the parlor by the fire with a glass of wine. Just as I'd gotten comfortable, a wicked hot flash assaulted me. I pulled off my sweater and my socks so that I sat in a camisole and jeans. Lucius hopped up in my lap and immediately curled up on my thighs. I sighed. I really needed to explain feminine hormones to him. For now, though, I stroked his head softly.

"You know," I said, "I never thanked you for saving my life."

"It was nothing," he said sleepily.

"Oh, it was definitely something," I retorted. "You sacrificed one of your lives to save me."

"I have five left," he said. "I'd gladly sacrifice them all for you."

That took me back. He had saved my life in the moment. And I imagined it was the kind of thing anyone would do if they wanted to protect someone they cared about. But in Lucius's case, it was all carefully premeditated. He'd known he would come back. And he had likely counted on that so that he would be able to thwart Paul's attempt to summon Camazotz. It was a calculated risk.

But it was something else entirely to say he would do it again and again until he had no lives left to give. I believed him, and that was a level of dedication I wasn't exactly accustomed to. I hadn't had good luck in the romance department, after all. So for Lucius to say something like that and to mean it – and more importantly, for me to accept it as true – was an unfamiliar sensation.

"Why?"

"Why what?" he murmured.

"Why would you sacrifice all of your lives to save me?"

"Because you freed me from the curse," he said. "And you are a far better mistress than Margaret Cartwright. You have a kind soul, and you are truly a good person.

"I'm surprised you have to ask."

I stroked his ear for a few seconds and had a sip of my wine.

"That street runs in both directions, Lucius," I said. "I couldn't have done any of this without you."

"Yes, you could have," he said with a yawn. "I helped here and there.

But you are the person that undid all the horror that Alexander Ellington wrought."

I drank some more wine. I supposed he was right. But I was still uncomfortable with the idea of taking sole credit. Lucius and Rhoda and Dorigen and Rusty Mueller had all helped, too.

"You're too modest," I said. A smile slid up my face. "I'm not sure that's allowed."

"What do you mean?"

"Well, you're a terrific familiar, Lucius. But you're really not much of a cat."

"There's no need to be insulting," he said as he drifted out of consciousness.

I couldn't help but laugh. This whole time he'd been insisting he wasn't a cat. And now when I'd suggested he was more of a familiar than a cat, he was still upset.

"I love you, Lucius," I said, chuckling.

"I love you, too, Bethany," he replied, his voice faraway.

And with that, he was fast asleep. I hadn't meant "I love you" in the romantic or familial sense. He'd misinterpreted what I'd said to him. But at the same time, he was right. I did love him. And after so many years of getting that emotion all wrong, it felt wonderful to have it right.

My phone rang. I looked to see who was calling and saw it was my mother. Despite it buzzing and playing its ringtone, it did not disturb Lucius's slumber.

"Hi, Mom," I said, answering the call.

"Hello, dear," she said. "I was just checking in on you."

I smiled. As usual, Mom was convinced that I hadn't recovered from an emotional blow like Andrew's email. It was sweet, and frankly, I could do with a lot more sweet in my life.

"I'm doing okay, Mom," I said.

"Just okay?"

I smiled again. She was so good at looking for trouble everywhere, but there was none to be found here.

"Actually," I said, "I'm doing great. In fact, I've never been better."

Afterword

Dear reader,

Thank you for joining me in Enchantment. *Midlife Melody* has been a blast to write, and I'm so glad you elected to come along.

From the beginning, this series has been about grief. It's a subject that we don't talk about much, and we generally don't think about it until we're dropped into the middle of it with no directions for getting out.

Grief is the most complicated of human emotions. And while the Seven Stages of Grief have been well-defined for years, what few of us understand before experiencing it is that those seven stages do not happen in any particular order. Worse, relapses into "previous" stages are common. I wanted a story that allowed myself as author and you as reader to explore grief in a sort of controlled environment, so we can better understand it.

To be true to that, Bethany has frequently taken several steps backward before moving forward again. And I deliberately blocked her Heart Chakra in *Mystic Harmony* to show how you can be feeling better and thinking you're moving on, only to have an unforeseen

AFTERWORD

trigger crop up that forces you back into a stage you'd "successfully completed." In my experience, grief issues strike without warning from completely unanticipated sources. It is a long road to fully moving past it.

The final Stage of Grief is Acceptance. It's hard to achieve and surprising when you get there. But the most important component of completing those seven stages is forgiveness. You have to forgive the person who caused your grief, and you have to forgive yourself for everything you believe you did. Whether that's forgiving an ex or a loved one who has died or family and friends from whom you're estranged, you can't get to Acceptance without letting go of the second stage, Anger. And releasing anger involves forgiveness.

The only thing that heals emotional wounds is love. Forgiving someone else is an act of love – maybe not for them, but definitely for you. You don't have to like them anymore or ever associate with them again. Or, if they've died, you can still be upset about their absence. But carrying a grudge or being resentful only robs what time we have left of its pleasure. Forgiveness, especially of yourself, is self-love. It is caring for your own soul. And it is the kindest gesture you can make to yourself.

That was the piece that was missing for Bethany. She resented her family for how they treated her. She resented her first husband for divorcing her in the wake of a miscarriage. And she hated herself for failing at everything she had attempted in her adult life. Until she let that pain go, until she forgave herself, she couldn't align her Crown Chakra. But once she did, true wisdom was possible.

Grief must be embraced. It reveals our truths and our weaknesses and our strengths. It is healthy and important and should not be avoided. For when we do allow ourselves to sit with that most complex of human emotions, we become wiser and perhaps even happier.

I've been grieving a long time myself. I wasn't sure it would ever get better. But it has, and Bethany helped me with that. I hope she's been helpful to you in some way, too.

Love,
Phoebe

AFTERWORD

P.S. (Readers are always on the lookout for good books. You can help them find ones you enjoyed by leaving a rating or review. Thanks!)

Acknowledgments

As always, I couldn't do this without a lot of help. I'm grateful to the following individuals for helping me make *Mystic Harmony* a reality.

Demetra Taylor: Everyone needs a good therapist. Demetra is the best I've ever had. She holds me accountable while sympathizing with my feelings. She helps me see new ways of looking at problems, enabling me to break the restrictive binary of right vs. wrong in favor of love and wisdom. Bethany couldn't have found peace without her, because I was struggling with similar issues. And though I always planned for her to come to the conclusions she did, I'm not sure I could have gotten her there authentically without Demetra's insight and care. Knowing that forgiveness was to the key to moving through grief doesn't help if you don't know *how* to forgive. I'm happier and healthier than I've ever been as a result of our work together.

My parents: It's impossible to express how profoundly influential my mom and dad were to this book, this series, and my whole career. I wouldn't be writing without my dad. I wouldn't be trying to say something meaningful without my mom. And they both unwittingly steered me into a love of fantasy fiction. I'm grateful for their support and for their inspiration. I'm not sure they always believed I could make a living at this, but they both gave me the courage to try.

Jen Lassalle: Jen helped me with the cover for this book, and her continued interest in *Midlife Melody* helps keep me encouraged. Drogo's expanded role in this this novel was for her.

Katerina Degratte: I'm still trying to figure out why this amazing person loves me. I've never had a partner who supported me as completely as she does. She gives me plenty of space while also remaining near-at-hand. She was one of the first people to truly accept me after I came out, and she continues to embrace the individual I am. On some level in the back of my brain, I understand that I am giving her as much as she does me. But it still seems lopsided in my favor. She loves me how I've always desired, and that makes all the victories more satisfying and all the losses easier to endure. I could not be luckier.

About the Author

Phoebe Ravencraft *is a non-binary fantasy author living and writing in Columbus, Ohio. Her preferred pronouns are she/her.*

She was raised on a steady diet of comic books, D&D, Broadway musicals, and Star Trek. She has a large collection of former jobs, most of which came with nametags. Writing is much cooler, since big-box retailers won't let you cast spells at work, and she can run on her preferred fuel of coffee, pie, and sarcasm.

When she's not gaming or binging geek shows on Netflix, she's scheming up her next literary adventure. She cohabits with a diabolical cat obsessed with the furnace closet, and two dogs who refuse to eat their own breakfast until they've had a piece of bread. She wishes she were more like Margo Hanson and less like Willow Rosenberg.

Printed in Great Britain
by Amazon